The Smuggler's Daughter

by

Caitlyn Callery

This is a work of fiction. Names, characters, places, and incidents are either the product of the author's imagination or are used fictitiously, and any resemblance to actual persons living or dead, business establishments, events, or locales, is entirely coincidental.

The Smuggler's Daughter

COPYRIGHT © 2023 by Hilary Mackelden

Cover Art by *The Wild Rose Press, Inc.*

The Wild Rose Press, Inc.
PO Box 708
Adams Basin, NY 14410-0708
Visit us at www.thewildrosepress.com

Publishing History
First Edition, 2024
Trade Paperback ISBN 978-1-5092-5370-8
Digital ISBN 978-1-5092-5371-5

Published in the United States of America

Dedication

To Tom Goodluck and Joyce Reed.
You taught me so much about the craft of storytelling.
And to dedicated teachers everywhere.
You're worth your weight in gold.

Chapter One

March 1818

Catherine Ashton sat beside her mother in the Potters' drawing room, and smiled and nodded at what she hoped were appropriate moments. Although Mrs. Potter spoke loudly, Catherine could barely hear her above the roar of all the other conversations filling the room. Glasses chinked as drinks were served, a group of gentlemen laughed loudly at some anecdote, and a pianoforte was played, though the tune was impossible to discern above the hubbub. Lanterns gave the room a warm glow, highlighting the stripes in the pink-and-purple wallcoverings, forming shadows on the pale pink carpet, and sliding off the silk dresses of the ladies, most of whom were here solely to greet the expected guests of honor, for it was well known that Lord Hadlow was at Hadlow Hall, and he had brought other single men with him.

"I wish they would hurry up and come," said Catherine's mother.

"They will be here," answered Ella Forbes-Smythe, who sat next to Catherine. "The drink is free. Hadlow and his friends could not resist if they wanted to."

Catherine dipped her head to hide her smile.

"That's unkind," Mama scolded Ella. "I'm sure they're not as bad as you believe."

"They will be perfect gentlemen," agreed Mrs. Potter. "There are four of them, you know. Lord Hadlow and three guests, so Mr. Potter said." She nodded emphatically. "And there is no need to be so scathing, Ella. Pockets-to-let they may be, but nothing a girl with a good dowry couldn't put right. They are, mostly, from respectable families; one could do worse. Obviously, none of them are meant for my daughter, since she is not yet out, and with looks and youth on her side as well as a sizeable portion, she should do a lot better for herself. But for some, Lord Hadlow, or one of his guests, would be quite a catch." She grinned maliciously at both Catherine and Ella. Catherine bristled and pinned her smile firmly in place as Mrs. Potter went on. "After all, it's not as if the neighborhood is awash with eligible gentlemen, is it? There's a veritable dearth of them now Viscount Frantham's heir has been snapped up by Amelia Bell."

She glared at the happy couple on the other side of the room, surrounded by ladies admiring Amelia's betrothal ring, and gentlemen congratulating her new fiancé.

Mrs. Potter's lips pursed as if she were sucking lemons before she seemed to remember herself, smiled, and said, "Other than Lord Rotherton, who doesn't seem to be in the market for a wife at present, these four gentlemen are the only ones you can choose from."

Ella muttered something. Lip reading to augment her hearing in the din of the room, Catherine thought she said, "God help us all."

"You don't approve of their arrival, do you?" asked Mama.

Ella shrugged. "It is not for me to approve or

disapprove Hadlow using his own home," she answered.
"If he chose to do it more often, perhaps he and his
wastrel friends wouldn't find themselves run to ground
until the quarterly rents come in and refill their pockets."

"You think they are rusticating?" asked Mrs. Potter.

Catherine mentally rolled her eyes. Of course they
were rusticating. Any friend of Lord Hadlow's would
only spend time in the country if forced to do so. They
were, invariably, inveterate gamblers who would sooner
be in London, soaking in the excitement, searching out
high-stakes games, and enjoying fine brandy to excess
whilst courting opera dancers by the score.

Not that Catherine was supposed to know about
opera dancers. Or the overindulgences of gentlemen, for
that matter. But she had endured two Seasons in Town
and she was not deaf, blind, or stupid. Plus, she had seen
the neglected and dilapidated homes of Lord Hadlow's
tenants, together with his untended fields and the
rundown state of Hadlow Hall. It was clear those were
not things on which the viscount cared to spend his
money.

"He hasn't come to set any major improvements in
place, I'll warrant," said Ella.

"Of course not! He is entertaining. He can't just
leave his friends while he goes off playing farmer, can
he?"

"Do we know any of the other gentlemen?" Mama
asked, and she glared at Ella. Catherine smiled,
sympathetically, although Ella did not look unduly
bothered by the implied scolding.

"As I said, there are three guests." Mrs. Potter
looked smug at the prospect of telling people things they
had not known before. "There's a Mr. Finch, who is the

second son of an earl. No fortune of his own, and no title, but he could do for some." She looked meaningfully at Catherine. Catherine pretended not to notice, but Mama stiffened. Mrs. Potter paused, but when neither of them spoke, she went on. "Then there is Baron Abberley and, of course, that gentleman who often comes here with Lord Hadlow, Mr. Colbourne."

"Baron Abberley?" Mama frowned. "I don't think I have come across him before." She turned to Catherine. "We didn't meet him in Town, did we?"

Catherine shook her head. She had never heard of him, which probably meant he was not received in polite Society. Catherine had, after all, spent two Seasons in London, and had been schooled in the names and backgrounds of every eligible bachelor.

"He's only just come into his title," said Mrs. Potter. "Mr. Potter says the previous baron died last year, while the present baron was abroad."

"How sad not have been here to say goodbye to his father." Catherine could not imagine being too far from either of her parents as they aged. It would break her heart not to be able to be with them in their final days.

Mrs. Potter waved a dismissive hand through the air. "Gentlemen do not have the same sensibilities as ladies when it comes to such things."

"I don't know that's true," argued Mama.

"Men are of a more practical nature," continued Mrs. Potter. "They accept their duty may make family ties a little more stretched. Besides, Mr. Potter says the previous baron was a recluse. Mayhap he didn't want anyone near, not even his son."

Which, Catherine thought, was even sadder.

"Perhaps the new baron is a young, dashing sort of

man," said Mama, hopefully.

Ella grinned. "Very likely. Why else would he be here with Hadlow and his other useless friends? And before the season has truly begun, too."

Mama looked as if she might give a scathing retort, but she fell silent as a footman approached Mrs. Potter and whispered in her ear. The lady looked surprised and a little alarmed for an instant before she covered it with a smile and excused herself. The noise in the room died to a buzz of murmurs as people turned to see. In the lull, men's laughter sounded in the hallway.

The door opened wider, and Lord Hadlow stepped into the room. Still in his mid-twenties, he might have been handsome once, but now his face showed the ravages of dissipation, his skin sallow and lined, eyes puffy.

He took a step and tripped on the threshold, grabbing the arm of a footman to stop himself falling. He glanced at the floor, then grinned and begged the servant's pardon.

"He's foxed," murmured Ella. She didn't sound surprised.

Mama said something in reply, but Catherine didn't hear it above the sudden drumming of blood racing past her ears. Her heartbeat quickened to a painful speed and she felt the color drain from her face. For there, in the middle of Lord Hadlow's companions, was Adam Mason. The man who, two years ago, had glared so contemptuously at her before storming out of her father's London house and slamming the door.

****

Adam was not surprised Hadlow had tripped over his own feet whilst trying to walk in a straight line. The wonder was the man had not fallen flat on his face before now. He had been drinking steadily all day, and had sunk enough brandy to fill a bathtub. He reeked of it, the sickly sweetness coating every breath until he threatened to inebriate everyone he talked to. His eyes were glassy, and he probably wouldn't have left the coach without falling into the ice-encrusted mud if Colbourne, in a manner that spoke of long experience, hadn't jumped out and stood ready to catch him. Freddy Finch had glanced at Adam, one eyebrow raised. Adam had shrugged his answer.

Perhaps they should have talked him out of attending the Potters' soiree, although he'd been determined to go. "Noblesse oblige and all that," he'd said, after Mr. Potter called to deliver his wife's invitation. "Got to do the pretty. Keep the neighbors sweet."

On top of which, Adam had his own reasons for wishing to attend. This soiree would shorten his job by weeks, allowing him to renew his acquaintance with Walter Ashton without arousing the man's suspicions.

He knew, of course, that at the same time as meeting the wealthy Cit, he would, in all likelihood, come face to face with the man's daughter. But far from seeing this as a problem, his superior at the Home Office thought it an advantage when Adam had tried to explain why he was not the right man for this job.

"Nonsense," Lord Fremont had said. "I can think of nobody better suited. Since you already know the family."

"She jilted me," Adam had pointed out, but he knew, even as he argued, this was a battle he had already lost.

"You had a lucky escape," said Fremont. "Besides,

you were merely a lieutenant then. Things will be different, now you have a title."

Adam didn't want things to be different because of his title. He had wanted Catherine to accept him for who he was—or rather, who he'd thought he was—not for the aristocrat he had unexpectedly become.

"If Walter Ashton isn't keen to renew your acquaintance now you are a baron," Fremont had continued in a breathtaking study in insensitivity, "you can renew your advances to the girl. No Cit's daughter will turn her nose up at the chance to become a lady."

Fremont clearly did not know Catherine Ashton. True, at the time of their courting he had been a nobody, with no fortune and no prospects, but Adam did not think the change in his circumstances would lead to a change in her mind.

In fact, seeing her now, staring at him across the crowded room, he knew it wouldn't. Her heart-shaped face was pale, none of the usual soft pink in her cheeks. Her pallor made her thick chestnut hair seem darker, and her eyes, those deep brown eyes a man could lose himself in, were wide with horror. Her back was unnaturally straight, her shoulders stiff. If Adam had harbored even the slightest hope that she'd be pleased to see him, it was now dashed on the rocks of reality.

Which did not bode well for his mission: to get close to her father and discover whether he was just a prolific smuggler or if he had also turned traitor.

****

Time seemed to slow as Catherine watched the four men enter. The sounds around her faded, and the people blurred and dimmed until there was only herself on one side and Adam on the other.

In some ways, he hadn't changed a jot in the two years since she had seen him last. He was still tall and lean hipped, his shoulders broad, although now they were encased in a dark evening coat rather than the scarlet dress uniform he had worn to such devastating effect in London. His hair, the color of ripe wheat, curled around his brow and touched his collar. His eyes were in shadow, although she remembered very well that they were the grey-blue of the sky on a misty winter's morning. His cheeks and jaw were well defined, his legs long and powerful.

He moved and she noted one difference about him; he no longer limped. The battle injury he had collected at Quatre Bras had obviously healed well.

But why was he here?

Somebody moved between them, breaking the spell. Time sped up again, and the room, the people, and the noise rushed back in. Mrs. Potter laughed nervously as the viscount righted himself, and told him that many people tripped over in that spot, and he might rest assured she would have it seen to forthwith. Beside her, Mr. Potter's face remained devoid of expression, though Lord Hadlow beamed, as if his hostess had just handed him the moon on a platter. Beside Catherine, Ella gave a longsuffering sigh.

Lord Hadlow swayed, and his friend, Mr. Colbourne, threaded his arm through the viscount's, lending him support. It was an innocent gesture, the sort of thing any man would do to help an unsteady friend, but it seemed out of place somehow, probably because Mr. Colbourne looked like the last person from whom one would expect it. He was a big man, not particularly tall, but broad, with a severe haircut and a nose that had been broken at least once and left misshapen. His shoulders strained the seams of his expensive coat as his meaty fingers gripped Lord Hadlow's arm tightly, and he led the viscount away from the crowds, toward a window alcove, where they spoke in agitated whispers. Catherine turned away, not wishing to be seen gawping at the spectacle of gentlemen making exhibitions of themselves in the polite room.

As she turned, her eyes met Adam's, and for an instant, he seemed to pull at her, holding her fast in his stare. His mouth was a thin line, his jaw stiff, managing to convey a wealth of hurt and anger. She shuddered and forced herself to look away, gazing instead on the man beside him.

She had met Mr. Finch a couple of times when she was in London. The second son of the Earl of Seaford and Adam's best friend, he had been charming and polite to her then, though she doubted he would think well of her now, after she had caused his friend pain.

The door closed behind the gentlemen, the shadowed movement catching Catherine's eye. She frowned as she realized all the newcomers had entered now. There was Lord Hadlow and his friend, Mr. Colbourne, Mr. Finch, and…

Baron Abberley? Adam was Baron Abberley? How could that be?

The Adam Mason she had known in 1816 was the son of a gentleman farmer. His father had not been poor, although neither had he been rich, and he certainly hadn't been a peer of the realm. Nor had there been the slightest hint that he had any expectation of ever becoming one. How then, could Adam have done so?

He had never mentioned any connections, as he

might have been expected to when talking to her father about his prospects. Not that it would have swayed Papa's opinion, but a hopeful suitor emphasized every advantage. Even had the connection been distant, surely someone would have mentioned it. In London, everyone knew everybody's family, going back three or four generations and several times removed.

Was he truly the baron he claimed? Or was this a fraud of some kind? If it was, it must be with the cooperation of Mr. Finch, for his close friend would surely know the truth. But then, the Mr. Finch she'd met in London was something of a prankster, so perhaps his approval of whatever was going on did not mean much.

But though Mr. Finch might have perpetrated such an outrageous fraud, Catherine was certain his quieter, steadier friend, Adam Mason, would not. He would no more have proclaimed himself a peer than he would have said he could fly. Adam was honest, honorable. An officer in the king's army and proud of it. Although, by the look of him, he was not in the army any longer.

Because now he was Baron Abberley?

Why would a man lay claim to a barony that wasn't his? What would be gained? Why would Adam and Mr. Finch engage in such a deception?

She told herself she didn't care. Whatever the truth of the matter, it was not her business and would not ever be, unless and until any of her friends looked to be in danger of being hurt. Deliberately, she turned her head, said something inane to Ella, and put Adam Mason from her mind.

Or, at least, she would have put him from her mind, had not Lord Hadlow shaken his arm from Mr. Colbourne's grasp and sauntered toward Catherine and her companions, a silly grin on his face. Behind him, Mr. Colbourne pursed his lips, though both Mr. Finch and Adam followed the viscount.

His lordship's grin widened as he called, "Ella Bella. You look ravishing."

Ella gave him a look of contempt. The noise level in the room dropped again. Adam and Mr. Finch exchanged uncertain glances, and Mr. Colbourne sighed.

Lord Hadlow executed an unsteady bow. "Ladies," he continued, "allow me to make my friends known to you." He bowed again and staggered as his balance shifted. "I say," he called out, "floor's dashed uneven in here, Potter. Need to get your builder back in to put it right."

He introduced his friends, all of whom bowed very properly to the ladies. Adam's eyes met Catherine's as he smiled and inclined his head. Catherine felt her cheeks heat. Her breath caught in her throat and her pulse skittered, jarring her.

"How are you, Ella Bella?" Lord Hadlow carried on, cheerfully.

Under her breath, Ella said, "Sober." Aloud, in a cool and disapproving tone, she answered, "Busy with my planting. Has yours begun, my lord?"

"No idea." Lord Hadlow waved his hand, dismissively. "Ask my steward. He'll know."

"You haven't got a steward," she replied.

Lord Hadlow smirked and opened his mouth, but before he could say anything, Mr. Colbourne took his arm again, excused them both to the ladies and steered the viscount back to the window.

"Delighted to see you again, Miss Forbes-Smythe," said Mr. Finch to Ella. "May I?" He pointed to an empty seat beside Ella. She inclined her head, and he sat, then engaged her in conversation. With a gesture and a questioning look, Adam followed suit and sat beside Catherine.

"Good evening, Miss Ashton," he said, softly, managing to move the chair close enough for intimate conversation, yet maintaining a respectable distance at the same time. "I hope you are well."

"I am, thank you. And you, sir?"

He inclined his head. "Never better."

She raised an eyebrow. That could not be true. If it was, he would not be here in Rotherton, hiding from his creditors. He looked around the room, as if searching for something further to say. A sadness welled within her, tightening her chest and making her throat heavy. Two years ago, they had never run short of conversation, finding pleasure in the smallest of exchanges, laughing at things nobody else would have understood, let alone found funny.

"Your parents?" he asked. "They are well?"

"Yes, they are. And…" She stopped before she could return the question. He had a title, which might mean his father had died. His mother had been dead before she met him and, to her knowledge, he had no other family.

"You are no longer in the army," she observed, looking to where his scarlet Regimentals had been replaced by a well-fitting, navy-blue tailcoat over a royal blue satin waistcoat that did nothing to hide the latent power in his body. Which she should not be noticing. At all. She cleared her throat and returned her attention to his face.

"Not for over a year now," he answered.

****

Adam grimaced as he said the words. Not for over a year. There had seemed little point in remaining a soldier. Napoleon had been defeated once and for all, exiled to St. Helena and guarded well so he could never escape again. That left serving soldiers with a stark choice. They could leave Europe for peacekeeping duties in more inhospitable climes, such as India or the Caribbean, or they could quell the growing unrest amongst factory workers calling for better pay and conditions, and deter men who wanted universal suffrage. Both were causes with which Adam had some sympathy and he did not relish the idea of putting them down. So he'd sold his commission and headed home, expecting to take up the life of a gentleman farmer. Only to have his entire world turned upside down.

He had never expected to become a baron. He didn't want the title now it was his. It called into question all he was, all he had known and believed and wanted, and left him confused and angry.

Ironically, two years ago, he would have given his eyeteeth to have it, for it might have meant Catherine's father looked on his suit with favor instead of contempt. The lady herself might have smiled at his proposal, instead of staring at him with such horror.

But then, it would not have been Adam she was accepting, would it? It would have been the prospect of being "Lady Catherine," of acceptance by the *ton* as one of their own, and of being the mother of a future lord. Adam, the man, would have been of no consequence.

All in all, he realized, Fremont was right. He had had a lucky escape.

Across the room, Catherine's father, Walter Ashton,

talked jovially with the other gentlemen. He turned his head and looked over at his daughter, saw Adam, and his smile died. His eyes narrowed, and his face showed contempt. Adam gave him the slightest nod, and Walter looked away, letting him know Adam's elevation did not signify with him.

But then, why would it? Ashton might want a title for his grandson, but he didn't want to pay too heavily for it. As far as that man knew, the newly minted Baron Abberley was wading through the deep waters of the River Tick, one step ahead of his creditors. Ashton would not want such a man for his daughter, unless and until Catherine was at her last prayers.

Of course, to some, that was exactly where she was. She was twenty-one, with two Seasons behind her. Her name had not been associated with any particular gentlemen, and there'd been no expectations of an announcement, although that didn't signify. The gossips hadn't known about the time he spent in her company, either. All-consuming though it had been to him, it meant nothing to anybody else.

Including the woman he now sat beside. The woman who watched him as if she expected him to speak. The same way the rest of the group watched him.

Freddy Finch arched an eyebrow in that annoying way of his. Clearly, someone had asked something while Adam was woolgathering, and now they awaited an answer. Which served him right for being rude enough to allow his attention to wander, but since castigating oneself did nobody any good, he stared at Freddy instead, willing him to rescue him.

"My friend is a very thoughtful man," said Freddy. A grin spread across his face. "He likes to think through every answer before he gives it."

If the company had not included ladies, Adam would have responded. As it was, all he could do was glare at Freddy. Beside him, Catherine sat demurely, hands folded in her lap and her eyes lowered. Adam wished she would look at him, smile, and show some interest in whatever he was going to say.

"It's not a bad thing to think before you speak," said Miss Forbes-Smythe.

"Be that as it may," Freddy answered, "he must give us his opinion of the late Miss Austen being identified by her brother as the writer of those wonderful novels."

Miss Austen? They were discussing the identification of a lady novelist? Aloud, Adam said, "I see no reason why a lady cannot write books as well as a man. Better than some men. But if Miss Austen did not wish to be known, her brother might have respected that."

"Mayhap he wished her to be recognized for her work," argued Miss Forbes-Smythe, leading them into a lively debate. Adam didn't take part. He wasn't listening to them. He was too busy watching Catherine. He could swear she had just given him a look of approval. The first he had seen from her in two years.

Chapter Two

Freddy and Adam spent the requisite amount of time with the ladies before moving on to other people. Their reception was mixed. Some, notably more mature ladies with unmarried daughters in their wake, were happy to meet a baron and the second son of a belted earl, no matter what their characters or the state of their finances. With breathless voices and nervous laughs, these ladies made them welcome and expressed hope of making their further acquaintance with much nodding of turbaned heads. Their husbands were less impressed, ranging from politely indifferent to downright hostile, depending on how much the gentleman thought buying the connections of these wastrels was likely to cost him.

Adam took a glass of wine from the tray of a passing footman and sipped at it while he pretended not to mind the looks of open contempt. These people's opinions should not matter to him; he was not here for them. His only reason for being here, both at this soiree and in Rotherton itself, was to renew his acquaintance with Walter Ashton. So he smiled politely at the others and inched ever closer to Catherine's father, although he also braced himself for a very definite rejection, if the glares of distaste being levelled at him by that man were any indication.

It looked as if Ashton would avoid him all evening, until the Earl of Rotherton came over and greeted Freddy like a long-lost brother. Rotherton was tall and lean and moved with a languid grace. Even his hair flopped lazily across his forehead, as if it was too much trouble to keep to his scalp. Yet, as he greeted Freddy and made his bow to Adam, there was no mistaking the keen intelligence behind his eyes.

"Abberley," he said. "From the Welsh Marches, is it not?" Adam cocked an eyebrow. It wasn't often he heard the area he hailed from referred to by its ancient name.

"It is in that vicinity," he agreed. "Worcestershire."

Rotherton nodded. "What brings you to Sussex?"

"Hadlow invited me, and I had nothing better to do." It was the answer he and Freddy had decided they would give to curious locals, and was accompanied by a lazy shrug of his shoulders. Rotherton nodded, but he didn't look fooled at all.

Surprisingly, he seemed to know Adam's destination, because he subtly steered him to the gentlemen conversing near the windows. Hadlow and Colbourne sat nearby. They still talked quietly, although Hadlow's body language was less belligerent and Colbourne seemed more relaxed. Unlike Walter Ashton, who tensed when Adam approached, straightening his spine so much it was a wonder it didn't snap.

A few weeks ago, Adam would have thought the man avoided him for purely personal reasons, that he was worried Adam might wish to renew his addresses to Catherine. He hoped that was still Ashton's reason, although now he was concerned there was more to it. If Ashton had the slightest inkling he was under observation, or that Adam worked for the Crown, he would make sure to keep his distance and the mission would be doomed.

Praying that wasn't the case, he followed Rotherton, who introduced him and Freddy to the gentlemen.

"We've met," growled Ashton.

Adam bowed his head in acknowledgement. "Mr. Ashton. I am glad to find you well."

"I didn't realize you had a title."

Would it have made a difference? Adam doubted it. Ashton had decided, two years ago, that Adam wasn't up to snuff, and a barony would never be enough to change the man's mind.

"I recently came into it," he said.

"You never mentioned you were even in line for it." Was it Adam's imagination, or did Ashton sound annoyed about that? Did he regret dismissing Adam's suit out of hand? Anger rose within him and he had to work to keep his expression neutral. Baron or not, he was the same man with the same feelings, and it was galling to know a title might somehow make him more desirable.

The really galling thing, though, was not Ashton's previous refusal of his suit. He understood completely that a man wished only the best for his daughter, and a soldier on half pay with no prospects to speak of was not what any father would consider the best. Adam could have worked to overcome Ashton's concerns, to show him that he could, and would, provide for his daughter, had that daughter not also rejected him out of hand.

He had been devastated by the look of horrified distaste on Catherine's face when she turned down his proposal, saying she had no interest in marrying a mere soldier, and if they could not remain as friends, it would be better to sever the relationship completely. He'd been unable to speak, unable even to breathe as she lifted her chin and stared squarely at him as if defying him to gainsay her.

Unable to do so, he'd done the only thing he was capable of doing in that moment. He'd turned on his heel and marched from the house, not waiting for the footman to open the door for him and taking a satisfaction he was not entirely proud of in slamming it shut behind him.

Adam remembered, all too well, the days after that, when he truly thought his heart would stop beating, so sharp and intense was the pain. As a soldier, he'd been in numerous battles, and injured more than once. But nothing, nothing, had ever compared to the wounds from his petticoat encounter.

And now, her father implied that his title might have spared him that? Well, if the minx was such a mercenary social climber, Fremont was right; he *had* had a lucky escape.

He wanted to curl his lip in open contempt of the title-chasing Cit. But he couldn't. There was far more at stake than his petty personal revenge. "I never expected to inherit," he said, in answer to Ashton's accusatory statement, and was amazed at the nonchalance in his tone. Perhaps he could do this after all.

"Oh?"

Before Adam could answer Ashton's curiosity, Mr. Potter joined the conversation. "Abberley," he mused. He rubbed his narrow chin with his thumb and forefinger, as if they might dislodge whatever it was that puzzled him. "Abberley," he repeated, then shook his head. "I seem to remember the name, though I'm da—" He shot a quick glance at where his wife now sat with two other ladies of mature years, "I'm dashed if I can think why." He watched Adam, clearly expecting him to remind him of what he had once heard. Something Adam would never willingly do.

Rotherton stepped into the conversation then, changing the subject and drawing the attention away from Adam and his title. "Anyone here heard anything about a boxing match at Offham?" the earl asked in his lazy, I-don't-really-care-but-I-must-ask voice.

"Offham?" asked Freddy.

"Near Lewes," supplied Mr. Potter. He turned to Rotherton. "I didn't know that was in your jurisdiction, my lord."

Rotherton sniffed. "Ordinarily, it isn't. But Lord Hamsey recently met with an accident and, until he recovers, I am holding the line. Which is all very well and good in the ordinary way of things, considering how tiny the villages are in that area. But just when one starts to think all will be well, one hears a rumor that someone's taken it into their head to set up a mill there. Outside the Blacksmith's Arms, if you please." He sighed in a longsuffering way. "I do wish people would refrain from such activities. I mean, I could ignore the actual fight, boys will be boys and all that, but one just knows it will inevitably lead to trouble, which will lead to arrests, and that's always such deuced hard work for me."

"A fight, did you say?" Hadlow joined the group, more sober now Colbourne had made him drink several cups of coffee. The idea of a prize fight animated him. "Where? When? Who is fighting and what are the odds?"

"Bertie," warned Rotherton, giving him a stern look.

Hadlow grinned and blinked slowly in an imitation of innocence. "I only asked."

"You only asked in the presence of the magistrate who is trying to find out about this fight for legal reasons.

Don't involve yourself, Bertie. I don't want to have to arrest you."

Hadlow grinned. "I wasn't planning to fight."

Rotherton gave him a sidelong look. "I shall pay my respects to the ladies," he said, and he moved away, then sat down next to Mrs. Potter, who gave him a frighteningly wide smile.

"He's such a stick-in-the-mud sometimes," complained Hadlow, sounding more like a recalcitrant child than a peer. Adam wanted to defend Rotherton. His father, or rather, the man he had thought was his father, had been friendly with the local magistrate, and Adam knew the man had had difficult decisions to make between upholding the law and allowing some leeway to people whose lives would otherwise be miserable and harsh. Doubtless, Rotherton walked the same fine line. However, such a defense would not be in keeping with the character of a devil-may-care wastrel, so he said nothing.

"You can't blame him," said Mr. Potter. "He can't condone boxing matches. They're illegal."

"Boxing is not, and never has been, illegal in England," pointed out Colbourne, who, with his misshapen nose and over-muscled build, looked as if he would know better than most.

"As a sport, no," said Mr. Potter, rather pompously. "But they don't encourage actual matches. And certainly not ones in the grounds of a tavern, where one might encounter any manner of riffraff."

Colbourne threw Potter a look of contempt, and Hadlow laughed. "Teaching your grandmother to suck eggs, Potter? I'll have you know, Alfie Colbourne here has forgotten more about boxing than you will likely ever know. Used to be one of the fancy, didn't you, Colbourne?"

Because he was watching Colbourne at that moment, Adam saw annoyance pass across his face. It was gone again in an instant.

Potter was intrigued. "You did? Perhaps you should accompany us, then. You can tell us about the fighters, give us pointers when it comes to laying down our blunt."

"Who are the contenders?" Colbourne's voice was soft, at odds with his bruising appearance.

"Tom Springson," answered Potter. "He is billed as the All-Sussex Bare-Knuckle Champion."

Colbourne nodded. "He's useful with his fists. Didn't know he was county champ."

"It's not an official title. Not like the All-England is."

"Who's his opponent?" asked Hadlow, eagerly.

Potter grinned. "Anyone who wants to be. Springson is being paid to take on all challengers. There's twenty guineas for anyone who can put him down for a count of five."

"Won't happen," said Ashton. "Springson's a scrapper. There's a good reason he's the champ."

"You could take him, Alfie." Hadlow smiled brightly.

"I'm retired."

"Wouldn't want to go up against Springson anyway." Potter grinned. "As Ashton says, he's a scrapper. Throws the hardest punch you can imagine. I've heard it described as being hit by a tree."

"Colbourne could beat him," insisted Hadlow. "Could you not?"

Colbourne gave a nonchalant shrug. Adam got the impression the man didn't care whether people thought he could do it or not. Which meant he probably could.

"Never beaten," continued Hadlow, determinedly. "In, what was it? Twenty-seven fights?"

"Twenty-eight. But I haven't fought a match in nigh on three years."

Hadlow waved a hand, dismissively. "Twenty guineas is a sizeable purse."

"I've earned bigger. But then, I've earned smaller, too."

"I have a splendid idea," said Hadlow. "A way for all of us to make a little blunt out of this."

Freddy groaned softly. Adam shared the sentiment. Bertie could no more resist wagering on something like this than he could resist taking a breath.

"Nobody knows Alfie in this area, do they?" he asked and Freddy groaned again. Hadlow either didn't hear him, or chose to ignore him. "So the odds against him beating the champ should be long. If we bet on him, and he wins, we all win."

Adam grimaced. A wager between gentlemen, for an amount a man could afford to lose, was all well and good. But this was different. Hadlow intended betting against working men, who could ill afford it, and whose women and children might well go hungry because they'd lost their wages to someone who was, in effect, cheating them.

"We could clean up," Hadlow finished.

"Or lose your shirt," warned Ashton.

Bertie tapped the side of his nose and gave a sly grin. "Won't happen. Trust me."

"I suppose it might be fun…" Potter's voice trailed

off. Adam glanced at him and saw he was looking at his wife, who sat on her sofa, her bright pink dress straining to contain her generous figure. She glared at her husband. Potter swallowed hard, and continued, "for some of you. But gambling, that sort of thing, it's not for me, you know." He smiled, sheepishly. His wife glowered at him for a few seconds more, then turned back to the conversation with those around her.

"I might attend," said Ashton. "If the weather's good."

"What about you two?" Hadlow turned to Freddy and Adam. "Finch? Abberley?"

It was a perfect opportunity for Adam to talk to local men in a setting where they would not be suspicious of him. And if Ashton was there, Adam could watch him, see who he met with.

"Why not?" He drained his drink, then turned to put down his glass. Which was when he saw Catherine. She stood a few feet away, her hand poised, ready to tap her father's arm to gain his attention. But the look of disgust on her exquisite features was aimed squarely at Adam.

****

Catherine could not believe what she had heard. These gentlemen—she used the term loosely—planned to wager on the outcome of a fight. They wished to amuse and enrich themselves on which of two men could damage, hurt, and perhaps even kill the other.

She knew little about prize fighting, only what she had overheard when local boys got together and, full of bravado, forgot to keep their voices down. They spoke of bare-knuckle fighting as "manly" and discussed things such as "drawing a man's cork," or "planting him a facer," and "giving their opponent a fiver." They talked of broken noses and cauliflower ears, and men knocked senseless. It all sounded barbaric to her.

It certainly was not a subject for gentlemen to discuss at a polite soiree, in company of their wives and daughters.

True, these men had not known Catherine was standing nearby. Mama had sent her to ask Papa if they could go home. Mama was never one to stay late at a party; in fact, given the choice, Catherine thought she would have been content to be at home, sitting quietly by her own fire, embroidering. Catherine suspected it was Mama's reluctance to socialize more than she had to that had caused Papa to say he would not fund another Season for his daughter.

Not that Catherine minded. Oh, unlike Mama, she had enjoyed the balls and soirees, musicales and theatre trips, the At-Homes and slow, meandering tours of Hyde Park in the fashionable hour. She missed the friends she had made and the fun of visiting the shops in Bond Street, whether actually spending money or just admiring the goods in the window displays. But she was also aware that the principal object of a young lady's Season was to find a husband, and where Catherine was concerned, that endeavor was doomed. There was only one man she had ever been interested in and, since she could not have him, she had no interest whatsoever in the business of marrying.

She'd had such high hopes and dreams at the start. She and Adam met at a card party a few weeks into the 1816 Season. He'd been dashing in his scarlet coat, a black sling encasing his arm, his right leg still a little stiff from where it had been broken under a dying horse in the final days of the war. He sat beside her, neither of them particularly interested in the games of whist and piquet going on around them, and they talked and laughed for hours, silly social chit-chat that meant nothing but which, to them, seemed as profound as any scientific lecture. Other people were there with them, of course, and doubtless joined in the conversation, but Catherine had no recollection of them. All those people, the music that was played, the cheers of winners and groans of losers at the various tables, the gossip and *on dit*, all were as inconsequential to her as mist, and as hard to remember the next day as a dream after you've woken from it.

That night, she lay in bed, staring into the darkness and replaying every moment she'd spent with the dashing soldier. She hugged herself tightly, a silly grin breaking across her face, the urge to squeal with delight almost overwhelming her. Nobody had ever made her feel the way Adam had. No one came close, not one of the gentlemen Mama put in her path, their manners pretty, their dancing elegant and their smiles full of practiced sincerity as they told her their well-rehearsed lies about her charm and her looks, when they really meant they liked her dowry.

Adam hadn't flattered her. He hadn't spouted dreadful poetry or paid homage to her eyes or struggled to compliment her hair. He'd spoken to *her*. He'd treated her as a person, someone who said things he was interested to hear, whose opinion mattered. By the time she fell asleep, she was in love.

For two months, all was wonderful. They met at events and entertainments, rode in an open carriage in Hyde Park, drank tea in Mama's sitting room, managing to speak privately even though they were surrounded by other callers.

And then had come that fateful night, at the Featherington's soiree.

Catherine attended with her mother, who hoped to put her in the way of some eligible bachelor or other, but the only person Catherine was truly aware of was Adam. By now, he no longer wore the sling, although the slight limp in his walk suggested his leg still gave him pain. All in all, however, he was recovered enough that he would soon re-join his regiment. The idea that he might be sent away from London, perhaps to France or Spain, or, God forbid, even farther, to the Caribbean, or even to India, caused a deep ache in Catherine's chest.

That was the night he kissed her.

They had found a small alcove, a place hidden from prying eyes but where they could still claim respectability. Both knew that, at any moment, someone might happen upon them and raise the hue and cry, demanding to know what they thought they were doing. In the moment, it didn't matter.

It was her first kiss, and it was everything she dreamed it would be. He stared at her for a long moment, his eyes darkening until they were almost black. All talk between them died. There was nothing to say. The room faded, the sounds of laughter and gaiety disappearing, the nearby people nothing more than a swirling mass of color that did not signify in any way. His gaze lowered until it rested on her lips. Instinctively, she licked them, just the tip of her tongue, moistening them before her top teeth caught the plump flesh of her lower lip, betraying her nerves. His eyes flared, and his hand caressed her cheek, his touch warm and gentle.

Catherine could not say if he pulled her nearer, or if she moved into him, but suddenly they stood so close that when she breathed, the front of her gown brushed against his woolen coat. She felt the heat of him, smelled the clean, fresh sandalwood of his cologne, the mint of his tooth powder mixed with the sweet fruit scent of the brandy he had drunk. His breath was slightly ragged, as was hers, and she saw the soft, rhythmic flutter of his pulse just above the collar of his uniform. He swallowed, his eyes moving from her lips to her eyes and back.

Then he kissed her.

His lips were warm and soft against hers, reassuringly gentle, yet thrillingly masculine. He tasted of brandy and the sugar-covered sweets the Featheringtons had served. His jaw was firm, his skin slightly rough, that of a man who spent time outdoors. His arms went around her, warm and strong, protective, and yet dangerous too.

She wrapped her arms around his shoulders, letting him know she welcomed his kiss, wanted it, wished it could go on forever. Of their own volition, her hands moved up, away from the strength of his back, over the column of his neck and into his hair. His lips curved against hers as he smiled, and a low growl worked its way up from his chest. He pulled her closer, closer, until she hardly knew where he began and she ended.

His lips left hers and she made a small moan of protest that turned halfway into a sigh of delight as he kissed her jaw, working his way up toward where her blood pulsed beneath her ear. It stuttered, its rhythm lost to the magic of his touch.

Suddenly, he pulled back and let her go. For an instant she stood there, her face raised to him, eyes closed, disappointment coursing through her. Her lips tingled. She wanted to cry out, to beg him to continue, to never stop.

The room returned, the noise, the people. Mr. Finch stood in front of her, half hiding her from everyone else at the soiree, talking loudly, his tone bright and jocular.

"Then he said, surely, he would have been better off to use a donkey." He laughed at his own punchline. Beside him, Adam laughed, too, before he turned his head and winked at Catherine. With a start, she realized what had happened and joined in, hoping the sound of her laughter was more convincing to other people than it was to herself.

Two ladies who had made their come-out alongside her approached. They bestowed upon the gentlemen smiles which were bright and eager, but which faded when they saw Catherine.

"Good evening, Mr. Finch, Lieutenant Mason…" said the taller of the two, her voice trailing off for an instant before she recovered. "Miss Ashton, I didn't see you there."

Catherine responded, they exchanged pleasantries, and the ladies moved on. Catherine sighed with relief. Her mind refused to work properly and all social small talk escaped her, because all she could think of was The Kiss. She fought the urge to bring her hand to her mouth, as if perhaps by touching her lips she could gather it, hold it close to her, stop it flying away into the evening.

When the ladies were out of earshot, Adam thanked Mr. Finch for his timely warning and Catherine blushed as she realized he, if nobody else, knew exactly what she and Adam had done. She couldn't meet his eyes when he bowed and said, "Your servant, Miss Ashton," before moving away and mingling with other guests in the suddenly stifling room.

"With your permission, I will call on your father in the morning," Adam said, and Catherine nodded before he bowed and moved away.

For the rest of that evening, Catherine floated on air. The world was brighter, its colors sharper. The perfume of the evening, a blending of the myriad scents worn by the ladies, and the intoxicating sweetness of the hothouse flowers arranged in vases around the room, was beautiful, clean and fresh, filling her with joy and hope.

And then, the carriage ride home. The consternation on Mama's face, the disappointment in Papa's eyes. It was not, they said, a match that could bring happiness, unequal as it was in every way. Over the slow hours of that interminable night, they persuaded her that Adam could never hope to provide the life Catherine was used to, and though she said now that it didn't matter, a few months of hardship and privation would certainly change her mind. Besides, what of Adam? If she loved him, would she want him to grow bitter and resentful, his pride and self-respect eaten away by the knowledge that, through her dowry, she was keeping him when it should be the other way around?

By the next morning, Catherine had accepted the folly of the match, and the fact that both would be happier in the end if it never took place.

Once that was agreed, Papa had one last suggestion. It was the one that nearly broke her.

"I could refuse him permission to court you," he said, his smile sad and sympathetic, "but he needs to break cleanly with you, to walk away rather than hanging around our door, hoping to change my mind, and causing you both undue suffering." She must refuse him, Papa had said. She must make him think she did not want his attentions, that they were no longer welcome.

It was the hardest thing she had ever done. Afterward, she'd lain on her bed, crying until her eyes were swollen and her head pounded with a sick ache. Mama had held her, crooning soft reassurances, until the storm subsided and Catherine was able to show her face again.

A week later, she heard Adam had sailed for the continent to rejoin his regiment. She re-took her place in society and, but for the hard, cold glances Mr. Finch gave her whenever their paths crossed, the entire thing might never have happened at all.

But happen it had, and it had colored her judgment so completely that no other gentleman could garner her interest at all. She danced when they asked, exchanged the requisite small talk, thanked them politely when they returned her to Mama's side. But the smile she gave them never reached her eyes, and soon they began calling her "the arctic Miss Ashton."

She hadn't cared. Their opinions meant less than nothing to her.

Now, two years later, here he was, and he wasn't at all like she'd thought he was. The decent and honorable officer she thought she knew was actually a rake, a gambler, and a wastrel who would happily wager on men being hurt. Worse, he would put his money on a man who was, to Catherine's way of thinking, entering the contest wearing false colors. Why, it was almost cheating!

It seemed her parents had been right to discourage a match with Adam after all, because Catherine could never be happy with a man who could behave in that despicable way.

Chapter Three

It was the early hours of the morning. Adam was getting ready for bed. The room he'd been given was sparse, with very little furniture to break up the space: a bed with an oak base and a mattress that sagged in the middle, covered by a royal blue counterpane above white cotton sheets that had seen better days. A small fire had been lit in the fireplace, but the room was much bigger than it could hope to warm, and the emptiness of the space, combined with the draught coming through the rotting, splintering window frames made what heat it generated struggle to make the slightest difference.

He took off his coat and unbuttoned his waistcoat, then unwound his cravat. Cold air touched his throat and he shivered. March it might be, but winter hadn't done with them yet. He hoped the snow that had plagued them in January and February was finished. It should be, especially here in the South. Sussex was not as warm as Adam might have liked it to be, but the weather here was certainly milder than it would be in Shropshire, where he had grown up, or Worcestershire, where he had his own seat.

Adam pulled his banyan over his shirt and stared out of the window at the grounds of Hadlow Hall. There was only a sliver of moon and its light was meager, but even so, he could see the tall grasses where most people had carefully manicured lawns. The graveled drive looked smooth and even in this light, though Adam knew it was rutted and holed, with clumps of grass growing between the stones and pebbles. When they had first arrived, he had maneuvered his horse along the drive carefully, thankful it was daylight and he could see the potholes before the animal put a foot into one of them. Tonight, in the carriage, they had been bounced about, thrown into each other, grunting at the discomfort and clinging for dear life to the leather grips on the carriage walls. Hadlow had said, without irony, that he must get the surface fixed, his tone altogether too cheerful, and not the least embarrassed by the ruin of his estate. Which was just as well, Adam supposed, because he knew, as they all did, that the viscount had no real intention of fixing anything; the man had neither the blunt to pay for repairs nor the desire to get them done.

As soon as he'd heard of the upcoming bare-knuckle fight at Offham, Hadlow's interest in Mrs. Potter's soiree had completely disappeared and he had made excuses for all of them to leave, so he could plot and plan his get-rich-quick scheme with the rather more reluctant but seemingly resigned Colbourne.

Adam would have liked to stay longer. He told himself it was so he might observe Ashton a little more, perhaps even encourage the man to talk with him. But, deep down, Adam knew it wasn't the real reason. The real reason had stood to one side, dark eyes flashing furious fire, lips pursed in distaste and disapproval of them all. He had longed to take her arm and lead her to a private corner where he could make her see he wasn't the reckless gambler he portrayed. Knowing he could not do so made his chest ache until he wanted to weep and wail and howl at the moon.

"When this is over," he muttered, then shook his head. When this was over, her father would likely be under arrest, and Catherine would hate Adam. He pressed his forehead against the windowpane and closed his eyes. The icy glass soothed as it cooled his skin, but at the same time, it sent a sharp pain through his head, like the pain he'd felt once when he'd eaten ice. He grimaced and pulled back, and after a moment the pain in his head subsided. The pain in his heart was not so easily remedied.

He must stop harking back to their time together in Town, stop torturing himself with thoughts of what might have been. What was done could not be undone. Besides, there was no reason to hold onto the hurt and regret, was there? It clearly hadn't been true love for, surely, God would not be so cruel as to inflict true love on one person when the other felt nothing. This was infatuation, not love, and infatuation was both temporary and survivable.

Things would improve now that he and Catherine had met again, for the first time since she'd rejected his proposal. A barrier had been breached. It stood to reason that, from now on, things would be easier. They could both go about their business as usual, unfazed by the other's presence, knowing they meant nothing to each other.

Although, if Adam proved instrumental in bringing her father to book for the crimes of smuggling and treason, he certainly would not mean nothing to Catherine. He would become the object of all her hatred.

The thought pained him, although not as much as the realization that, if Walter Ashton was convicted, his daughter would also be ruined. She would never be received anywhere, ever again. It wouldn't matter that she was innocent, had known nothing of what her father was doing. She would be guilty by association, and that would be that.

Of course, she had already had a small taste of ostracism from Society. As the daughter of a Cit, a tradesman who had been grudgingly admitted to the higher echelons because of his wealth, Catherine had never been universally accepted. Some of the highest sticklers in the *ton* had refused to have anything to do with her at all. It astounded Adam that people who thought themselves so much better than others could be so ill-mannered and lacking in basic decency. Those people, so high in the instep they were in danger of toppling over, had not accepted him, either. At least, they hadn't until they learned he was a baron. Even then, there were some who remembered the story of his parents and refused to acknowledge him. Adam found it difficult to care for their opinions. The Catherine he'd known two years ago would have felt the same way.

However, it was one thing to refuse to care that they cut you because your birth didn't measure up to their snobbish expectations. It was quite another to have them talking behind their hands because your father had been hanged for betraying his country. Absently, Adam, massaged his chest with the heel of his hand, trying to dull the pain. He wished with everything he had that Ashton could not be guilty of the crimes of which he was accused.

Why should he not be innocent? Adam straightened and stared out at the darkness, his thoughts whirling, desperately trying to make the circle into a square.

There was no ironclad guarantee that Walter Ashton

was the villain, was there? True, Adam's superior was convinced of it, but Lord Fremont had made his judgment on what was, at best, circumstantial evidence. It could be wrong. And if it was wrong…

Adam catalogued the evidence he'd been shown. Firstly, they knew someone in Sussex was controlling the plot to free Napoleon Bonaparte and reseat him on his throne. That person was using smuggling as a cover for his treasonous deeds, but according to Fremont, they had based their operation away from the actual coastline, working slightly inland instead. Which made sense. Things that happened on the coast attracted attention from the militia to such an extent that any plot would have been quickly discovered. On top of which, men taken in raids at the coast would give up information on larger crimes, if only to save themselves from the noose.

A few miles inland, things were not so frenetic, which was why the bulk of the smugglers' business was conducted as much as twenty-five miles from the sea. It was a well-organized operation. Once the goods were landed, Tubmen carried them away from the beaches to be stored in barns and stables, church crypts, and the Lord alone knew what else, until they could be sold and distributed. These Tubmen crossed the South Downs at night, secure in the knowledge that, once they quit the seaside areas, they were unlikely to be caught. There were just too many trails, too many ways a man could go, and never enough militia to find them.

It was reasonable to assume, then, that the head of the operation would also stay inland, leaving the risk of arrest to those lower down the order.

Adam knew Fremont's attention had been drawn to the area around Rotherton earlier in the year when a group of men attempted to assassinate both Lord Liverpool, the Prime Minister of England, and the Duc de Richelieu, the Prime Minister of France. That plot had been thwarted and the leader of the group, a man called Sykes, taken to London, where Fremont hoped to interrogate him and learn who gave him his orders. Alas, Sykes had died in mysterious circumstances before he could even think of giving up any information to them.

All Fremont knew was that the traitor was a man of some standing, wealthy enough that income from his lucrative smuggling activities would not raise questions, and he operated in or around Rotherton. More, his name began with an A but he was known to his cohorts as "the Miller." Ashton, who had made his fortune by building and operating textile mills, fitted all the criteria.

Which did not, in itself, make him their man.

Adam groaned. He was clutching at straw pieces here, he knew. Fremont was vastly more experienced in intelligence work than Adam, and had access to information Adam knew nothing of. If he was convinced of Ashton's guilt—and he was—he was probably right. Freddy, too, seemed to think Catherine's father was their villain. Adam's wish that it was otherwise did not make it so.

It was his duty to uncover the evidence that would put paid to the plot once and for all. A duty he would carry out or die in the trying. Even if it broke his heart.

He turned from the window and moved to his bed, shucked out of his banyan, then pulled it back on when he heard a light scratching on his door. It couldn't be a servant, since Hadlow kept none who lived in. The viscount employed people who came daily from the village to do whatever was necessary, and even then he could barely afford more than a couple of them. Adam had no servants of his own, partly to maintain the lie that he was as pockets-to-let as Hadlow, but mostly because he was used to fending for himself and saw no reason to change. Cautiously, he opened the door, then stood aside so Freddy could enter.

"Morning," whispered Freddy. "Fancy some company?"

Adam closed the door softly and moved to the dresser, where there was a bottle of brandy and some tumblers. He held up the bottle to ask if Freddy wanted some. Freddy nodded.

"Thought you were playing billiards with the others."

"I was," said Freddy. "I took a pony off Bertie in very short order." He shook his head. "The way he cannoned those balls around, I'm surprised the house is still standing. He managed to hit everything but the pockets."

"Has he been drinking again?"

"Does the sun rise in the morning?" Freddy sighed. "I called it quits at twenty-five pounds, though he wasn't happy with me for it. I'm surprised you didn't hear his complaints all the way up here." He mimicked Hadlow's petulant tone. "Bad show, Finch, old fellow. How's a man supposed to recoup his losses if you walk away?"

Adam chuckled. "Where is he now?" He had a vision of Hadlow taking off into the night, desperately searching for somewhere else to lose his money.

"Sleeping it off. Colbourne had to more or less carry him to his chamber, where now he lies, snoring loudly and building up to one beauty of a hangover in the morning."

"And Colbourne?"

"On the terrace, smoking a cheroot. He is not a happy man. In the billiards room, he left Hadlow in no doubt he was angry with him."

"Can't say I blame him. It was clear he didn't want to fight. Bertie more or less pressganged him. Hardly the behavior of a gentleman, was it?"

Freddy laughed. "Bertie is no gentleman. Never has been." He sauntered over to the window, gave the gardens a cursory glance, then turned and sat on the window ledge, his shoulders leaning against the glass. "On the other hand, God bless him, he's serving his country well, even if he doesn't know it."

That was true. If Bertie hadn't been short of funds and ready to leave London on a repairing lease, Adam and Freddy would have found it much harder to come to Rotherton and begin this investigation.

"I saw you talking with Ashton," said Freddy. "Did you manage to speak to him privately?"

Adam shook his head. "Only in the group, and only on the subject of the fight. Hardly what you would call an intimate conversation."

"He wasn't unfriendly, though?"

"He was polite and proper. But if his eyes had been pistols, I would be in my grave now."

Freddy frowned. "You don't have a quarrel with him that you didn't tell us about?"

"No." Adam shook his head. "There is nothing between us, other than that I am the man who thought himself worthy to court his daughter, and he is the gatekeeper who wouldn't allow me over the drawbridge." Adam's jaw clenched at the memory.

Two years ago, Walter Ashton had listened to

Adam's suit, his face polite, giving away nothing. After their interview, he had allowed Adam ten minutes with his daughter, alone and unchaperoned. Adam hadn't needed even five.

He had walked into the Ashtons' morning room, his heart beating eighteen to the dozen, mouth dry, the rehearsed words trying to slip out of his head. It had taken everything he had to get them spoken without sounding like an incoherent fool.

Only to be shot down by Catherine.

"She is beautiful," said Freddy, now. "Back then, her father would have had higher hopes for her than a half-pay soldier."

Adam gritted his teeth and pushed back the hurt. "Yes."

"Of course, you're a peer now, with more than a decent income."

That should not matter. And besides, "Ashton doesn't know that."

"But he does have to consider his options. Her options. Which are more limited now. She is practically on the shelf."

Adam glared at Freddy. He didn't say anything, partly because there was nothing to say and partly because he didn't trust himself to be civil. Catherine had hurt him, he couldn't deny that. And it was true that two Seasons and no meaningful offers did not improve her prospects, but Freddy did not need to point that out.

Freddy saw the look Adam gave him. "My observation offends your sensibilities." He sighed and moved away from the window. "I appreciate you once cared for her, but…we need to get closer to Ashton, Adam. By any means possible. You must see, his daughter is a perfect way of doing that." Freddy stared steadily at Adam, daring him to disagree.

A long half minute passed. Then Adam stood and went to the dresser to refill his glass. He sipped at the brandy before saying, softly, "it seems wrong, Freddy. This…" he waved his free hand through the air, "I know what you and Fremont think. I appreciate you both have a wealth of experience in this work, while I am very much the novice, but I cannot like it. Whatever her father may have done, the lady herself is innocent. It seems wrong to… It's not the action of a gentleman."

"Ours is not a work which can always be gentlemanly," answered Freddy. He sat on the edge of the bed and the mattress shifted, lifting up on the far side. "I do understand your reticence, my friend. If you wish to walk away from this assignment, I will completely understand."

"Then what?"

"You can return to London and someone else will take your place." He grinned. "Me, for example."

"You?" Adam almost shouted the word. He grimaced, then repeated it, more quietly but still just as filled with outrage and shock. "You?"

"Why not? I don't have a personal history with the lady to make me uncomfortable. And, according to my father, I am no gentleman, so that would not signify, either. I'd be happy to do it."

Adam tensed. His jaw clenched tight and his shoulders hunched, setting off a headache. His cheeks heated, letting him know his color was up, but when he spoke his voice was soft and low, his tone dangerously even. "You will leave her alone."

Freddy nodded. "As you wish."

"I will do my job. Nobody need do it for me."

Freddy watched him for a moment, then wished him goodnight and slipped out of the room.

Chapter Four

Catherine and Mama were already at the breakfast table when Papa strode in, his face full of thunder, anger in every swing of his arms and every click of his boot heels against the polished wood floor. He had clearly been out for his morning ride, for he wore his riding clothes, and his cheeks were red where the wind had chapped them. It boded ill indeed if he was in a black mood after a gallop across his lands, for such exercise almost always put him in the best of humors.

A footman stepped forward to offer him coffee and was waved away, impatiently. Seeing his master's mood, the servant had the good sense to place the coffeepot on the table before bowing and making himself scarce. Catherine wished she could do the same.

"Oh, dear," murmured Mama. Louder, she said, "Good morning, my dear. Did you enjoy your ride?"

"I did." Papa did not sound as if he meant it.

"Where did you go?"

Papa waved his hand through the air, as if to say it was of no consequence, picked up a slab of bread and slathered butter onto it. He stabbed the butter knife back into the pat of butter. Mama winced, reached over and pulled the knife out, wiped the blade across the top of the pat to clear it of excess butter, then carefully and quietly laid it onto the dish. Catherine lowered her gaze to her plate and concentrated on her own bread and jam.

When she looked up again, Papa was staring at her intently, as if she were a specimen he must study. She glanced at Mama, who shrugged an I-don't-know at her. Trying not to let her consternation show in her expression, Catherine quickly thought through the last day, trying to remember having done something that might have made him angry. Nothing came to mind. She took another bite of bread and waited for him to talk about whatever had put him in such a mood. Mama poured herself another dish of tea and sipped at it slowly, obviously doing the same thing.

They did not have long to wait. After a few seconds, Papa put his elbows on the table and rested his chin on his fist. Through gritted teeth, he asked, "Did you know that…that…*upstart*…would be at the Potters' last night?"

Catherine chewed slowly and pondered how best to answer. She was tempted to adopt an expression of dumb innocence and pretend she didn't know who the "upstart" was, but such disingenuousness would only serve to make Papa even more angry, and neither she nor Mama would want that.

She should, she supposed, simply give him the truth, that she had had no more warning of Adam's arrival than anyone else, but if she did that, it would permit him to insult Adam when he had done nothing to warrant it. Papa was being rude and Catherine was not inclined to join him in it.

"Forgive me," growled Papa. "That was a stupid question. Of course you didn't know he was coming. How could you have known?"

"You should eat before everything is too cold, dear," said Mama. She sat in a relaxed manner, her expression nonchalant.

Papa narrowed his eyes at her. "I suppose the Potter woman did not think to warn you either?"

"Why would she?"

That was a perfectly reasonable question, Catherine thought. With the exception of Adam's particular friend, Mr. Finch, nobody outside the family had any idea that she and Adam had once harbored hopes of anything other than friendship.

Papa grumbled something under his breath. Catherine picked up the teapot and poured herself a second cup of tea. She kept her movements light and relaxed, although light and relaxed were the last things she felt.

Ever since she'd seen him across the room last night, she'd been unable to purge Adam from her thoughts. She'd taken in every detail of his appearance, searching for differences in his looks and wondering what those differences might mean. His hair was a shade longer than she remembered—did that mean he was not taking care of his appearance? His gray eyes, which had once sparked with natural and ready humor, seemed more serious now, and the skin beneath them was darker, suggesting he sometimes didn't get enough sleep, although it was not so dark she would think he never slept at all. Was it the worry of gambling losses that kept him awake at night? Or had he been restless because he anticipated seeing her again? He must have known the chances of them meeting would be high, for Society here was limited, and everyone could be expected to attend every gathering.

Did she want him to have been anxious about their meeting? On the one hand, it might mean he still thought of her and cared for her opinion. Then again, after the way they had parted, perhaps he viewed her with contempt, and any concern he'd had over it was because he was still angry.

He had sat next to her and engaged her in polite, albeit stilted, conversation. But then, he'd had no choice really, after Mr. Finch paid attention to Ella. If Adam had ignored Catherine, it would have been noted, and the reputations of both of them would have suffered.

There had been a time when she knew exactly what he was thinking, how he felt, what he would do next. If only she still possessed that power! Last night, it was as if he had hidden himself behind a curtain and she had no way of drawing it back.

"What do you mean, why would she?" Papa responded testily to Mama's question, pulling Catherine's attention back to the here and now. "You ladies tell each other everything, do you not?"

Mama rolled her eyes. "Not everything."

"Don't be absurd," Papa argued. "You know as well as I, if a man wishes to know what is happening to his neighbors, he must ask his wife."

Mama fixed him with a deadly glare. "One thing is certain, Mr. Ashton," she said, and Catherine winced. If he was "Mr. Ashton," he was in trouble. "You need not worry that you will learn anything from this wife. If you have finished breaking your fast, Catherine, perhaps you might wish to accompany me into Tunbridge Wells? I feel the need for rather more shops than Rotherton can supply." She wiped her mouth on her napkin and stood. She truly was upset. She only needed to shop when she needed to let Papa know he had gone too far.

"Just a minute," protested Papa. "We haven't

finished our conversation."

"Is that what we were having?"

He sighed. "I apologize. I spoke—unwisely." Mama raised an eyebrow. "Of course I did not mean to imply all wives are gossips." She glared at him, and he winced. "My annoyance got the better of me."

"I could tell."

"Please, sit down, my sweet."

Catherine lowered her head and concentrated on keeping the grin from her face. Mama gave Papa one last dark look, ensuring he definitely knew who had won this little spat, then she sat down.

"Mrs. Potter mentioned her husband had called upon Lord Hadlow," she said, as if their previous conversation had not been interrupted. "She said his lordship agreed to come to her soiree and he would bring his guests."

Papa held up the teapot, silently asking her if she would like more tea. She nodded, and he poured some into her dish. He made the same offer to Catherine, who shook her head.

"The guests would include Mr. Colbourne. That was a given, since he always comes with Lord Hadlow when he visits his estate. They seem inseparable, do they not? Although, they are nothing alike. Hadlow is all 'hail fellow well met,' and 'call me Bertie,' whereas Mr. Colbourne…" She shuddered. "There is something about him… I don't say he's not a gentleman or anything like that, but I cannot warm to him."

"Quite so," said Papa. He smiled, but it did not reach his eyes. "Mrs. Potter had told you Colbourne would be there. Did she mention anybody else by name?"

Catherine was shocked at the implication in Papa's question. Did he really believe Mama would have withheld the news that Adam Mason was in the area and likely to be at the soiree, had she known it herself? She knew all that had happened two years ago, and she might know Papa would be angry and Catherine embarrassed.

"She did," said Mama. Catherine gasped. Her own mother had led her into an ambush? Why would she do such a thing? Mama sipped her tea, then continued, "She mentioned Mr. Finch who, let's face it, is not a surprising addition to the party. The man's good for nothing at all, really. Spends his time and money on the most regrettable pastimes. Even his own father despairs of him, or so the *ton* would have it." She smiled at Catherine. "An earl's son he may be, but that is one member of an aristocratic family I would *not* want showing an interest in you."

"Catherine is far too sensible to find herself linked with that scoundrel," said Papa, and his testiness crept back into his tone. "What of Mason?"

Mama shook her head. "She made no mention of Mr. Mason. She did say Baron Abberley was the final member of the party, but I was not to know that he and Mr. Mason were one and the same person, was I? Rest assured, if I'd had the first idea of it, I would have said something to you."

Papa massaged his forehead with his fingers. "You did not know it was him," he muttered.

"I have just said so."

"Mrs. Potter likely didn't know either," he continued, more to himself than to his wife and daughter. "And even if she had known his given name, she would have no reason to link Adam Mason with Catherine. She knows nothing of their unfortunate history." His head snapped up, his eyes narrowed. "But *he* knew." He slammed his fist on the table, making the crockery rattle and causing both Catherine and her mother to jump visibly. "*He* knew."

Mama gave Papa a look that said she thought his wits had deserted him. "Of course he knew. How could he not know? He was one of the principal players."

"That's not what I meant." Papa waved his hand, as if to erase her confusion. "He knew we lived in this neighborhood. He knew, or, at least, he should have suspected, we would be in attendance last night." He turned to Catherine. "Am I not right? He knew this is where we hail from?"

Catherine tried to remember if they had discussed such things. She'd known he hailed from Shropshire, where his father had a farm, but she didn't think he'd told her the name of the village, or even the nearest town. Likewise, she had said she lived in Sussex, but little else about her home. Their time together had been too precious to waste it on such inconsequential details.

"I don't think so," she said at last. "I am certain he would not have deliberately sought me out." *Not after the way I rejected him.*

"You see," said Mama. "That he should turn up here with Lord Hadlow, it's just coincidence."

"I don't believe in coincidence." Papa sounded churlish now.

"Oh, for goodness' sake. The man was invited by Lord Hadlow. It is hardly his fault his friend lives close to us."

"Of all the places he could have gone, all the people who would welcome him, he chose our neighbor?" Papa shook his head. "No. That is one step too far for me." Mama raised a disbelieving eyebrow, and Catherine blinked, slowly. Papa firmed his jaw in his most mulish expression. "I tell you, he planned it. His presence here is not random chance."

Mama nodded. "Yes, dear."

Papa narrowed his eyes at her. "He will bring shame on us." He shook his head in despair. "I thought we had seen the last of that worthless guttersnipe."

Hearing Adam described in such a derogatory way made Catherine wince.

"You cannot call him a guttersnipe when he outranks you." Mama took a piece of plum cake and concentrated on cutting it into tiny portions as she spoke, so she did not see the frustrated way Papa pursed his lips. "He is now a baron," she said. "A member of the House of Lords."

"I know." Said through gritted teeth as Papa glowered at Mama. Catherine wondered if she should get up and leave the room before they began to argue in earnest, then decided it was probably more prudent to stay where she was and not draw attention to herself.

"I don't think you may call a member of the nobility a guttersnipe," continued Mama. "It's probably a hanging offense." She grinned and held up a tiny piece of her cake. "Imagine that. Lieutenant Mason, a member of the Upper House."

Papa's lips curled into a sneer. Catherine closed her eyes and wished Mama would change the subject. Mama nibbled at the cake. "I wonder if he has voted on any of the laws affecting us," she said.

"Bills." Papa growled the word. Mama blinked and looked blankly at him, and he gave her his most supercilious smile. "The Members vote on bills, which then become laws."

"There is no need to be pedantic. And my point still stands. When you see him again, you will have to call him, 'my lord.' "

Papa's face darkened, and his eyes glittered. Mama ate her cake and contrived to look wonderfully innocent, while Catherine wished she wouldn't tease him. Papa's sense of humor was not as strong as Mama's at the best of times, but when it came to the subject of Adam Mason—*Baron Abberley*, she corrected herself, with a mental click of her tongue—Papa would see no humor at all.

Catherine did understand his feelings, to an extent. When he launched her into Society, he'd had high hopes of a good match. A half-pay soldier was not what he'd envisaged at all. Neither would he be happy with a lord of the realm who had no money and a penchant for gambling that made it necessary for him to take to the country on a repairing lease before the new Season had really begun.

However, she did have to wonder why Adam's presence made Papa as angry as it had. He had no cause for concern that she could see. After all, she had rejected the man, and left him in no doubt she would never encourage him to renew his suit. At the time, it had broken her heart to do so, but now she knew how he had fared since leaving the army, had seen for herself the man he had become, she knew she had made the right decision.

"You show respect to Lord Hadlow, or a dozen other wastrels with titles," Mama pointed out. "You must do the same with him, now he, too, is a lord."

"Ha!" Papa pointed an aggressive finger at her. "You only have his word for that. For all we know, this is nothing more than a Banbury tale concocted by Mason for his own nefarious purposes."

"Lord Hadlow believes him. He wouldn't have invited him if he didn't."

Papa snorted his derision. "Hadlow is a sot. He'd believe anything anybody said if they bought him a drink. Look at how he was last night. Completely under the weather before he even arrived at the Potters'." He took a deep breath to calm himself. "I remain unconvinced that he truly is a peer."

"He must be, dear," Mama said, her voice too sweet. Catherine rolled her eyes again and sipped her cooling tea. It seemed her parents were determined to fight this one to the bitter end. "There is no doubt," continued Mama, still in that sickly sweet tone. "He has a coronet with sixteen pearls on it, and a robe with a miniver cape. I saw it once, when—"

"You know very well I do not mean Lord Hadlow," bellowed Papa. "I *know* he's a viscount. I'm speaking of Mason." He hammered the table with his forefinger several times, emphasizing his point. "How do we know he is a baron? How do we know the barony even exists? I certainly never met any previous Lord Abberley."

"Both Mr. Potter and Lord Rotherton said they had heard of him."

"If the title exists, it doesn't mean it's his. Any Tom, Dick, or Francis can claim a title. But how do we know the Privileges Committee have even seen his claim, let alone agreed it?"

Catherine stared at her father in disbelief. Had he just accused Adam of lying about his title? Catherine herself had been surprised at his elevation, that was true, but she had never seriously questioned the veracity of his claim. There had been a moment last night when, in her shock, she had wondered about it, but she had immediately discounted any suspicion. Adam was an honest, honorable man, and she could not imagine him lying about such a thing.

"Let's examine the facts," said Papa, counting off the reasons for doubt on his calloused fingers. "Lieutenant Mason, as we knew him, was an officer in His Majesty's army. Now, I don't doubt he did his duty and acquitted himself well then, for was he not wounded at— Where was it? Waterloo?"

"Quatre Bras," said Catherine, quietly.

"Thanks to those injuries, two years ago, he was kicking his heels in London and, with Napoleon on his way to St Helena, he was, like every other officer in the town, surviving on half pay. He had no prospects whatsoever. The man did not even have the money to buy himself a captaincy, let alone anything else."

"One cannot buy a barony," argued Mama.

"One can't inherit it, willy-nilly, either. Mason was a nobody. Son of a nobody. His father was a gentleman farmer in—Shropshire, wasn't it?" He glanced at Catherine for confirmation. She nodded faintly, then looked away. Somehow, verifying Papa's summary of his family and his expectations seemed disloyal to Adam. Which was absurd. She owed the man no loyalty, so there was no need to feel guilty. Her duty was to her father and nobody else. Telling herself that did not make her feel better, though.

"A farmer from Shropshire," continued Papa. "Gentry, perhaps, but nothing more. Then, suddenly, the man is a lord?" He barked a short laugh. "If you believe that, please feel free to bid on the goods in my Puffer's auction."

"Walter Ashton! In front of Catherine." Mama gestured with a nod of her head and a wink of her eye that she did not want such things mentioned in front of her daughter. Although, Catherine thought, there was no need to worry about corrupting an innocent mind. Catherine was well aware of the Puffers in London, who enticed the gullible and the greedy to part with their cash by setting up legitimate-looking auction houses and tempting them to bid on lots being sold at extraordinarily low prices. It was only after parting with their cash that the buyers learned the goods they'd bid on either did not exist or they were not being sold by their true owners. By that time, of course, the auction house, the sellers, and the dupe's money had disappeared. Catherine had learned of the practice when one of the girls who'd made her come-out with her had been forced to go home suddenly, after her brother lost his entire fortune to the Puffers.

"My apologies, madam," said Papa, insincerely, paying lip service to Mama's objections. "The fact remains, Mason's sudden elevation is suspicious, to say the least. Had you even heard of a Baron Abberley before now?"

Mama grimaced. "No."

"Precisely." Papa grinned, triumphantly.

"I heard the previous baron was a recluse," said Catherine, before she could stop herself. Papa glared at her. Her cheeks heated and the hairs at the top of her forehead prickled, letting her know her blush was widespread, and very bright.

"How very convenient." Papa's voice was low and steady. He had not appreciated her interjection. She lowered her eyes and wished she had said nothing.

After a few moments during which she could feel his eyes on her, his gaze as sharp as sticks poking at her, he sniffed and turned back to Mama. "As I was saying," he held up his hand again, "his father was a nobody, who did not have a title to hand down." He folded one finger into his palm. "Nobody knows of the previous baron because he was, supposedly, a recluse." He folded a second finger. "I spend a lot of time in the city, in company with men who make it their business to know everybody else's. Their continued prosperity relies on them knowing what's what. Yet I have heard nary a whisper about a new Baron Abberley." He folded his thumb across the bent fingers, holding them in place and denoting his third point was made.

"I find it hard to believe that a man can lay claim to a title that isn't his." Mama frowned at Papa. "Surely, checks are made on such things?"

"Of course they are." Papa sighed, irritated, and looked away from his wife and out the breakfast room window. His demeanor suggested he was silently counting to ten and praying for patience. Careful not to react, not wishing either parent to believe she took the other's part, Catherine followed his lead and gazed out of the window herself. It was a sunny day, although the grass on the lawn still showed patches of white where the frost had lingered. Bare trees ringed the gardens, their branches and twigs a dark tangle against the bright sky. Here and there, clumps of mistletoe hung, huge untidy cankers. A magpie glided across the garden and landed in a tree, his feathers stark black and white. In her head, Catherine gave compliments to the bird's wife, as her nursery nurse had taught her to do.

Papa turned back to the table, his voice calmer, his tone less belligerent. "Certainly, there are checks and balances," he said. "The entire fabric of the country would disintegrate if there were not. But these checks can only be brought to bear if they are invoked." He leaned forward and pointed his forefinger at Mama, emphasizing his point. "What if the man did not approach the Privileges Committee for verification of his claim? Or, what if he did and they denied him? How should we, here in Rotherton, know of that?"

"We are but fifty miles from London—"

"We may as well be five thousand miles away at times. The *Times*, when it reaches me, is already two days old. The latest *on dit* is no longer the latest by the time we hear of it. And if a man wished to hide something from his neighbors, well, he would have more chance of success here than he would have in London. Under the circumstances, what is to prevent a man who is not a peer in London from coming into this neighborhood and announcing he is Lord this or Baron that?"

Shocked, Catherine could not hold her tongue. "I cannot believe Ad—Lieutenant Mason would do any such thing!"

"And if he would, we are not bumpkins to be easily gulled," added Mama. Her eyes narrowed and her jaw tightened, her fury at the perceived insult plain.

"I did not say you were," Papa told her, and he gave her a mollifying smile. "Although you will surely own that there are some within our acquaintance who might be fooled?"

"Lieutenant Mason is an officer and a gentleman," insisted Catherine. She no longer cared if Papa grew angry with her for defending the man. He did not deserve to be maligned in this way. "He would not lie about such a thing, of that I am certain."

Both her parents studied her far too closely now. She felt her color rise again, and her mouth dried so that when she swallowed, her throat was dry and painful. She looked down at her empty plate, placed her hands demurely in her lap and waited for Papa to scold her for her impertinence. Although, she decided, whatever he had to say about her outburst, she would not apologize for it. She believed wholeheartedly in what she had said, and she would say it again, unless and until Adam proved her faith in him unfounded.

But Papa did not scold her. Instead, he walked to the window, where he stood, hands clasped behind his back, his attention on the winter garden. "Mayhap he is, in truth, a baron," he conceded, at last. He turned back to his family. "If he is, it still does not make him a better man."

"No," agreed Catherine, carefully. "But it does make him a truthful one."

"Nonetheless, I say he is not to be trusted. Oh, don't give me that look of outrage, miss," he said as Catherine opened her mouth to argue more. She shut it again as he went on. "You must know I am right. One has only to look at the company he keeps to see he is not out of the top drawer."

"He's a guest of Lord Hadlow," began Mama.

Papa swiped a hand through the air, cutting off her words symbolically as he spoke over them. "Hadlow is usually found in his cups, deep in debt, and wagering his last farthing on which raindrop will roll faster down a windowpane, or something equally stupid, while

Mason's friend, Finch, is a wastrel of the first order. An earl may have sired him, but he lived to regret it. Rumor has it he cut the lad off without a penny, and not before time, if you ask me." He strode back and forth along the length of the table, much as Catherine imagined a naval captain would pace his poop deck. "I grant you, the other man with them, Colbourne, has displayed better manners than either of those two members of the nobility, but really, saying that is damning him with faint praise. And what's more, Colbourne is not, and never has been, a gentleman."

"Not a gentleman?" exclaimed Mama. "He is a friend of Lord Hadlow."

Papa rolled his eyes and muttered something that sounded to Catherine like, "Give me strength." He smiled at his wife and said, "I hesitate to tell you this. It is not really the sort of thing one discusses with ladies, but, well, needs must, I suppose."

By which, Catherine took him to mean that Mama would not be satisfied until he had explained what he meant.

"Reference was made last night," continued Papa, "to the way Colbourne made his money and managed to rise through the ranks of society." He looked around as if frightened that eavesdroppers lurked in the corners of the room, lowered his voice, and said, "Prize fighting."

Mama gasped and covered her mouth with her fingers. Having been near enough to hear the conversation last night, Catherine was not shocked, or even surprised, by her father's revelation.

"My point is," said Papa, and he returned to his pacing, "a man is known by the company he keeps, and look at Mason's, or Abberley's, or whatever he calls himself. His friends are a drunk, a rake, and a man who fought for money. All of them now intent on wagering money they do not have, on the outcome of a fight between Colbourne and some other uncouth ruffian! Throwing good money away like it was nothing! It is simply not to be borne!"

On this point, Catherine and Papa were in complete agreement, though she suspected their reasons were different. Papa was fond of telling her and Mama, usually when denying them the funds to buy something outrageous, that he had started with nothing and made his way from there through hard work, determination, and judicial spending. He looked positively nauseous whenever he heard of money being frittered away.

Unlike him, Catherine had never had to struggle with economic hardship, but she abhorred the waste, all the same. She had seen the poor in London, and even here in Rotherton she saw people breaking their backs for pennies, their faces pinched, cheeks hollow, starving themselves so their children might eat. She had seen, too, the old soldiers, their uniforms tattered, eyes glazed with lack of hope. Some missed limbs, others wheezed and coughed.

Those men struggled while their former colleague wagered on which of two men could land the nastiest blow upon the other. Not only that, but he and his friends were not content with beggaring each other, and planned to take money, unfairly, from people who had very little to start with.

Yes, Catherine knew that many of those people would wager on the fight, with or without Adam and the other so-called gentlemen. If they lost their shirts, they really had only themselves to blame. But that did not mean Adam and the others were exonerated. For sport, they planned to take every penny the working men had, and they didn't care that wives and children would go hungry.

The thought sickened Catherine. That Adam would take part in such an act hurt and distressed her, more even than being persuaded to refuse to marry him had done.

"No," said Papa, and he curled his lip in disdain, "those…gentlemen are not an asset to the neighborhood. I, for one, will be glad when they quit the place and return to their careers as rakes and reprobates in London. Until they do, though," he turned to Catherine, "you are not to leave this house unaccompanied, do you hear? You will take a maid *and* a footman with you at all times. I will not be able to rest easy if you are unprotected."

"Yes, Papa," said Catherine, meekly. After all, what else could she say?

Chapter Five

Catherine walked into Rotherton accompanied by her maid and a footman, as Papa had ordered. The air was cold and crisp, with a nip that made her nose tingle and her eyes water, and her breath formed small white puffs in front of her.

The puddles in the lane were frozen, and mud ruts, formed by carts and pony traps, were solid. Either side of the lane, small fields were dotted with sheep, fat with fleece and lamb, while shepherds worked to clear ice from water troughs, or to spread winter feed for their flocks. Small copses broke up the landscape, many of the trees bare, although here and there were evergreens, dark and lush against the starkness of the winter countryside. Long threads of old bramble tangled at the tree bases, and here and there, dark green ivy enveloped the trunk of an older tree. Dry stone walls separated the fields from the lane, broken every now and then by a five-bar gate or an occasional stile.

Nearer to the village, the fields gave way to houses, large homes at first, set in well maintained gardens, then smaller cottages in rows of three and four where children played in tiny front gardens and waved at Catherine as she passed. She smiled and waved back.

Her maid, Mary Ann, and the footman, Peter, walked a few feet behind her. They did their duty, giving her countenance and providing protection, which seemed absurd in a place where she had always felt safe, but Papa's orders must be obeyed, or he might forbid her to go out at all.

If Peter had not been there, she might have found the walk more enjoyable. Mary Ann was the same age as Catherine, and she was usually happy to walk beside her mistress, chattering and laughing with her in a familiar way that made the housekeeper frown. Today, however, Mary Ann spoke with Peter, and Catherine was left with her own company.

She grimaced, annoyed at herself. It really was too bad of her to feel envy for servants, who worked long hours, constantly at the beck and call of their masters. "You are an ungrateful wretch," she muttered, "if you begrudge them this." She walked on, determined to enjoy her outing and planning which shops she would visit.

At the start of the High Street, Catherine stopped and waited while a swineherd encouraged half a dozen pigs across the road and into a pen beside the butcher's shop. A cart rattled by, its bed loaded with manure, the sickly sweet scent of it rising on steam. Two men in laborer's clothing stamped their feet and blew on their cupped hands while they talked amiably to a stout, older man in a good quality coat, a woolen muffler wrapped around his throat.

Seeing him brought Adam Mason to mind. His father was a farmer, just like that man, or rather, he had been. For Adam to have come into the title, she assumed his father must have died. Once again, she wondered why Adam had never made mention of the title before. Even if the previous baron had been a more distant relative, surely he would have mentioned the connection to the father of a woman he hoped to marry.

Perhaps Papa was right: Adam had never mentioned the connection because it did not truly exist. Papa was a shrewd man. He was successful because he saw behind the facades of other men, and it helped him make astute decisions. If he thought Adam was a fake, it might be true.

Her mind went back and forth on the question as she walked. Adam was an honorable man who would never pretend a title. But then, why had he not mentioned it? Had he not known about it? How could that be? A man would know if his family included a peer. Unless, of course, it didn't, and he had invented the connection. But then, Adam would never do that. He was an honorable man. And so the thoughts went round again.

By the time she reached the village center, Catherine's head swam, and the only conclusion she had been able to come to was that if she wanted an answer, she might have to ask Adam herself.

She could imagine how that conversation would go. One could not just approach a gentleman and ask him, "Are you truly a baron, or have you lied to us?" and expect him to answer in a mild, good-natured way. But how else was she to discover what she needed to know?

The answer came in a flash of inspiration. In Papa's study, she was sure she had seen a copy of *Debrett's Peerage*. It was an elderly copy, of course. Like most of Papa's books, it had been included when he bought the house from a bankrupt baronet fifteen years ago, so it had to be at least that old. However, it would give her information about the barony, and might even help her to solve the puzzle. It would certainly be less fraught than asking Adam Mason.

Happier now, Catherine approached the first shop

on her list with a definite bounce in her step. Mary Ann and Peter had to increase their pace to keep up with her.

****

Adam had not slept well, though he knew it had nothing to do with the sad sagging of the elderly mattress, nor the creak of the old, worn ropes underneath it. Those ropes had played a veritable symphony of squeaks and groans throughout the night, and more than once he had braced himself for them to break and dump him, unceremoniously, on the floor. That they held had not been thanks to him, for he had tossed and turned all night, his movements straining them to the limit.

He was still awake when dawn lightened the sky and sent a probing shaft of light through the gap between the thin curtains. Taking it as a call to rise, he threw back the covers and climbed out of bed, then tensed in shock when his warm feet touched the icy floor. He put on his leather slippers and went to the dresser to wash.

Twenty minutes later, dressed in his riding clothes, he carried his boots along the corridor, not wishing to disturb his friends. The servants had not yet arrived from the village, so he cut himself some hard bread and chewed on it as he walked to the stable where there were four horses: the riding hacks he and Freddy had brought, and the rather more showy carriage horses that Hadlow had, so far, managed to keep from his creditors.

The stables were quiet, and far too cold, but the straw was flesh and clean, indicating that somebody attempted to look after the animals. He smelled fresh manure, and the earthy, dusty scent of old wood mixed with the mustiness of the horses. They shifted in their stalls and watched him, their brown eyes full of friendliness and hope. He greeted them with soft words and patted the long noses of each one in turn. They shook their heads and snorted, returning his Good Morning greeting.

He saddled his horse and led it out of the stable into the frosty morning.

The sun was almost completely risen now, and it coated the day in a beauteous glow. The sky was a gold blue, the clouds tiny, ranging from a luminescent cream tinged with the gray blue of shadow to bronze-tinted silhouettes. Trees reached upward, their leafless branches a dark lace, and the overgrown grass was crisp white with the barest hint of green showing through. A small herd of roe deer foraged in a field, most eating, though one stood by, head up, alert for danger. Birdsong ranged from high-pitched chirps and rhythmic whistles to the mocking ha-ha of a crow. A magpie sat on the stable roof and scolded Adam with its jarring, almost mechanical chatter.

He mounted up and headed out, away from the rutted driveway and uneven, overgrown park into the lanes surrounding the estate. He would have preferred to canter and ride out the fidgets that bedeviled him, but he would not risk the horse's well-being, and there was nowhere near that he knew of where such exercise would be safe.

Over the next hour, he wandered the byways, meeting not a soul as he turned up this road and down that, until he wasn't absolutely certain where he was or how he would get back. Not that he was bothered; it shouldn't be too hard to retrace his steps and, if push came to shove, he was bound to meet someone eventually, and then he could ask for direction.

He found chalk cliffs, rising up on either side of a

large, grassy meadow. Beyond the meadow, he could just see a fast-flowing river, roaring and racing toward the larger River Ouse, and the sea at Newhaven.

Adam stopped at the gate to the meadow and looked toward the river. He'd been tempted, for a moment, to dismiss this tributary as too fast and difficult to navigate and, therefore, of no use to the smugglers he sought. However, on reflection, he doubted it was usually as high or as fast as this. Early March had brought a lot of rain, following the snows in January and February, and many of the lower-lying parts of Sussex had flooded. Even the bottom half of Lewes, the county town, had suffered when the Ouse burst its banks two weeks back. As winter turned to spring, this river would slow, and then this meadow, sheltered, almost hidden between two cliffs, would make an excellent place from which to load and unload contraband.

"Let's take a closer look, shall we?" he murmured to his horse before dismounting and heading into the meadow.

Ten yards in, his foot sank into marshy ground, the wet mud coming halfway up his boot. He grunted his distaste, pulled his foot from the quagmire with a loud squelch, and retreated to the gate, where he rubbed his boots against the thickest clumps of grass, trying to clear the worst of the mud from the ruined leather. The horse eyed him as if it thought he was an idiot for even contemplating walking across the saturated ground.

"You're right," he said, and he patted the animal's neck. "They don't call it horse sense for nothing, do they?" The horse gave a soft snort and shook his head, as if agreeing. Adam remounted and moved on.

Ten minutes later, the horse suddenly changed its

gait. Adam dismounted and checked the animal's feet, then cursed when he saw it had thrown a shoe. Luckily, there seemed to be no stones or nails embedded in the horse's foot, and no damage that he could see. Provided he got it to a farrier fairly soon, all should be well. Leading the horse, he trudged along the narrow lane and hoped he would find civilization again without too much delay.

Luck was definitely on his side, he thought, as he turned another corner and recognized the hump-backed bridge that crossed the river on the outskirts of Rotherton. "Nearly there," he told the horse, and led it into the village.

The High Street was busy with people shopping, while traders greeted them from doorways or rearranged their displays to make them more appealing. A cart rattled along the street, banging and creaking as the wheels hit potholes. Children ran in front of it and the carter shouted gruffly at them. A milkmaid negotiated the pavement, covered wooden buckets balanced from the yoke across her shoulders. She turned into the yard of the Golden Goose. A boy pulled a trolley loaded with bread and pastries, their warm, fresh smell making Adam's mouth water. Behind the houses, a cockerel crowed.

Outside the forge, a group of youths laughed and shouted, and threw stones, clearly tormenting something, most likely a poor, stray dog. Angry, wondering why anyone would ever think doing that was fun, Adam moved forward to stop it, and saw it was not a dog they attacked but another youth. In his late teens perhaps, the tormented young man was skinny, arms and legs spindly and too long for his body, and his cheeks were hollow.

His hair was uneven, as if someone had tried to hack it short while he fought every cut. His clothes were ill fitting, his trousers ragged, no stockings covering the legs between trouser hem and the top of ankle boots that were cracked and split. The lad's shirt was torn and his tattered jacket was far too small, and everything was badly stained with mud and grass and Adam could only guess what else.

He made for a gap in the circle of boys surrounding him, but it closed as he reached it. He looked around for another way out. His arms cradled his chest and his shirt squirmed and wriggled, betraying the fact that something sheltered in there. A stone hit his shoulder and he yelled like a whipped dog. The youths laughed.

"Come on, Ned," called the boy just in front of Adam. "Let's see you dance." He raised his arm, ready to throw the stone he held, then whirled around, surprised when Adam grabbed his wrist and held it firmly, stopping the throw.

"Give me that before you hurt yourself," said Adam. He had learned a long time ago that most men responded to quietly spoken words better than they did to parade-ground shouts.

"Let go of me," answered the boy. "You can't just grab me."

"And you can't throw stones at people." From the corner of his eye, Adam saw other boys drop their stones and back off. Their victim seized his chance. Still clutching whatever was inside his shirt, he took off down the side of the forge and disappeared. The other boys muttered about getting back to work and moved away, until Adam and his prisoner were the only people left.

"Let me go!" The boy pulled and squirmed. "What

did it have to do with you, anyway?"

"I don't like to see people throwing stones at others."

"We wasn't hurting him. We just…"

"What's going on out here?" bellowed the farrier. He swaggered from his forge, wiping sweaty hands on a dirty cloth. Brawny, coated in soot, he smelled of smoke and leather and horseflesh. "Jed?"

"This man's attacking me, Pa," cried the boy. The farrier's eyes narrowed. He tensed, his muscles bulging, and Adam prepared himself for a nasty beating, though he refused to show any fear, nor did he intend to back down. If he did, things would only get worse for the skinny youth, and anyone else who got in the way of this boy's delinquency.

"Do you tell him the truth of it, or do I?" he asked the boy.

The farrier frowned, uncertain. His bluff called, Jed lost most of his bravado. "We weren't doing nothing, Pa."

The farrier studied Adam. "What does he call nothing?"

"He was attacking another boy." Adam's lip curled, contemptuously. "Couldn't even do it in a fair fight, either. Had to have half a dozen of his mates backing him."

Jed had the grace to look shamed, even as he tried again to pull himself free.

"Shouldn't go in mob-handed, boy," said the farrier. "Not if the other lad was on his own."

"Pa!" Jed was clearly unhappy that his father agreed with Adam.

"On the other hand, there's always two sides to a

story. What did the other boy do to you?"

Adam stared at the man, astounded. Several boys against one, and the farrier thought there might be justification for that?

"It was only Ned, Pa. And it was his own fault. There was a bird with a broken wing. Stupid idiot swooped in to save it. He got in the way, that's all."

The farrier grinned. "Boys will be boys," he said. Adam glared at him, and the grin faded. "This gentleman is right. You've got no call to be attacking Ned. If I've told you once, I've told you a thousand times, you shouldn't mock the afflicted." To Adam, he said, "I'll make sure it doesn't happen again, Mister...?" He cocked his head to one side, expectantly.

In the year since he had come into it, Adam had never thrown his title around. He saw no reason to do so. But now and then, he was beginning to realize, there might be a certain satisfaction in it. This, he decided, was one such time. "Lord," he corrected the man. "Lord Abberley."

The farrier swallowed and bowed his head slightly. When he spoke again, his tone was more respectful. "Apologies, my lord. He won't do it again. You," he pointed at Jed, "get in there and pump my bellows. Then you can go and find your sister, and tell her to come home and make us a meal."

Adam let go of the boy, who moved reluctantly toward the forge. As he passed, his father clouted him, hard enough to knock him down. Adam winced, realizing where the boy had learned to attack those weaker than himself.

"Don't you worry, my lord. I'll see to it he's kept busy. He won't go for poor Ned again." The farrier smiled, obsequiously. "Can I do anything else for you, my lord?"

Wishing he could say no and take his trade elsewhere, but knowing that was not a choice he had, Adam led his horse to the forge. "He threw a shoe," he said.

Five minutes later, the horse was in the farrier's pen, and Adam strolled along the High Street toward the Golden Goose, where he hoped to buy a jug of ale and a hot pie, then sit in a corner seeming to mind his own business while listening to the unguarded conversations of the other patrons.

He stopped dead, his plans changing when he saw Catherine Ashton step out of the haberdashery and start walking along the road, a maid and a footman in her wake.

Chapter Six

Adam watched Catherine walk from the haberdashery to the bakery and go inside while her servants waited on the pavement. The footman said something to the maid and she gave him an eager smile. If they were there to give Catherine countenance, they were doing a poor job of it, far too wrapped up in their own flirtation to pay much attention to her. Not that he would have thought she needed them in the middle of rural Rotherton.

She looked well. Last night, he had noted her beauty, which had grown in the last two years from a girlish prettiness to an elegant maturity. Her face had lost the roundness of adolescence, her features more defined, and there was an added confidence in the way she carried herself. This morning, in full daylight, that confidence was even more on display, in the way she walked with her head erect and her shoulders back, just the hint of a sway in her hips. Her pelisse was a deep red that accentuated the soft creaminess of her skin and the bright roses in her cheeks from the crisp air. Dark curls escaped her bonnet, which was adorned with cream satin flowers, and a wide cream ribbon, the ends of which fluttered behind her in the breeze.

Instinctively, Adam took two steps toward her before he thought about what he was doing and hesitated. Once, he would have flown to her side without a second's thought, and she would have greeted him gladly. Now? What was the protocol for meeting the woman you once hoped to marry?

He was thinking about this too much. They were friends. They had renewed their acquaintance last night and it would be rude to ignore her now. So he would go to the bakery and greet her. Because it was the mannerly thing to do. And because it would help him investigate her father. There was no other reason for being in her company. None whatsoever.

Adam reached the bakery as Catherine came out, clutching a paper bag dotted with stains from the cream on the cakes inside. The footman took it from her, and she smiled her thanks. The mischievous dimple still winked on her cheek.

She saw Adam. Her smile wavered, just for a moment, and there was a catch in her step so small that someone who did not know her well might not have seen it. Then, the uncertainty vanished, and the polite Society lady, unfazed and unruffled, returned.

"Mr. Mas—I'm sorry, my lord," she said. Her voice was low and husky and made the words seem like a caress.

"Miss Ashton." He bowed as she curtseyed.

She gave him a half smile. "You are about early this morning, my lord."

"As are you."

"I keep country hours."

He nodded, and looked around as nonchalantly as he could and said, "It's a charming village."

It's a charming village? Was that the best he could come up with? His wits had flown out of his head and nested in the fustian tree.

"It's larger than most of its neighbors," she replied.

He nodded.

She looked away.

Seconds ticked by in silence.

Say something. "It's a nice morning, for March."
Not that.

"Yes."

They strolled along the pavement, the awkwardness between them growing with each step. He wracked his brains for something to say. Her frown suggested she did the same thing. Her servants walked at a respectable distance behind them. People bustled from shop to shop. Children ran along the road and played in the mouths of alleys. A boy in ragged clothes furtively took an apple from the greengrocer's display. The shopkeeper cuffed his ear and snatched the fruit back, and the boy ran off.

Several times, Catherine opened her mouth as if to say something, then closed it again. Finally, she said, "I didn't know you were in line for a barony."

You and me both. A bitterness filled him, leaving a nasty taste in his mouth.

"When did you come into your title?"

"Last summer." He didn't want to talk about this. It still hurt too much.

She hesitated, glanced at him, and asked, "Who held the title before you?"

There was a complicated question. The factual answer was, of course, his father. But that didn't seem the right thing to say. For one thing, she would think he meant the man who brought him up, the man he'd told her so much about. Then he would need to explain that that man was still hale and hearty, tending his farm and licking his wounds from the tongue-lashing Adam had given him once the truth emerged.

Besides, he could not think of the previous baron as his father. Could a man really be a father when all he had done was sire him? He had had nothing to do with the loving and nurturing, the teaching and training and discipline that shaped the man Adam had become.

"My lord?" Catherine prompted.

Adam took a deep breath, cleansing the sourness from his thoughts and his emotions. "It is a long and convoluted story."

She hesitated for a second before she continued, "I was surprised to see you here. I didn't realize you and Lord Hadlow were friends. Has that happened since you came into your title?"

Why was the blasted woman so fixated on his title? Was it all she cared about? If so, she was in for a disappointment because Adam did not wish to talk about his bloody title. He would rather everybody else did not talk about it, either, although he could not stop them. If he said nothing, perhaps the gossip would die down, although he felt only faint hope of that. From what he had been told, it had taken years for the tabbies to stop last time, and his father—his real father—had never recovered from their cruel words.

"I do not wish to discuss my title," he said, curtly.

Catherine's eyes narrowed with suspicion. She thinned her lips and drew in a deep, determined breath through her nose. "My lord," she said, enunciating each word carefully. "Adam. We were friends once. It is as a friend I feel compelled to speak with you. You should know people are…*some* people are…speculating about you. Please, be careful. It will not be easily forgiven if you should…if you should treat them…if you should dissemble."

He raised an eyebrow. Why would she mention dissembling? She could not possibly know the real reason for his presence in the neighborhood, could she? If she did, was it because she was aware of her father's nefarious activities? Was she involved? Oh, Lord, he hoped not. He did not think he could bear that. It would be difficult enough to arrest her father and have her hate him for it. He didn't think he could survive arresting her as well.

"For myself," she carried on, "I can think of no good reason why you would be untruthful, but the reason, or lack of one, does not mean people will not wonder. You yourself told everyone your father was a gentleman farmer, a member of the gentry. You never once said he was a lord, nor that anyone within your family was one, either. With no previous hint of it, people are saying— well, I think you can guess what people are saying."

So she wasn't talking about his reasons for being in Rotherton. Then what…?

"I know very little about the nobility," she said, "and even less about the law, but I would be astounded to discover it is not illegal to claim a title that isn't yours."

She did not believe he held a title! She had just called him a liar, to his head. Did she truly think so little of him that she believed he would perpetrate such a fraud?

"You think me a criminal?" he asked, through teeth clenched so tight his jaw ached.

Her eyes widened. "No. No, I—"

"So be it. Far be it from me to contradict a lady."

"I didn't…it wasn't—"

"I daresay you are also right about the

consequences. Lying about a peerage would doubtless bring the wrath of the Lords down upon one's head, together with the full force of the judiciary and, I expect, of the Regent himself. 'Twould be a worse crime than murder. I wonder you don't report me and claim whatever reward they offer for the apprehension of so dangerous a blackguard."

"Adam—"

"Not wishing to sully your reputation further by imposing my company on you, I will bid you good day." He gave her a curt bow and made to move away. She reached out and held his forearm. He stopped and glared, pointedly, at her hand on his sleeve.

"I never said I thought you untruthful."

"It's difficult to interpret your words in any other way."

"If that is how they sounded, I apologize. Don't go." Tears pooled in her eyes, making them shine. "Adam, please. I am sorry."

He forced down his anger. It would do no good to be on the outs with her. "Fine," he said, then made a conscious effort to relax the muscles in his neck and face. "Abberley is a legitimate title, and I am the legitimate heir. I don't know why you would believe otherwise. Do you truly think me such a low person that I would…" He waved his hand, indicating what he did not wish to say.

"No," she replied. He raised an eyebrow and she blushed, then closed her eyes, a pained expression on her face. "No, I don't. But when I heard the speculation, I wanted…I have insulted you badly. You must hate me."

"I don't hate you." He smiled, although it felt more like a grimace, and he wondered that she didn't run from him when she saw it. "Shall we cry pax?"

She nodded, and looked relieved as she put her hand through the crook of his arm.

"Now," he said, keeping his tone light, "I saw you leave the bakery, so perhaps you can answer a question for me? I have a yen for Shrewsbury cakes. Do you know if they sell them, and if so, would you recommend them?"

"I would. If they haven't sold out. Everything they make is excellent."

"Good. For I must also buy buns for Freddy, and *langues du chats* and marchpane for Bertie."

"Is Lord Hadlow a close friend?"

"No," Adam answered. There was no point in lying about it, for Bertie would tell the truth if he was asked. "I hardly know him at all. I met him for the first time two weeks ago."

"Just two weeks? Yet he invited you?" She colored, her cream complexion turning a rosy pink that somehow darkened her eyes until they were almost black. "I am sorry. It is none of my business."

Adam shrugged. "It's not a secret. To be honest, Lord Hadlow did not invite me himself. He invited Freddy, and Freddy invited me. You may recall, he is my best friend."

"I do. You met in the army."

"Aye. We served together in Portugal and Spain. I am aware many people think him a fop, but there is no one I'd rather have at my side in face of the enemy. Matter of fact, he was the first person I told when I came into the barony. He gave me a lot of good advice. A second son he may be, but he knows as much about running his estate as his older brother does."

Catherine looked thoughtful. "I am surprised you

were allowed to join the war, if you were the heir. About a year ago, I met Mr. Wingfield, who complained bitterly that he could not compete with the officers in their regimentals, and the only reason he wasn't wearing them himself was that he was not permitted to purchase a pair of colors."

Adam laughed. "Methinks he did protest too much." He put his hand over hers on his arm. Even through his gloves he felt her warmth, and there was a strange tingling in his blood, like the crackle in the air when lightning strikes. He almost pulled away in surprise. The last time he had felt such a sensation was…the last time he held her hand. He'd touched hands, and other parts, of several women since, and not once had he experienced anything like it. Until today.

"You think he was permitted to join the army after all?" she asked, wide eyed with shock.

Who? Oh, yes. Wingfield. "No," he answered, "he probably wasn't permitted. The heir apparent rarely is. But, no matter what they may say, some of them are not unhappy about that."

She frowned. "You were allowed to go. Did you defy your family's wishes?"

"I did not. Fact is, Miss Ashton, until a year ago, I was not aware of the title. I certainly had no expectations of it." He watched her carefully. "I did not deceive you two years ago."

She cocked her head to one side and studied him.

His irritation rose again. "Why would I keep such a prospect to myself, when knowledge of it can only have aided my suit at that time?"

Catherine stopped dead, turned to face him squarely, and fixed him with a cold stare. "How so, my lord?" Her

79

voice dripped ice, although why she should take offence was beyond him.

Adam returned her stare steadily. "Miss Ashton," he said, "I am not a fool, and neither are you. We both know your father wanted a title for you at that time. He might have done what he could to persuade you to accept the match if he had known of mine."

She lifted her chin, haughtily. "It would not have made one iota of difference."

He huffed a soft laugh. "Of course it wouldn't."

She took her hand from his arm and glowered at him. "You have a high opinion of yourself."

"In the last year, I have met enough young ladies and their marriage-minded mamas to learn that a title makes a great deal of difference to a man's worth."

Her jaw clenched, and all her angry feelings were displayed clearly on her face. "You believe that because some feather-headed goose in the *ton* bats her eyelashes at you, all women will do the same? I have met some pompous, arrogant braggarts before, but you, sir, are beyond belief."

Adam frowned. When put like that, it did sound arrogant and pompous.

"Let me tell you, so there can be no further confusion. I would not have accepted your suit had you been next in line to the Regent himself! By implying that I would, that my affections could so easily be bought, you wrong me, and show that you, yourself, are no gentleman."

The anger and hurt of the last two years surfaced suddenly, spiking his temper. "I never claimed to be one. But then, turn-around for turn-around, madam. A true *lady* would not cast aspersions on my character in a public street!"

Adam regretted the words as soon as they left his mouth, but it was too late. Catherine gasped, and all the color drained from her face. He took a deep breath and bowed his head, unable to look at her. "I apologize. There was no call for me to say that."

She swallowed, hard, and her chin trembled, but the tears did not fall. She held her head high and when she spoke, her voice was steady. "Let me be absolutely clear," she said. "I would not accept your suit, under any circumstances. Even if I did want a nobleman for my husband, you would not qualify. There is more to being noble than having a title, and I am afraid, my lord," she sneered his title and he flinched, "you, and your current companions, fall sadly short. I would never wish to ally myself with a rake and a gambler. And not a particularly good gambler at that!"

"Another accusation?" He glared at her, his teeth gritted. "On what do you base this one?"

She smiled. It did not reach her eyes. "You are here, are you not? Avoiding the duns?"

That took the wind from his sails. He could not refute her accusation, although the urge to tell her the truth, that he was not recovering from large losses, that he never gambled to excess, his coffers were full and his life in good order, was almost overwhelming. Being unable to say these things to her caused a pain in his chest so sharp and piercing it almost took him to his knees.

She was so close he saw the tiny flecks of green in her dark brown eyes, the individual lashes, the small pock mark beside her eyebrow, legacy of a childhood bout of chicken pox. An errant curl had escaped her pins, and the breeze floated it across her face. He itched to reach out and capture it, gently stroke it back into place before he leaned in and kissed her. He needed the strength of a titan not to do so.

For an instant, she looked as if she wanted the same thing. If she moved toward him, even a fraction of an inch, he knew he would be lost. Then, she shuddered. He blinked, the moment lost.

Back straight, head haughtily high, Catherine turned to walk away. He did not want her to go. Not on such angry terms. He reached out and his fingers encircled her narrow wrist. She startled.

"Miss Ashton?" asked her footman, moving forward. "Is everything all right?"

"Yes, thank you, Peter," she answered. Her voice quivered. Adam glanced at the man, who frowned a warning at him.

"Miss Ashton has regained her balance, my lord," Peter said, firmly. "I thank you for aiding her, but she does not need your help anymore."

The men stared at each other for perhaps two seconds longer, and then Adam let go of Catherine's arm. He gave her a curt bow and walked away.

A few yards on, he looked back. She stood on the pavement, watching him. Their eyes met for the briefest of moments before she turned her back on him and marched in the opposite direction. Peter gave Adam a threatening look before he and the maid followed her.

A sadness descended, so thick he thought it might suffocate him, and he had to take several deep, slow breaths to regain his equilibrium before he made his way back to the forge where, he hoped, the farrier would have finished shoeing his horse.

The heat hit him as he walked in through the double

doors at the front, and it took a moment for his eyes to grow used to the dim light after the bright day outside. It was a fair-sized building, but its low roof and the charcoal-covered walls made it seem smaller. Half the space was taken up by a large firepit, the coals within it glowing deep red. Above it was a huge set of bellows hanging from the ceiling. A large bucket sat beside the pit, filled almost to the brim with clear water, and a set of tongs sat in the bucket. Around the walls hung tools: hammers, tongs, and crowbars, along with horseshoes of varying size. On the floor was a weathervane, solder at the iron cockerel's neck showing where it had been repaired. There was a scythe, a firebox for a small fireplace, and a narrow gate with decorative scrollwork. This farrier was clearly talented, and in demand.

He was, however, nowhere to be seen. Nor was his bully-boy son, though they could not have gone far, for the coals still burned brightly, indicating they had been stoked recently.

A narrow door at the rear of the building let in daylight, so Adam made his way toward it. As he approached, he saw a corner of a corral, in which three horses stood patiently, his ride among them. Perhaps the man was out there, dealing with one of the animals. Adam walked to the door, meaning to go outside, but just before he reached the point where he would be seen, he saw the farrier talking to a man wearing the same livery as Peter, Catherine's groom. One of Ashton's men, then.

As Adam watched, the man pulled a piece of paper from his pocket, glanced around as if looking for spies, then handed it to the farrier. The farrier also looked around furtively, read the paper, then stuffed it into the enormous pouch on the front of his leather apron.

Adam watched them closely. It could be nothing more than a business transaction, he told himself, but if it was above board, why the cloak-and-dagger looks?

"I didn't think it would be so soon," said the farrier, gruffly. "Not this close after the last one."

"The miller says it's time. So it's time."

"I'm telling you, it's too soon." The farrier put his hands on his hips, and his huge biceps stretched his sooty shirt sleeves. His face was grim as he stared at the liveried man, who shrugged nonchalantly.

"He's thought of that. He…" A sudden gust of wind whistled around the door, drowning out the man's next words. Silently, Adam swore. As the wind died again, the liveried man pointed at the farrier's pocket. "Burn that." The farrier gave him a look that said the command was unnecessary. "I'll see you later," and the liveried man turned toward the door into the forge.

As quickly and quietly as he could, Adam hurried to the front door. Once there, he adopted an indolent stand and called out, "Halloo? Anybody here?"

The liveried man came in through the rear door, saying loudly, "If you come out in the next day or two, we'll have six horses need reshoeing."

"Right you are," answered the farrier, following him in and also talking louder than he needed to. He grinned at Adam. "Your horse is all done, my lord. Right as rain."

The liveried man tipped his hat to Adam as he passed and walked into the street while Adam followed the farrier through the stifling forge and into the crisp, cold air of the corral beyond.

Chapter Seven

All the way home, Catherine relived those minutes with Adam. Her mood veered from anger and frustration at the way the conversation had gone, to shame at her part in their argument, to happiness that he had been willing to stay despite the offense she had caused him. For she *had* been offensive. She should have known Adam Mason would never lie, especially about something as momentous as a title. He had too much integrity for that, no matter what Papa might think.

He said he hadn't known he was in line for the title two years ago. Catherine found that strange. Even stranger was the fact that nobody else in the *ton* had mentioned it, either. If there was one thing everyone in Society seemed to know, it was everybody else's family history. Most of the older ladies—the ones who sat on the periphery of an event and kept an eye on debutantes and frightened the life out of the men who wished to court them—were able to list a person's antecedents for several generations. It was the first thing they mentioned about anyone. Yet nobody had connected Adam Mason with Baron Abberley. There had to be a reason for that. Looking up the title in the old edition of *Debrett's* might give Catherine some hint as to what that reason was.

She would do it discreetly, though. Papa seemed to have taken Adam and his friends in severe dislike, so he was unlikely to be pleased if Catherine showed any interest in him or his family. The last thing she needed was any more unpleasantness with him. So she waited until after nuncheon, when Mama went to her room for a rest and Papa left for an appointment with his steward. Then she made her way to the study.

It wasn't a large room, and it had a cluttered, overcrowded feel. Dark curtains hung at the window, cutting the light from outside and giving the place an air of gloom. In front of the window stood the large rosewood desk that dominated the space. Its top was inlaid with dark green Morocco leather, on which rested an intricately carved brass inkstand with two crystal inkwells and a clipper for trimming quills. A small pile of papers sat neatly to one side, a candleholder to the other. Behind the desk was a sturdy chair, upholstered in green leather to match the desk, while a chest of drawers, in which Papa kept his most important documents, stood to one side. On top of this chest was a decanter, half full with brandy, together with several rummers and a carafe of water. Other chairs stood on the rug in front of the desk. A stone fireplace took up one wall, a set of brass fire tools on one side of the hearth and a small pile of sweet-smelling pine logs on the other side. Above the fireplace was an enormous picture of the family as they'd been ten years ago. Catherine remembered sitting for it and struggling to remain still long enough for the artist to take her likeness. In the picture was a small dog they'd never owned, and they sat under a chestnut tree that had never grown where it was depicted.

The other two walls were lined, floor to ceiling, with bookshelves. Old books were crammed onto them, their covers faded, the gold leaf titles chipped. A few had frayed and tattered spines. None had been taken from the shelves in years, and they made the room smell musty and old. Catherine wrinkled her nose against the smell as she set to, reading the spines as best she could in the dim light.

It took twenty minutes to find *Debrett's Peerage*, a heavy tome two inches thick. She had to use both hands to carry it to Papa's desk, where she was grateful to put it down. The book was eighteen years old, hopelessly out of date, and in most households it would have been thrown out and replaced many times. Considering how keen her parents had been that she marry a title, she was surprised there wasn't a more recent copy, but this book would probably tell her what she needed to know.

The entry for Baron Abberley listed the fourth baron, Robert George Moore, who was born in 1754, meaning he would have been sixty-four years old now. That was a great age for working men struggling to keep their families and make ends meet, but it was still young for a member of the aristocracy. Briefly, she wondered how he had died, then read on.

In 1786, he married Miss Helen Mason, daughter of a gentleman farmer. Catherine tapped the page with her fingertip, making note of the connection with Adam's family, although it was tenuous, since the Masons were on the distaff side and would not, under normal circumstances, inherit.

The baron's son was, according to this entry, born in 1788, and was christened Adam Robert. She blinked. Two cousins with the same given names? It wasn't unheard of. She'd even known a family who, having lost one child named George, had a second baby and called that one George, too.

The baron's son, Adam Moore, would be thirty now.

The same age as Adam Mason. Three months after the birth, the baroness died. Next to this was a note saying the baby's whereabouts were unknown and he may have died with her, although this had not been verified by the note writer.

No other family on the paternal side was listed. The fourth baron had been an only child, as had the third baron. There were no other heirs. Reading this, Catherine surmised that, if the baby had indeed died with his mother, the title would have become extinct unless the baron had remarried after this book had been published. If he had married again, Adam could not be the son of any second union, though. He was far too old.

Try as she might, she could not see how Adam, son of a gentleman farmer and nephew of the baroness, could possibly be the baron's heir. It made no sense and left her no more enlightened than she'd been when she came in here to look.

Not that it mattered, she thought. How a man came to his position was irrelevant. It was what he made of that position that was important. Sadly, it seemed Adam wasn't making much of it at all. He'd let it go to his head, and the quiet, sensible, frugal man she'd fallen in love with was now a rake who gambled and drank and mixed with wastrels like Lord Hadlow.

Catherine would never have thought of Lord Hadlow as the sort of company Adam would choose to keep. Which went to show how little she had truly known the seemingly respectable army officer she had met. But if *that* character had been an act, it had been a good one. There had been no hint of its falseness. Was he an actor to rival Edmund Kean?

She put the *Debrett's* back on the shelf, slapped the

dust from her hands, and made her way to the drawing room, where she tried to distract herself by hemming handkerchiefs, but her mind was so full of the enigma of Adam Mason that she had to unpick her work and start again. Twice.

"I don't even really wish to know about him," she muttered as she threaded her needle for the third time. And if she said that often enough, she might come to believe it.

****

Adam spent the rest of the day pondering what he had seen at the forge. The exchange between the farrier and Ashton's servant might have been completely innocent, a payment of a debt, perhaps, or a list of instructions for a future job. But the way the men had looked around was anything but innocent, and why would they go out into the cold corral rather than stay in the warm forge to conduct their business, if it was legitimate?

In the end, Adam decided his best course of action would be to watch the farrier. If the man left his home late at night, Adam would follow him and see where that led.

After dinner, while the others played billiards and tried to drink the cellar dry, Adam excused himself, saying he wasn't feeling quite the thing and would have an early night. Then he changed into dark clothing and tried to sneak out of the house.

The front door was locked and barred for the night. It would be noisy to open it, and he couldn't take the risk that someone would hear. Instead, he went through the dining room and out onto the terrace. He was surprised the French window in the dining room had not been locked. Perhaps it had been an oversight. He would make sure to lock it when he returned.

It was a cold night, frost already forming on the stone parapet bordering the terrace. Silhouetted rhododendron bushes were dotted about the gardens, shaggy and unkempt, like badly groomed sentinels guarding the house. In the distance, a fox barked.

Adam was halfway across the terrace when he saw the tiny red glow of a cheroot and realized he was not the only one out here. Cursing silently, he slowed and, instead of going down the stone stairs to the gardens, he moved closer to the smoker, who stepped out of the shadows and made himself more visible.

"Colbourne," greeted Adam, as nonchalantly as he could. The man wore his dinner coat, which could hardly keep him warm out here.

"Abberley," replied Colbourne. His voice gave no hint of what he thought.

"Are you not cold?" Adam hoped the man would say yes and go back inside, so that Adam could continue on his way.

"I'm not warm," said Colbourne. "But Bertie doesn't like me to smoke indoors." He chuckled. "He doesn't like the smell." He drew on his cheroot again. "Thought you'd gone to bed."

"I had," said Adam. "It wasn't helping. I thought some fresh air might be of use." Colbourne nodded but didn't reply, so Adam went on, "A walk would do me good." He turned to leave. Colbourne would assume he was walking in the dark garden, and he could get on his way.

"I've been restless, too," said Colbourne. "Daresay I could walk the fidgets out of me."

Adam's heart sank, but he could not object without raising questions in Colbourne's mind. So, accepting there was a chance he might not get to the farrier's home tonight, he accompanied Colbourne down the stone staircase and along a gravel path, full of holes and weeds, which cut between two lawns of long grass, bramble branches, and nettles. For a few moments, they strolled in silence. Colbourne did not seem in any hurry, and Adam tried not to show that he was.

"Served with Finch on the peninsula, didn't you?" asked Colbourne, and he flicked the stub of his cheroot into the grass.

"Yes," said Adam.

"Bond that can't be broken, friendship like that." He pulled his gloves from his pocket and put them on.

"That's true. You a military man?" Adam would be surprised if he was, but one never knew.

Colbourne laughed. "Not me."

"You spoke as if you had experience of battlefield comrades."

"You don't just get those in a war between countries. Even civilians can have your back when you need them to."

Adam nodded. "You've needed them to?"

"Once or twice. I should think everyone has at some time." There was a short silence before he added, "Hard to see Finch on the battlefield. Doesn't strike me as the warrior type."

Much as he wanted to defend Freddy, it was not what his friend would want. Freddy had taken great pains to cultivate his image.

"There were a lot of dandies in the officer's mess," Adam answered, carefully. "Gentlemen who joined the army because they liked the uniform, and the effect it had on ladies. But once they were out in the field, they quickly learned they had to fight or die, just like the rest of us."

Colbourne nodded. "Acquitted himself well, did he?"

Saved my life. "I never heard anyone complain. Which cannot be said about every officer."

"I can imagine." He studied Adam for a moment. "And you? What kind of officer were you?"

Adam gave him a sidelong glance. Colbourne walked with his shoulders hunched against the cold wind. He had expected to be outside only as long as it took to smoke a cheroot and had not put on his warm coat. He must regret offering to accompany Adam now. Pity he had not thought about it before he prevented Adam's errand. A small and childish part of Adam was glad the man was paying for that with his discomfort. It wasn't a feeling he was proud of, but it was, nonetheless, hard to push away.

"The sort of officer who came through it, along with as many of my men as possible."

"Can't ask for more than that."

They walked on, their boots crunching on the gravel so their footsteps sounded like the march of a hundred soldiers. An owl swooped silently past them, its white wings bright in the moonlight. Halfway across the grass, it dived. There was the tiniest shriek, and then it climbed again, its beak full.

"What about now?" asked Colbourne.

Adam frowned. "I'm not in the army now."

"Do you miss it?"

"I am a different man now."

"What about the Frenchies? Do you still hate them?"
Strange question, "We are not at war now."

"True. But it must be difficult not to hate someone who's tried to kill you."

Adam could not see where Colbourne was taking the conversation. If, indeed, he was taking it anywhere. It might be nothing more than small talk, easier on the ear than silence. "It was nothing personal," he replied. "I don't hate a man because he did his duty to his country."

"And they do make damn fine brandy. Hard to hate a nation that makes something that good." Colbourne cleared his throat. "It's getting colder. Shall we go in?"

They walked back in silence, and entered through the French door into the dining room. Colbourne pulled it shut and locked it. "Feel better for that walk?" he asked.

"Yes, thank you. A good night's sleep and I shall be right as rain." Adam hoped Colbourne would return to the billiards room. If he could slip out now, he might still be able to watch the farrier.

"I think I'll have an early night myself," said Colbourne. Mentally, Adam cursed.

Together, they walked upstairs and along the landing, parting at Adam's room. He went inside, closed the door, and waited a few minutes, giving Colbourne time to get to his own chamber.

After he thought enough time had passed, Adam opened his door and looked out onto the landing. Colbourne stood there yet, staring out of the window onto the moonlit gardens. He turned to Adam.

"Oh, it's you." Adam grinned, hoping it looked friendly. "I thought I heard something."

"Sorry," said Colbourne, flatly. "I will try to be

93

quieter."

Adam returned to his room and started to undress. He wasn't going to get out of here tonight. He just hoped tomorrow night would not be too late.

Chapter Eight

At ten the next morning, as the gentlemen sat down to breakfast, someone knocked on the door.

"Deuced uncivilized for someone to be calling at this hour," said Bertie, as he went to answer it, muttering about the need to find a footman.

"Deuced uncivilized to be up at this hour," agreed Lord Rotherton as he came into the breakfast room. He put his gloves, cane, and greatcoat on a spare chair and rested his hat on top of them.

"Do you want breakfast? I'm sure there's plenty." Bertie waved an expansive hand at the credenza, its surface filled with covered dishes, then helped himself to bacon and mushrooms.

Rotherton narrowed his eyes in suspicion. "That depends. Did you cook it?"

Colbourne, Adam, and Freddy laughed at Bertie's look of horror. "Do I look as if I cook breakfast?"

"Not edibly. But I know you haven't had the chance to hire staff yet, so…" Rotherton shrugged.

"I have engaged the services of Mrs. Hargreaves. She comes up from the village every morning at some ungodly hour, makes us breakfast and a cold nuncheon, then goes away again."

Rotherton nodded. "If Mrs. Hargreaves prepared it, I will eat." He served himself a plateful of food and sat down.

"What brings you out so early?" asked Freddy. A good question since, from what little Adam knew of the earl, he didn't think he would have roused himself to come here without a good reason.

"I'm on my way to Rotherfield," he said. Rotherfield was a large village on the outskirts of Tunbridge Wells. It had a well-established watch house with a holding gaol, something Rotherton lacked, and the only reason the earl would go there this early.

"Have you arrested somebody?" Bertie peered at the door as if he expected to see a prisoner standing there. "Where have you put him?"

"I haven't arrested anyone." Rotherton took a bite of sausage. "Mrs. Hargreaves has to be the best cook not employed in a household this side of Paris."

"Worth her weight in silver," agreed Bertie. He grinned. "Not that she'll get her weight in silver, but who said life was fair?"

"As long as she's paid what she's worth." Rotherton's voice was light, but Adam detected a steely warning in the words.

"Why are you going to Rotherfield, if you're not going to the gaol?" asked Colbourne. He reached for the marmalade pot and spooned some onto his toast.

Rotherton cut into a slice of bacon. "I didn't say I wasn't going to the gaol. I am, as it happens, but not until I have eaten my fill of this wonderful breakfast."

"But why, if you've no prisoner to deliver?" Bertie picked up the coffee jug and looked from one guest to another. "Coffee, anyone?"

"I'm meeting with the watch. They don't know it yet, but I have it in mind to give each of them a hard and painful kick in the rear end. Lord knows, they deserve it."

Colbourne pushed his cup to Bertie, who poured coffee into it. Adam and Freddy exchanged surreptitious glances.

"They're less effective than a sundial in the shade," continued Rotherton. He put another morsel of bacon into his mouth, then used his fork to point at his listeners. "I've heard of towns where constables are being given their position on a permanent basis. They do it as their only job. None of this elect-them-for-a-year-and-hope-they-have-time-for-it nonsense. There's a lot to be said for employing somebody properly, in my opinion."

"Bit radical, isn't it?" Bertie poured coffee into Rotherton's cup.

"Has there been some trouble?" asked Freddy.

Rotherton cleared his plate and sat back. "The captain of the coast guard says there were two ships off Hastings last night, but by the time his men had reached the town, the vessels were gone, as had whatever they were landing. It's his belief—and I tend to agree—that the contraband came over Ashdown Forest and into this area. Where the watch may have intercepted it, if they'd done their duty properly." He shook his head. "They'll wish they had. I intend to have them out this morning, and they'll search every nook and cranny for it."

Bertie laughed. "Lot of trouble for a couple of kegs of brandy and a length of lace."

"If that was all," said Rotherton, as he drank his coffee, "I would happily turn to the wall along with everyone else. God knows, some families around here could do with a little extra income, and I'm not so heartless as to deny them. But we're not talking about the odd ten bob earned here or there. The captain thinks this particular operation rivals the Hawkhurst gang at the height of their activities."

Adam raised an eyebrow. Even in Shropshire he'd heard of the Hawkhurst gang. In the middle of the last century, they'd been the biggest and most vicious smuggling gang in the country. They'd not only smuggled goods on an industrial scale, but they'd ruled the Kent and Sussex coasts by terror, carrying out beatings, torture, and murder. They'd been so powerful that, when the coast guard seized a large shipment, they'd simply raided the customs house and retrieved it.

"A huge quantity of illicit goods coming this way, and not one member of the local watch saw or heard anything." Rotherton tightened his jaw. Adam glanced at Freddy again, but Freddy watched the earl. Colbourne stared into his cup and nodded, as if agreeing Rotherton was right to be angry.

"Mayhap they truly didn't see or hear anything," said Bertie. "I have no experience with smugglers myself, but it occurs to me that, by definition, they need to be discreet in their comings and goings. If making a noise could get me the drop, I'd be quiet, too."

"Nobody's that quiet, and nobody is invisible. Even a smuggler's lantern gives off a sliver of light. A man keeping a sharp eye would see it. And if he had, I would not need to be awoken at the crack of dawn and forced to listen to a lecture from a jumped-up militia man about doing *my* job properly!"

Adam sipped his coffee. Frustration rose within him. If he had been able to reach the farrier's home last night, he might have seen what was going on. He would have had the information for Rotherton, to say nothing of the proof Fremont needed to arrest Walter Ashton.

That thought made him falter, and he almost dropped his cup. The coffee inside sloshed over the rim, coating his skin. Not hot enough to scald, it still stung for a moment. He carefully put the cup down and wiped his hand, staining the white napkin.

Part of him was glad he had been prevented from his errand last night. Although he wanted to put paid to crime as much as the next man, and he especially wanted to bring traitors to justice, he didn't relish the thought of bringing shame and ruin on Catherine's family. If only Fremont had listened when he tried to recuse himself. Alas, the man was, like so many Englishmen of his class, single-minded in his actions, determined in his plans, and completely unable to accept any viewpoint that didn't match his own. He could no more understand Adam's reluctance to do this than he could flap his arms and fly.

Adam would do his duty, of course, but he couldn't shake the thought that maybe, just maybe, Fremont was mistaken. Ashton was, by all accounts, a hardnosed businessman, and an ambitious social climber, but Adam had a hard time imagining him a traitor. An opinion nobody else involved in the investigation seemed to share. They wanted evidence of Ashton's guilt, and that was what they would seek. Adam was the only one who would also be looking for evidence of his innocence. For that reason alone, he must continue his search.

"This won't do." Rotherton threw his napkin onto the table, pushed back his chair, and stood. "Thank you for the excellent breakfast. I will see you anon." He put on his coat and gloves, and left.

"What was that all about?" asked Colbourne, after he'd gone.

Bertie shook his head. "I have no idea. Game of

billiards?"

While Bertie and Colbourne played billiards and made an early start on the brandy, Freddy and Adam exercised their horses in Hadlow's park. The sky was blue, streaked with white clouds that held no hint of rain. The first buds showed on bare branches where pigeons and magpies sat, preening themselves and arguing. A squirrel darted from one tree to the next, startling some of the birds into flight. The grass in the park was bright green and, on the distant horizon, fields and meadows stretched out, strips of green and brown, some hemmed by dark hedges or gray stone walls. Beyond the fields rose the Downs, small hills that, from here, were a bruised blue.

Freddy reined his horse in and looked around at the scenery. "I take it the farrier was not involved last night?"

"I don't know." Adam explained how Colbourne's presence had altered his plans. Freddy swore and Adam nodded. "My sentiments, exactly." He sighed. "I can continue to keep watch on him, but is it worth it? They won't run on consecutive nights, will they?"

"Who knows? They're a greedy bunch, if they're bringing in the amount Rotherton thinks, and two ships does support that. They may be bringing in as much as they can, as quickly as they can."

"I'll look for a foolproof way to leave the house unseen, then."

"Mayhap you won't need to. We're going to Offham tomorrow to see Colbourne give this "Sussex Champ" a pasting. Bound to be men there who might well be involved." Freddy shrugged. "Flowing ale, a few shillings in winnings, loosened lips."

Adam's horse fidgeted and he leaned forward to pat its neck. "You think he'll really fight?"

"He says he will. It's what he does. How he made his money in the first place. And, I believe, he enjoys it." He frowned at Adam. "What's the matter?"

Adam grimaced. "Betting on him like this…it feels like cheating."

"Make sure you lose some, then. If this champ is as good as they say, he's bound to put down a few challengers before Colbourne darkens his daylights. Bet on those men. Which isn't a bad idea, when you think on it. They're more likely to talk to a man who's lining their pockets than to one who's emptying them." He wheeled his horse around. "Race you back to the stables?"

"No. This fine beast has been eating far too many oats. He needs a longer ride."

Freddy headed back to the Hall. Adam watched him go, then moved in the opposite direction. "All right, old chap," he said, softly, "let's get some of the fidgets out of you, shall we?" and he gave the horse its head.

****

Whenever Catherine was troubled, she liked to ride. There was something about being on a horse, the fresh air in her face while solitude enveloped her, that always helped get her thoughts into sensible order. After tossing and turning all night, mulling over her meeting with Adam yesterday, a ride was exactly what she needed, so after breakfast, she changed into her dark blue riding habit and made her way to the stables. She hoped Jem, the stable boy, didn't have too many chores today, as she would need him to accompany her, per Papa's instructions, and she didn't want to overburden him.

She clicked her tongue impatiently. It was ridiculous

that a woman of her age could not take herself for a ride across her family's land without an escort. However, Papa was adamant and, considering his mood since the Potters' soiree, Catherine knew better than to defy him.

Briefly, she wondered whether it was the presence of all the gentlemen that unnerved him, or if it was just because Adam was among them. Papa had never seemed to worry much when Lord Hadlow had come to the country before.

Not that Papa needed to worry about Adam. Yesterday, he'd made it plain he no longer harbored any finer feelings for her. He had been civil, and even said he wanted to cry friends, but there had been nothing to suggest anything more. Especially after she had insulted him, first calling him a liar, then a gambler and a rake. She blushed to think of how rude she had been. There were times, she thought, that her tongue could shear iron.

There had been an instant when she thought he might kiss her. They had stared at one another, enthralled, oblivious to the street and all that was happening around them. His eyes had darkened to the color of the sky at dusk, and his gaze had softened as he leaned toward her, and she leaned toward him. A delicious shiver ran through her, longing, anticipating…

Then he had changed his mind. Blinked. Stepped back, cleared his throat, and donned the persona of detached gentleman once more.

Catherine had been exceedingly happy that he had done so before it was too late. She did not want to be kissed by anyone, and most especially not by Adam Mason. She had no interest in that man, whatsoever. She would not even think about him. He was no longer in her thoughts. At all.

She strode determinedly to the stables, planning the route for her ride. Depending on how long the head groom could spare Jem, Catherine wanted to ride across Papa's park, giving the horse a good run, before walking it along the lane to cool it down, coming round in a big circle, in through the front gates and back to the stables. If that didn't lift her mood, nothing would.

Preoccupied with these thoughts, she rounded the corner into the yard, then stopped when she saw Mr. Colbourne at the stable door, in close and quiet conversation with Milton, Papa's steward. From the looks of them, their conversation was serious. Although Milton was taller than Mr. Colbourne, the other man wore an air of menace, his head forward, his jaw set, arms akimbo and gloves tight over the knuckles of his fisted hands as he glared at Milton. Catherine could see from his expression that the steward was intimidated. As well he might be, since he was an employee and was clearly being berated by a member of a higher class.

Catherine looked around for her father but didn't see any sign of him. If he had been, he would surely put a stop to this conversation. He detested bullying of any sort. As did Catherine. And since Papa was not here to protect his man, it was up to her. She moved toward them.

She was almost upon them when Milton saw her and turned his head, alerting Mr. Colbourne, who smiled and gave her an elegant bow. "How do you do, Miss Ashton?" he said.

"Good day, Mr. Colbourne." She pushed every ounce of her social training into acting as if she had seen nothing untoward. "Are you here to meet with my father?"

Mr. Colbourne's smile faltered, then brightened again. "We don't have an appointment, but I did hope to see him. In his absence, I spoke to Milton, instead." He slapped the steward's shoulder. Milton, tall but thin, without a discernible muscle to his frame, took a step forward under the force of the blow. Mr. Colbourne merely grinned. "I have no horse, and your father keeps a fine stable. I thought to buy…" He looked around the yard, then pointed at a stall where the top half of the door was open and a huge horse stood, watching them with a gaze of absolute contempt. The animal's coat was so black it shone blue in the wintry daylight. "That one," finished Mr. Colbourne.

The stallion snorted and tossed his head, as if he understood the gentleman's words and derided them. Catherine agreed with the animal.

"Alas, Milton here doesn't believe I can persuade your father to part with him."

"Mr. Milton is correct," she said, emphasizing the word "mister." Her father might address the steward as a servant, but Catherine wanted this man to give him more respect than that.

Mr. Colbourne sighed. "Pity. That is a fine horse. I would give a pretty price for him." He looked back at Catherine, his lips curled back in a semblance of a smile that made her shudder. She raised her chin, defiantly.

"Midnight is not for sale, sir," she said firmly.

He stared at her for a full minute. It unnerved her, but she met his gaze with a steady one of her own, refusing to give him the satisfaction of seeing her cowed.

"He can name his price," he said at last.

Catherine drew herself up to her fullest height, which, she was surprised to see, was not far short of his.

She had known Mr. Colbourne was shorter than most men, but there was such a latent power about him that he seemed bigger.

"Midnight is not for sale," she repeated. "Not for any price. My father would not sell him were he offered the crown jewels in exchange."

Mr. Colbourne watched her for a few seconds more, then nodded. "Ah, well. Thank you anyway, Miss Ashton. Milton."

She watched him walk away until he turned the corner at the far end of the stable block and disappeared from view. She then turned to Milton, who gave her an obsequious bow. "I'll be getting on, miss," he said. From his demeanor, she half expected him to tug at his forelock.

What was the matter with the men around here? Either they were like Mr. Colbourne and even Adam, too arrogant and self-assured for their own good, or they were too subservient for hers. Was there no happy medium?

Milton walked toward the estate office.

Catherine went into the stable, in search of Jem.

****

Catherine and Jem gave their horses a good run across the park, then walked them, as she had planned, along the narrow lane that ran outside the south wall of Papa's land. They reached the junction, and she hesitated, deciding which way to go. If they went east, they would come to the hamlet of Frantham, and beyond that, Frantham Manor where, recently, Catherine's friend Amelia and her fiancé had foiled a plot to kill the Prime Minister and start a war. Catherine did not know all the details of what had happened, but she did know

Amelia had been in mortal danger.

"Rather her than me," muttered Catherine. She wasn't built for adventure and derring-do, thank you very much.

"Did you say something, miss?" asked Jem.

"Nothing important. Just thinking aloud." She smiled sheepishly, then turned west. Eventually, this route would lead her to Rotherton, although they would reach the front gates of Papa's estate long before the larger village came into sight.

They were almost at those gates when a lone rider on a bay gelding came toward them. He stopped and tipped his hat. "Good day," he said, with a broad smile.

"My Lord," she replied. She lowered her eyes and willed herself not to blush, though she could already feel the burn in her cheeks. Why did she always seem to color up when she encountered him? It was ridiculous and embarrassing, to say nothing of humiliating.

Clearly, he had no such problem, for his tanned face did not change its shade at all. "You look well today, Miss Ashton." The way he said her name, emphatically and with his eyebrow raised, told her he had noted the formality of her greeting and wasn't pleased by it.

Her cheeks grew even hotter.

"May I accompany you?" he asked, and turned back the way he had come. She nodded and walked her horse beside his. Jem fell back a few lengths, close enough to chaperone but far enough away that he would not be party to their conversation.

****

Adam had not expected to encounter Catherine on his ride today—although, he admitted, some part of him must have hoped, for why else would he have ridden along the lane beside her home? It had not been a conscious decision, but that meant nothing.

He'd been deep in thought, wondering how best to proceed with his mission. He suspected the farrier was involved with smuggling, if nothing else, and he would watch him as he'd said he would, although if the smugglers had landed cargo last night, they were unlikely to do so again for several nights. On the other hand, perhaps the farrier would lead Adam to where the goods were stored. It would certainly help Rotherton in his attempts to stop the crimes in this area, although it wouldn't necessarily lead Adam and Freddy to their prey.

"What brings you out here?" Catherine asked him as they walked their horses along the narrow lane. Carts had made two deep tracks either side of a raised middle, all of which was covered in a dark brown sludge where strong storms had deposited silt and soil. On one side of the road was a dry stone wall, about four feet high, marking the boundary of Ashton's parkland, which undulated softly over the downland hillocks. Here and there, the landscape was broken up by a mature elm or oak tree, or a small copse of newer trees with more slender trunks. The chimneys of the Ashton home were just visible on the horizon, thin streams of smoke rising from some of them.

On the other side of the road, beyond a grass verge and a deep ditch through which water trickled, there was woodland where a mix of evergreens and deciduous trees grew in haphazard rows.

"We're quite a way from Hadlow Hall," continued Catherine, and he nodded.

"I was exploring," he said. "I don't know the area,

and when people mention somewhere—a house, a village, a landmark—I like to picture it in my mind, don't you?"

"It hadn't occurred to me before, but yes. When someone mentions something, it's easier to make sense of it when you can envisage the scene." She studied him for a moment. "Did someone mention something that happened here, to pique your interest?"

In for a penny, thought Adam. "I saw Lord Rotherton this morning," he said. "He was unhappy because the smugglers were out and about last night."

She frowned. "Why would that make him unhappy? His jurisdiction does not stretch to the coast. And, by definition, I would think smugglers would need to be at the coast."

"To land their ill-gotten gains, they would," he agreed. "But apparently, they bring them inland to hide them, and that *is* in his jurisdiction."

"Ah, yes." Catherine smiled. "I have heard that. They say the coast guard is too good at patrolling the coast, so they have to come further inland."

"It's a common occurrence, then?" He kept his voice light as he feigned innocence.

"I don't know, to be honest. But if Lord Rotherton thinks so, I suppose it must be."

Not the answer he'd fished for, although for his personal peace of mind, it was the best answer she could give. Still, he'd have to satisfy more than just himself that she was not involved, so he pressed on. "It intrigued me," he said. "I wondered, where would one hide contraband in this neighborhood?" He tried to seem nonchalant while he watched every move, every expression on her face. It made him feel sly and underhanded.

"I never gave it much thought."

"It's not really something to exercise most people, is it? But it was driving poor Rotherton to distraction."

"So you thought to explore the neighborhood to see if the villains left a keg or two of brandy in the middle of the road?" Catherine laughed, and her eyes sparkled the way they always had in his memory.

He shrugged his shoulders. "The stuff has to be somewhere. Probably in the most unlikely place. For instance, I heard of a gang in Essex who hid it in the crypt of the local church." Adam grinned. "Puts a whole new perspective on the idea of the church being full of spirits."

She rolled her eyes at his schoolboy humor. "That won't happen here, for I cannot imagine the Reverend Mr. Burgess allowing illicit goods within fifty feet of any church over which he presides." Having met the man at the Potters' soiree, Adam agreed. Catherine laughed and continued, "Any smuggler coming within half a mile of his domain would likely find himself sermonized half to death, if not excommunicated altogether."

"Do they have excommunication in the Church of England?"

"He would introduce it." She bit her lip guiltily. "That was unkind of me, wasn't it?"

"Not if it's the truth. And I won't tell, if you don't." He gave her a conspiratorial wink. "Not the church, then. So, where? What about the cellar of a local house?"

Catherine looked surprised. "I think people would know if their cellar was commandeered."

Her astonishment at his suggestion was so innocent he began to relax. Her father may yet be guilty, but Adam would wager Catherine knew nothing of it.

"The householder would have to be in on it," she said. "Their upper staff, too, for anyone with a cellar big enough to hide the goods must have staff." She frowned. "Although, surely, anyone with a house that big would never be involved in such goings-on. Think of the scandal if they were caught!"

She had a point. People wouldn't want to risk anything being found in their own homes. "Where then?" he asked.

"A barn? Stables?"

"Busy places. Somebody would be bound to find it there."

"Mayhap they bury it, like pirates' treasure."

He narrowed his eyes at her, skeptically. "They're looking for easy money, not hard work."

They walked along the lane, coming up with other suggestions. They began sensibly, the ideas plausible, but as each was discounted, the suggestions became more and more absurd, until they'd laughingly discounted the duck house on Lord Frantham's pond, and the weathervane on the church spire, the summer house behind Rotherton Assembly Rooms, and the flower gardens at the center of the square in Crompton Hadlow.

"It can't be there!" She laughed, a clear, joyous sound he hadn't heard for far too long. He hadn't realized how much he'd missed it, and he wished he could trap it in a box and take it with him, so he could take it out and listen to it when she was once more gone from his life. The thought that they must part again, and this time she would not only send him away but hate him too, caused a sharp pain in his chest, as if someone had pierced him with a sharpened blade.

"If one wanted to hide something and keep it secret," she continued, "one must put it somewhere people don't visit. Somewhere like…" She thought for a moment, her brow furrowed. "Marshy Meadow." She grinned triumphantly. "Nobody goes there. There's nothing to go to, and even if there were, people would steer clear, what with the tales of ghosts and demons attached to the place." She moaned in what she clearly thought was a ghostly way.

Adam froze for a fraction of a second before he pasted on a smile and acted as if this was yet another joke, although he thought it might, at last, be anything but. He didn't know where this Marshy Meadow was but, according to Catherine, it was isolated, and the tales of ghosts were exactly what smugglers might use to keep away nosy but superstitious locals.

"Marshy Meadow?" he asked, hoping he didn't sound too eager.

"Wasteland down by the river. There's nothing there, except the aforementioned ghosties." She laughed again. "Which would, if you think on it, make it the perfect place for the smugglers. Lord Rotherton would never catch them there, would he? His men would be too frightened to go near after dark." She frowned, thoughtful. "Although the smugglers would probably feel the same way, so they wouldn't go there to hide the goods in the first place."

"This Marshy Meadow sounds fascinating."

Catherine grimaced. "It isn't. It's wet and muddy, and the perfect place to ruin your clothes and lose your boots when they sink in the quagmire."

"It's near here?" He kept his tone light, and prayed

she would think his interest was in the jocular spirit of their earlier talk.

"Not far." She gave him directions to it. "But I warn you, if you go there and find yourself up to your chest in mud, do not blame me."

They circled her father's estate, riding up one narrow lane and down another, moving single file along tracks that cut through hedges of hawthorn and holly bushes, broom, fern, and grassland, past beech and silver birch, bramble and nettles lying dormant at their bases. They skirted the outer edge of Rotherton and passed fields of ploughed soil waiting for seeds, and green meadows where horses, cows, and sheep grazed.

They were almost back to where they'd met when they saw the herd of deer wander out of the park, across the road, and then through gaps in the hedgerow and into the trees.

Catherine peered after them, then gasped in delight. "Oh, look!" she said. "The first flowers of spring." She scrambled from her horse, the skirt of her habit riding up against the saddle, showing off her dainty half boots and the slender calves above them. Adam watched, appreciatively, until Jem cleared his throat. Then he looked away across the landscape and tried to seem innocent.

"Could you hold her for a moment, please, Jem?" She smiled sweetly at the groom as she handed him her reins.

"Yes, miss," said Jem, his reluctance clear in his tone. Catherine either didn't notice or chose to ignore it as she moved across the road, jumped over the narrow ditch, and headed into the trees. Jem looked uncertainly after her.

"I'll see that she is safe," said Adam. He dismounted, handed over his own reins, and followed her into the woods.

Chapter Nine

The sandy ground was uneven beneath his feet as Adam made his way between the trees. He side-stepped tangles of last year's bracken and bramble, and roots that had forced their way up through the soil. Here and there were patches where the day's heat had not been enough to melt the ice in the tree's shade. Farther ahead, he could see the dark blue of Catherine's habit.

She crouched next to a bed of crocus, their yellow and purple flowers bright against the icy ground. "Isn't it lovely?" she asked, her voice hushed with reverence at the wonder of nature.

"Indeed, it is," he answered, though he wasn't looking at the flowers. Her dark hair was held in a sleek bun nestled at the nape of her neck, just below the brim of her blue top hat. A few strands, which had come loose from the pins as she rode, reached down over her neck to her shoulder, and a curl lay against the side of her cheek, a contrast to her creamy skin and dark wine lips. Her riding habit hugged her slender body and showed off the enticing curves of her breasts. His heartbeat galloped at the sight, his breath shallow, his mouth dry. He swallowed, hard.

She smiled at the flowers. "It always feels like the long, cold winter is over when I see something like this."

He felt the same.

Catherine pulled off one of her gloves and reached

out with her long, fine fingers to stroke the edges of the petals. Adam almost groaned out loud as his stomach kicked and his thighs hardened. He fisted his hands at his sides, the leather of his gloves tightening across his knuckles.

She shifted slightly and picked up a tiny part of her skirt, not enough to show him her legs but more than enough for his mind to paint pictures of them. Long and slim, well-shaped from frequent horse riding and ballroom dancing, he wished he could caress them as gently as she caressed the flowers, his fingers teasing the soft flesh until she trembled and…

"My hem is dirty." She laughed. "My maid will be cross."

Adam shook himself and banished the images.

She glanced up. Their eyes met. She did not look away. Her gaze was sure and yet uncertain, innocent and yet all-knowing, and it drew him as a candle flame entices a moth.

He moved forward. One step. Two.

Catherine stood and faced him fully. The sound of the birds, the breeze, the tiny noises of the woodland, all disappeared as they drew closer, closer, until he could see the tiny flecks of gold and amber hidden in the rich chestnut of her eyes. He saw each long, dark lash framing them, the soft down of her cheek. Her lips parted, just a fraction. The scent of her enveloped him—lavender, mixed with the fresh wintry air on her skin and the linen soap on her clothes. Her eyes moved from staring into his and fixed on his mouth. His breath caught. Blood whooshed past his ear, a roaring, tumbling waterfall of sound. The beats of his heart wracked his body, so loud and strong he thought she must be able to see and hear them. His trousers tightened. There was nothing he could do to save himself.

Then she smiled, a mix of shy innocent and wicked wanton that almost sent him plummeting over the edge. She leaned in closer. Or mayhap he did; he could no longer tell. All he knew was they were together, toe to toe, breast to chest, the warmth of her reaching out to him, pulling him in.

Of their own volition, his arms went around her shoulders. Her skirts brushed his trousers, and he felt the shiver of it down to his soul. Her breath smelled of mint tooth powder, and the tea she'd drunk at breakfast. She tilted back her head and closed her eyes, and moved nearer. Her face was less than an inch from his now. He felt her soft breaths against his skin. Their lips met.

The kiss was gentle, barely there. Her lips were cold from the outdoor air, but her mouth was warm. A soft sigh escaped her, a sound of contentment. Encouraged, he kissed her again, pulling her tighter against him, his hands stroking her back through the wool of her pelisse.

Shyly, Catherine kissed him back. Her hands reached around his waist under his coat, and he felt the warmth of them against his back, building the desire within him until he thought he must expire from it.

Gently, he pressed the tip of his tongue against the seam of her mouth until she opened, letting him in. His tongue danced with hers, and he made a sound, deep in his throat, not unlike the purring of a cat. Catherine's arms moved up, over his chest, his shoulders, then wrapped around his neck. Her gloveless fingers played with the ends of his hair and sent soft, delicious shivers through his scalp and along his spine. Vaguely, he knew her hat toppled to the ground. They both ignored it.

Adam pulled his mouth from hers, and she moaned, but her complaint turned halfway to a mewl of delight when he nuzzled at her neck, his lips finding the pulse point behind her ear and nibbling at it until she melted against him. He touched her shoulder, stroked her arm, her side, then cupped her breast through her clothes. She arched her back, pushing herself farther into his hand.

There were too many layers. Too much clothing between them. Vaguely, he knew there was a reason for that, but he could not think what it was, and right now he didn't care. He wanted, no *needed*, to feel her skin against his skin, to see her, to touch her, to know every part of her.

He wasn't aware that he'd removed his gloves, but suddenly his fingers were free, and he felt the damp thickness of her woolen pelisse, the cold bone of the buttons as he slid them through the stiff buttonholes. He pushed open the coat, exposing her slender neck, and the soft mounds of her breasts peeking above the neckline of her dress, hinting at the fullness still hidden. Her chest rose and fell, rose and fell, accentuating her pebbled nipples. Adam wet his lips as every nerve in his body filled with electricity. He bent his head to kiss her again, his hands reaching out to undo the bodice of her gown…

Someone coughed loudly. Both Adam and Catherine started and, for an instant, she looked as confused and disoriented as he was. Then her eyes widened in alarm and she pulled away, turning from him, her back stiffly straight as she rebuttoned her coat. Adam took a deep breath and willed himself calm, then half turned, grateful that his greatcoat hid the telltale state of his trousers.

Jem stood a few yards away, his expression bland,

his face unreadable. "Begging your pardon, Miss Ashton, but we ought to be getting back."

Catherine cleared her throat, but she could not hide the tremble in her voice. "Yes. Yes, of course." She turned, her coat rebuttoned now, though there was a rosy glow to her cheeks that had nothing to do with the cold, fresh air. "I…er, I got carried away. Admiring the flowers." She gave Jem a smile that was dazzling, though it was filled with nervousness. Then, eyes fixed straight ahead, not making contact with either man, she marched back to the lane.

The stable boy watched Adam for a moment longer. His expression was carefully neutral, none of his thoughts and feelings on show, which somehow made them more obvious. Adam nodded his understanding, and Jem looked satisfied as he gave just enough of a bow to acknowledge Adam's status as a peer, but which left him in no doubt what he truly thought.

Jem followed his mistress back to the road, where Adam heard them mount up and ride away.

He stood for quite a while after she had gone, relishing the cool shadow of the wood and willing his body to come back under his control enough that he could walk away.

****

Jem helped Catherine back into her saddle and remounted his own horse, leaving Adam's bay tethered to a tree. She did not look back into the wood. She didn't dare. She couldn't believe what they had done.

Adam Mason had kissed her. Right there, in the open air, in a place where everybody and his wife might have seen them. More, Catherine had kissed him right back. She'd responded to the feel of his lips on hers, the faint rasp of the skin on his jaw, the warm strength of his arms wrapped around her, cocooning her. He'd tasted of coffee and the salty bacon he'd eaten for breakfast, and she'd smelled his cologne, fresh and woodsy, on his skin, the starch on his cravat, the musk of masculinity.

What might have happened next, had Jem not come upon them as he did? Oh, Lord! That was something she could not think about. She was not naive and completely in the dark about all that happened between men and women. Not only had she grown up in the country and seen enough animal behavior to have an inkling, but in London, despite what gentlemen and chaperones might think, the girls did not simply stand together and discuss hats and gloves. Some had older brothers and sisters, or maids who were willing to tell them what they wished to know, and even, now and then, enlightened mamas who thought a girl should not go to her marriage bed in complete ignorance. Those girls passed on what they had learned in shocked whispers. Other young ladies had read books they'd found in their family libraries, the kind of books their parents would be appalled to see them with. There were even one or two who, Catherine would not have been surprised to learn, had firsthand knowledge.

Catherine would like to think the kiss she had shared with Adam would not have gone further than it had. Common sense would have prevailed, Adam would have been gentlemanly enough to end it before it went too far and, anyway, she was not so shameless.

No matter what she would like, though, she knew those thoughts for lies. If she was honest, and with herself she must be or all was lost, she had to admit she had been caught up in the moment and would have given herself to him gladly.

Her eyes stung with tears of embarrassment and shame, and a huge lump blocked her throat, making it impossible to swallow. Adam must think her a complete wanton. Had he been disgusted with her? Horrified by her behavior, her eagerness? Her cheeks burned. Even the cool air could not calm them.

They were still burning when they rode into the stable yard, the steady clip of the horseshoes ringing against the flagstones. Jem dismounted and came to help her down. She did not meet his eye.

"I'll see to the horses, miss," he said, quietly.

"Thank you." Barely more than a whisper, it conveyed everything she needed to say to him. He nodded his head and she felt reassured, watching him as he led the horses away before she made her way into the house.

After changing into a woolen day gown in lavender, to which she added a cream-lemon scarf around her shoulders, Catherine went downstairs to the morning room, where she found her mother sitting by the fire, drinking tea with her particular friend, Mrs. Bell. They were clearly enjoying a good gossip, so Catherine turned, thinking to make her escape. Unfortunately, Mama looked up and smiled at her.

"Catherine," she said, her smile welcoming. "Ring for more tea before you sit down." Catherine did as she was bid.

"I had it from the viscount's valet," said Mrs. Bell, clearly continuing a conversation they'd started before Catherine arrived. She assumed they spoke of Viscount Frantham, since the only other viscount in this neighborhood was Lord Hadlow and, from what she'd heard, he had no servants at all, let alone a valet. She thought the ladies were discussing Lord Frantham's health, or mayhap, his son's upcoming wedding to Mrs. Bell's daughter, Amelia.

"Mr. Hicks," continued Mrs. Bell, referring to the valet, "has been dressing gentlemen for years, and he's been privy to some secrets, I can tell you."

"Such as?" Mama leaned forward, the better to hear.

Mrs. Bell waved her hand, dismissively. "He didn't say. He vows he'll take them to the grave."

Which, thought Catherine, was how it should be, if they were secrets.

"Actually, that's rather comforting, is it not?" Mrs. Bell echoed Catherine's thoughts. "Otherwise, where would we be? Imagine if servants could write books! All our secrets might be laid bare." She clapped her hands together and held them in front of her mouth in a gesture that was at once pleading for deliverance from such a betrayal, and horror that any servant of hers might even contemplate it.

"Well, he must have said something to you," reasoned Mama.

Mrs. Bell picked up her teacup, took a sip, then put the cup back into its saucer, deliberately. Her gaze darted around the room as if she were worried about eavesdroppers, before she took a deep breath, ready to impart an important piece of news that must never fall into the wrong hands.

"Mr. Hicks," she said, "said he was in service to a young man about town at the time 'it' happened. It was all the Quality could talk of for weeks, on account of her having been the toast of the Season, and him not only a nobleman but a hero. He distinguished himself in the

American Revolutionary War, apparently. According to Mr. Hicks, it was said that King George lost the war but Lord Abberley won all his battles. Quite dashing, Hicks said he was. But then, I suppose the current Lord Abberley is no slouch, either, is he?"

No, he isn't. Suddenly, her interest in their gossip was real.

The talk stopped when the maid brought in the new tray of tea, some fresh-made buns, *langues-du-chats*, and shortcake biscuits.

"What happened?" asked Mama, once the maid had gone again.

"The Belle of the Beau Monde, Miss Hermione Mason, married the heroic Lord Abberley. Everyone who mattered was there, and they all said how happy the couple seemed. Just one year after the wedding," continued Mrs. Bell, "they had a son. It seemed they lived a golden life. Everything they could want seemed to fall into their laps." She shook her head, sadly, tragedy writ large upon her face. "And then, it was all gone."

"How so?" Mama fixed her eyes avidly on Mrs. Bell's face. Catherine wanted to know, too, but she was at pains not to appear quite so eager.

"Three months after the son was born, the baroness was found dead in the folly at Abberley's estate. It was clear she'd been..." Mrs. Bell leaned farther forward, and her voice lowered to an almost silent whisper. "...done away with."

"No!" Mama was horrified and enthralled.

"And the couple had had what the witnesses called a "violent disagreement" just before. The servants said that after they quarreled, he took himself into the library and got very drunk, and she marched off into the gardens to be alone and calm herself. As you may imagine, the finger of suspicion soon pointed his way."

"But he loved her," Catherine blurted before she could curb her tongue.

Mama and Mrs. Bell shared an indulgent, knowing grin before Mama said, "You have much to learn, my love."

Catherine grimaced. That was what she was always told. Surely she would learn more successfully if, instead of saying that and keeping the truth secret, people explained what they meant?

"They never really suspected anybody else, so Mr. Hicks said." As Mrs. Bell went on with her tale, Catherine nibbled a shortcake biscuit, trying not to spill its crumbs everywhere.

"Did they arrest him?"

"They would have done, had he not been a peer. Anyone else would have been arrested and tried in a jiffy, but he had a title and, well, you know how these things go. There was no actual proof, you see, He swore his innocence and, though nobody really believed him, they weren't willing to try a baron unless the proof was indisputable."

"How awful, if he truly was innocent," murmured Catherine. Her heart ached for the bereaved baron and his murdered wife, and for their tiny son, whose life had been blighted from the start by the dreadful events.

"Then," Mrs. Bell paused, dramatically, "the baby disappeared."

"Disappeared?" Mama's eyebrows rose almost to her hairline.

"Disappeared?" echoed Catherine, shocked even though she already knew there was some mystery surrounding the child, his whereabouts and wellbeing, from having read the entry in *Debrett's*.

"Disappeared," confirmed Mrs. Bell. "Vanished without trace. As you might imagine, speculation ran rife. Everyone thought the baron had murdered his wife, and now his child, like some Bluebeard *de nos jours*. It was made worse because the baron said nothing. He ignored all the talk about his family. Eventually, the local magistrate said he had investigated and was content the child was alive and well, but nobody ever saw him again."

Could Adam be the infant son who'd disappeared? It all sounded very havey-cavey to Catherine, and it brought up more questions, without providing answers.

"What about his wife?" asked Mama. "Did they ever find the proof they needed about her murder?"

"Oh, yes. But it took twelve years and it was only solved when another poor woman died in the same way, in the same place. Luckily, this time the killer was caught in the act."

"The baron?" Mama's face was a study in horror.

Poor Adam, thought Catherine. To have his childhood blighted by all this. Was that why he'd taken his mother's family name? To avoid the scandal?

Mama frowned. "Surely we'd have heard of a baron being tried for murder?"

Mrs. Bell bit on a *langue-du-chat* and spoke around it. "It wasn't the baron."

"Then who was it?"

"I don't know, to be honest. Didn't think to ask his name. All I can say is, the villain was caught and, when questioned, he admitted to six more murders, including Lady Abberley's. Six more! Seven altogether. Can you

124

think it? I could not sleep nights to know somebody like that was about."

"Seven murders? And the local authorities did not realize?"

Mama had a valid point. Even the most simple-minded of watchmen had to have noticed seven people murdered in the same fashion in the neighborhood.

Mrs. Bell shook her head. "That is the most frightening thing of all. The local authorities didn't know because the victims weren't all killed in the same area." She put her hand to her chest. "He might have been anywhere. *We* might have been in danger of him."

Mama gasped. "Oh, my word!"

"Two of the women were killed on the Abberley estate," Mrs. Bell quivered with excitement now. "One was, of course, the baroness, but the other was only a nursemaid. Then there were three killed in the London stews, so we wouldn't know of them, would we? If the newspapers reported every crime that happened to those people, there would never be space for the important things."

Catherine gazed into the fire and decided not to ask what the papers might print that was more important than several murdered women.

"The last three were killed in…Lincoln? Leicester?" She waved her hand. "Somewhere. Again, all working class. The baroness was a mistake, I suppose. He probably hoped one of her servants would come by, rather than the lady of the house. Although, her class didn't stop him, did it?"

"They knew it was him, without a doubt?" Mama was clearly not willing to let go of the delicious scandal of a villainous baron until she had to.

"They did. Not only did the man confess to all the murders, but they found the baroness's ear fobs in his possessions. It seems he took a little memento from each woman he…you know." She shivered, dramatically. "Man must have been a lunatic."

Catherine thought that was a given, since who but a madman would even think of murdering seven women?

"Anyway," continued Mrs. Bell, "it exonerated the baron, and he was welcomed everywhere once more. Although he did not rejoin Society."

"That's understandable," Mama said. "They would have ripped him to shreds while he was under suspicion and, since he was a former darling, they would have taken great delight in doing it."

Mrs. Bell nodded sadly. "The so-called Quality really do delight in saying dreadful things about others, do they not? They prose on about the lives of their friends and talk of things which do not concern them at all." She shook her head. "Nothing better to do with their time, I suppose."

Catherine gazed down at her half-filled tea cup and fought the urge to smile.

"What of his son?" asked Mama. "Was the child ever found?"

Catherine looked up, sharply, then tried to cover her sudden interest by putting her cup onto the tray and taking another biscuit.

"I suppose he must have been," Mrs. Bell answered with a disinterested shrug. "Since he is wandering tame around Hadlow Hall. Mr. Hicks told me nothing else." She picked up a *langue-du-chat*. "Did you hear what Ella Forbes-Smythe said to Caroline Potter?"

No longer interested in their gossip, Catherine

allowed their voices to fade until she could not hear them at all. Her mind reeled with all she had heard. Her heart ached for the family that had lost so much, for the baroness who had died so needlessly, her husband wrongly blamed, the child who had grown up separated from both parents. Although, from what he had said when she'd known him in London, his upbringing had been a happy one. He'd spoken fondly of the man he called Father and hadn't seemed to feel cheated in any way.

There were, of course, still unanswered questions. How could there not be, with a story like this? For one thing, if the baron had been exonerated when Adam was twelve, why had he not reunited with his son? If he had, why had Adam not spoken of his father's title when he was offering for her? And if the baron hadn't returned for his son, why not?

Adam's name was Mason, but that was his mother's maiden name. Had her family taken him in and brought him up? Had the man he'd called Father actually been a grandfather, or an uncle? The questions swirled in her mind, tangling one with another, until she could make no sense of any of it.

If the opportunity arose, she would ask him to explain, and hope her questions—and the accompanying admission she'd listened to more gossip about him—would cause no further offense.

Chapter Ten

Adam left the woods and headed in the direction Catherine had indicated toward Marshy Meadow. Even though it was the middle of the day now and the sun was at its height, away from the shelter of the trees the air was sharp. His fingertips froze inside his leather gloves as he rode, and his face was cold, his cheeks stiff, the tip of his nose pinched.

A mile or so along the lane, he reached his destination and realized he'd been here before. The boggy grassland nestled between two chalk cliffs looked exactly as it had when he'd come across it the other day. On the road side, it ended at a drystone wall and a five-barred gate. On the far side, he could hear the river, booming and bashing the rocks.

"So this is Marshy Meadow," he muttered. The horse shook its head, rattling the bridle as if confirming he was correct. He reached forward and patted the animal's neck. "Doesn't look like the kind of place one would hide contraband, does it?" Then again, it didn't look like somewhere people would invent ghost stories about, either. He peered across the meadow, knowing from his previous visit that it was well named, and if he entered, he'd likely lose his boots, if not sink completely.

"It was just lighthearted banter," he murmured. Catherine had no more thought this place was likely to be the smuggler's hideaway than she'd thought they used

Lord Frantham's duck house. Another dead end.

He made to turn and ride away, but a movement caught his eye and made him stop and stare at the far end of the field. A figure darted across the meadow, without seeming to get stuck in the mud. At the cliff, the person scrambled up a few feet, then disappeared from sight.

There had to be a cave there. In which case, this place might well be what Rotherton sought, and might also lead to answers for Adam.

Adam tethered his horse and, with a deep breath and more than a little reluctance, set about moving across the Marshy Meadow. The ground under his feet squelched as water was pushed from the clay. It coated his boots with brown sludge, and he could feel the cold permeating the leather, although he was thankful that, so far, the boots held out the actual water. With graceless difficulty, he struggled to the cliff wall where, he hoped, the going would be easier. Couch grass grew in hard clumps, and green algae stained the chalk while, higher up, small plants and bushes clung precariously to the rock. Several times, he stumbled as his balance was compromised, and he held one hand to the cliff, for reassurance as much as actual help. His boots were ruined, thick with mud almost to the tops, and his breeches and greatcoat were splattered with globules of dark, foul-smelling clay. The thought occurred that this was a wild goose chase, for if he had difficulty moving here, so would smugglers.

But then, he argued with himself, mayhap that was what they wanted people to think. Mayhap there was a path through the bog, which they knew and he had yet to discover.

About halfway across, he found what looked like a well, a large, round wooden board covering it. *Why on earth would someone put a well here?* He struggled over to it. There was a wall around it, made up of large stones, and the wooden cover had seen better days, gray and warped with age, its edges misshapen where pieces had rotted away. Gingerly, he lifted it, surprised by how heavy it was, far sturdier than he'd expected.

The well under it was about twelve feet deep, and he could just make out the bottom, wet and slick, with a puddle of water that didn't quite cover the whole base. There was no contraband there. He maneuvered the board back into place and moved on.

He was almost at the river when he saw the figure re-emerge from the cliff wall, and recognized him as the youth who'd been bullied outside the forge. The boy still wore the same tattered clothes, gray with dirt and age. His hair was a mass of self-shorn clumps, his thin calves bare, his shoes no more than rags tied to his feet. He saw Adam and ducked quickly out of sight.

The farrier had called the boy "afflicted," and mocked him. There was a childlike innocence about him that Adam thought made him an unlikely smuggler. On the other hand, he might be exactly the kind of person the gang needed for the lowly work—easy to control, cheap, and too simple to be easily interrogated if he were caught.

As Adam approached where the boy—Ned, he recalled—had disappeared, he saw a fissure in the rock, about three feet above the ground. Tucked into a crease in the cliff, it would be easy to miss. From the opening, it went back a few feet before darkness hid everything. Adam stepped nearer to see more, then stepped back, startled and almost falling as he heard the growling of a huge dog.

He swallowed. "Ned?" It came out as a croak, so he cleared his throat and tried again. "Ned? Call your dog off. It's Adam Mason. I stopped those boys at the forge." He prayed Ned had the mental faculties to recognize him before he set the dog on him.

The growling continued.

"Ned? I mean you no harm."

The growling grew louder as it grew nearer. Ned appeared in the cave opening and glared down at Adam, his teeth bared, lips curled back, and growled again.

Adam blinked. There was no dog. Just a very talented mimic, making his feelings known.

He held up his hands, palms out, placating the boy. "I'm not here to hurt you," he said in the same voice he used with skittish horses.

The growling stopped, and the boy cocked his head to one side, contemplating Adam, before he darted back into the darkness and disappeared.

"Ned? Ned!" There was no answer. Adam cursed under his breath and climbed into the cave. If he found the boy guarding contraband, he'd have no choice but to make a citizen's arrest and hold him. He didn't want to do that, but he couldn't leave him free to warn his colleagues, so...

His thoughts came to an abrupt halt when he turned a corner and entered a chamber with a high ceiling. Light flickered on the cave walls from a flame burning in a sconce, giving the chamber an orange glow. There was the slightest smell of damp must, although the walls looked dry and there were no puddles on the floor. A small fire crackled merrily in the center, with what looked like a cooking pot suspended over the flames. In the pot, leaves and pieces of carrot and turnips floated in water. In one corner was a bundle of blankets.

"This is your home?" whispered Adam, appalled at the conditions in which the boy lived.

Ned growled again. Adam stood still, careful not to go forward, which the boy would see as a threat, nor to move back, which might be construed as weakness.

"Are you not cold here?" he asked. The growls softened. "Mayhap I can find you somewhere warmer." The growls grew louder again. "Or not." The growls subsided. "I am sorry to intrude. I'll leave you in peace." The growls stopped. He and Ned stared at one another for a moment before the boy turned away and stoked the fire, a deliberate show that he no longer considered Adam a threat.

Ridiculously pleased by that, Adam turned and walked away, out of the cave and back over the boggy ground. At the gate, he scraped off as much mud as he could, but he knew his boots were beyond saving. It was probably a good thing he had no valet, for any man worthy of the name would have Adam's guts for garters for treating his clothes like this.

Chuckling at the idea of having someone to dress him, Adam headed home, keeping to back lanes and quiet roads where he could, so he was seen by as few people as possible in his disheveled state.

****

"What happened to you?" Freddy sat in a wingback chair in the corner of the morning room where Adam had sneaked into the house, hoping that by avoiding the main entrances he could reach his room unseen.

"Why aren't you in the billiards room getting foxed with Hadlow and Colbourne?"

Freddy laughed. "Why have you been dragged cross

country on your arse?"

"I was chasing a lead."

"On the riverbank?" Freddy shook his head. "I hope it was worth it."

"It wasn't."

Freddy watched Adam, clearly expecting to hear more. Adam looked around, checking they were alone. "I found a cave," he said in a low tone. "Thought it might be something, but it wasn't. Turned out it's home for that boy, Ned."

"The lackwit?"

Adam felt an urge to defend and protect the boy. "He does not lack wits. He's not like everyone else, but that doesn't mean he's stupid. He's got enough nous to take care of himself, and he's built a nice stronghold in Marshy Meadow. No one will bother him there."

"Marshy Meadow?" Freddy frowned. "What made you look there?"

"Something someone said."

The bemused look faded and Freddy straightened, alert and ready. "You heard someone talking? Who?"

Adam grinned. "It was a comment made in jest when I mentioned Rotherton's investigation. I wondered where they might hide things from him, and several places were mentioned. Most of them highly unlikely."

"In jest?" Freddy watched Adam closely. Adam wanted to fidget, to look away from the probing stare. "By whom?"

"By Miss Ashton, if you must know." Freddy's eyebrows rose. Adam sighed, leaned against the windowsill rather than smear mud on one of Bertie's chairs, and told Freddy of their encounter this morning. As he relived their walk, their talk, the time in her company, a feeling of rightness descended and he couldn't help but smile.

Freddy smiled right back. "You seem to be getting on better than you thought you would."

Adam shrugged and stared out of the window at the weed-covered terrace and the overgrown park beyond. He did not want to discuss Catherine Ashton with Freddy. Or anyone else.

"Do you think she can lead us to proof of her father's activities?"

Adam scowled, and Freddy sat back, hands up. They watched each other for a moment. Adam's thoughts whirled in his head, too fast to catch as they tangled together, refusing to allow him to marshal them.

"I'm wet and I'm cold, and I need to change," he said at last, and he retreated from the room.

Half an hour later, he sat in a hip bath, the warm water soothing him, the smell of soap replacing that of the rain and mud and leaf mulch he'd dragged in. His mind was in turmoil, his emotions tossed and thrown like a ship in a storm. He'd sooner face the guns at Badajoz than have this dilemma. If Walter Ashton was betraying his country, he had to be stopped. Adam had sworn an oath to serve Britain, and he would do so, even to death. But if doing that duty hurt Catherine…

He snarled his frustration and slid down into the water, submerging his head, ridding himself of the last of the day's grime. If only everything was so easily washed away.

****

It was after midnight and Catherine couldn't sleep, even though she'd gone to bed earlier than usual. She'd been in a pother all day, and it had only grown worse after dinner, when the family sat in the drawing room, her parents talking while she and Mama embroidered. Catherine could not have said what they discussed as she mechanically made stitches, which would, undoubtedly, need to be ripped out tomorrow.

Two things vied for attention in her head. There was what she had learned of Adam's childhood and all that happened to his family. Her heart went out to the lost little boy he must have been, even though she knew her pity was the last thing a proud man like him would want.

More than that, though, she thought, over and over again, of the kiss they'd shared today in the woodland, wondering what it had meant to him. Was it just a kiss? A snatched opportunity to hold her, touch her, perhaps punish her for rejecting him? Or did it mean he still had feelings for her? And if he did, what would that mean?

Perhaps he thought that now he was a baron, she and Papa would look more kindly on his suit? Certainly, Papa had made no secret of the fact he wished her to have a title, but there were other considerations, too. Much as being a peer made a man eligible, Papa wanted Catherine to be safe and happy in her married life. He would want there to be a mutual liking and respect, if not actually love. He'd also want to be certain that any prospective son-in-law could, and would, look after Catherine and keep her well. Adam's very presence in Rotherton went against him in that. Papa did not want to *buy* a title for her, any more than he'd wanted her to marry a soldier and follow the drum. He would also not be happy to find he'd given over her dowry only for it to disappear into a deck of cards.

Yet, to her knowledge, Adam had never been a gambler before. Nor had he drunk to excess, or indulged in any of the pastimes that parted foolish young gentlemen from their cash. He had always seemed so prudent when they were in London. Catherine could not believe that was simply because he hadn't had the money to throw around, nor because of the fear of court-martial if a serving soldier created debts he couldn't pay. So how had he come to be here, on a repairing lease with Lord Hadlow, one of the worst wastrels in the *ton*? Could he really have changed so drastically?

It was a conundrum. It had consumed her all evening, until she pleaded tiredness and retreated to bed.

Being in her bedchamber was no better. Here, with nothing to distract her, thoughts of Adam, the kiss, and her confused feelings spun in her head like a child's top. She dismissed her maid, needing to be alone, then brushed her own hair. She thought she'd given it the requisite one hundred strokes that Mama said a lady's hair needed to make it shine, though her thoughts were so distracted she kept losing count. It was, however, relaxing and restorative to feel the steady pull of the brush's bristles working through.

She braided it as best she could without help and climbed into bed, but her mind would not relax. She tossed and turned, kicked off her blankets, then pulled them over her again, pounded her pillows, then smoothed them, until finally, as the grandfather clock in the hall struck twelve, she accepted she was not going to fall asleep.

With a heavy sigh, she climbed from her bed and wrapped her robe about her, then pushed her feet into her carpet slippers. The fire in her room had banked now, and there was a chill in the air, which made her shiver, tempting her to climb back between her toasty warm sheets.

"What would be the point of that?" she muttered peevishly, and she poked at the fire, sparking new life into it. When small flames licked at the coals, she lit a taper from them and put it to her candle, then sat and tried to read. It was no use. She couldn't settle to her book, either.

There was one last thing she could try. A drink of warm milk, accompanied by a couple of shortbread cookies, should do the trick. Taking her candle, she made her way along the corridor and down the stairs as quietly as she could and sneaked into the kitchen.

The kitchen was dark and quiet. Most of the center space was taken up by the large table where Cook kneaded bread, rolled out pastry, and did any number of other things. It was also where the servants took their meals, sitting on benches each side, while the butler and housekeeper sat in more comfortable chairs at each end. The wooden tabletop was spotless, as was the deep sink and wooden draining board, the red pantiled floor, and the huge oven that took up most of the far wall. It was to this oven that Catherine went now.

It took but a minute to pump the fire inside the stove and set a saucepan of milk on top before going into the pantry and carefully lifting down the cookie tin. She took two shortbreads and replaced the tin, added cinnamon to the now hot milk, and sat to enjoy her midnight feast.

Adam came to her mind again, but she held up her hand, determinedly. "We are not thinking of him now," she scolded. "Adam—*Lord Abberley*—has taken up entirely too much of my time and energy tonight as it is." She would think of anything but him. Her embroidery pattern, perhaps, or the gift she planned to make for

Papa's birthday, or her horse. No. Not her horse, for that made her think of the ride this morning and all that had happened then.

The new dress Mama had promised she'd have for Amelia Bell's wedding. She would think of that. She could doubtless think for hours about its color and style, what it would be made of, what accessories she would need, and whether Adam would think she looked well in it.

With a roll of her eyes and a frustrated sigh, Catherine drained her cup and turned to leave the kitchen but stopped when she heard a strange, muffled noise, like a thud and a scrape together. For a moment, she stood unmoving, listening carefully. All was silent.

"My imagination," she muttered and made to leave once more. It sounded again. This time, when she listened, it came a third time and she realized whatever it was moved around in the cellar, the door to which was between the pantry and the back door. It was very faint, and had Catherine not been sitting quietly in the kitchen, she wouldn't have heard it at all.

Nobody should be in the cellar at this time of night, surely? No one should be down there at any time at all, unless it was to fetch her father a new bottle. Since Papa wasn't a big drinker, that didn't happen often.

The noise sounded again. Mayhap an animal had fallen in and was frantically looking for a way out? Poor creature, she thought, but she could hardly raise the hue and cry at this time of night over a fox. Especially when she could probably deal with it herself. If she couldn't release it, she might at least be able to secure it and stop it doing too much damage until the men were up and about.

The last thing she wanted was to open the door and have the creature rush into the kitchen, where it would cause untold mayhem, and definitely rouse the entire household. So she opened the door as slowly and quietly as she could, hoping not to frighten it.

There was a light coming up from the cellar, a bright, steady light such as that from a lantern. Catherine frowned. Foxes did not light lanterns. Was somebody down there, stealing papa's wines? She decided she would sneak down, see who it was, and decide what to do about it from there.

A man laughed. Another shushed him. A voice she didn't recognize said, "What? Nobody can hear us."

Oh yes, they can. Catherine blew out her own candle and put it on the floor just inside the kitchen. If the thieves saw her light and realized she was here, they might be desperate enough to... She didn't want to find out.

Stealthily, hugging the stone wall, she crept down the stairs. They were coarsely made of wooden slats, with gaps where the risers should be. The wood was un-planed and uneven, and the balusters and the worn handrail were rough, too.

From about halfway down, she could see the entire cellar below. Pressing herself against the wall to keep in the shadow, she watched, confused, and more than a little frightened. The cellar was a hive of activity, and she recognized several of the men moving about. Her father's steward, Milton, stood to one side, directing the other men, who included the farrier from Rotherton, as well as Sayer, Papa's head groom, Frederick, the under-footman, and two of Papa's gardeners. All the men wore dark clothes, though most bore streaks of white, as if they had brushed against chalk.

Most of the wine racks stood in long rows around the walls, their shelves filled with dusty bottles of wine and spirits, but one wine rack stood at right angles to the wall, beside a doorway, beyond which she could see a dark passage where orange lights bounced and flickered. The men went back and forth to that door, collecting heavy-looking boxes and smaller caskets, large barrels and little kegs, which they piled in the cellar, where Milton directed them. Some of the men grumbled, and others scolded them. One or two made lewd suggestions, and Catherine blushed at words she barely understood.

Clearly, this was the contraband Lord Rotherton searched for. Not only that, but the smuggling gang she and Adam had joked about today seemed to include half her father's household!

The scandal, if news of this got out! Should their neighbors ever discover their home was lousy with miscreants and illicit goods, they would be ruined. And if they themselves fell under suspicion... How could Milton, Papa's trusted right-hand man, do this to them?

Another thought hit her like a bolt from the heavens. What if Papa knew? In fact, how could this happen here, in his house, if he did not know?

The thought that her father might be guilty made her stomach churn, and she took deep, slow breaths in an effort not to be sick. If he was not guilty, then he was being duped by his employees. That did not make her feel any better.

Now that Catherine had seen this, what was she to do? She could ignore it and plead ignorance, she supposed, but she had never been good at dissembling. And if she gave it away and Papa *was* involved...she might put his neck in a noose. The bile rose again.

Mayhap Papa was unwillingly involved, coerced by these men to do their bidding. It might be so. If she went to Lord Rotherton with this information, she might save him…

No. Catherine knew the local people called the smugglers "the gentlemen" and ignored their activities. People who heard them coming knew to turn to the wall so they could truthfully say they saw nothing if they were questioned. However, Catherine also knew "the gentlemen" were anything but. She had heard tales of their viciousness toward their enemies and those deemed to have crossed them. Beatings, maimings, and even killings were not beyond them. Going to Lord Rotherton with this information was far too risky, for both Papa and herself.

She could tell Adam. He was not the magistrate and thus wouldn't necessarily feel obliged to call out the militia to arrest Papa. And, being a man of the world, he would know what she should do.

But what if he insisted on calling in the authorities, obliged or not? Adam had been a king's man all his life. He'd served in the army with distinction, and valued honor, integrity, and loyalty to the crown. He would see this as going against all he had fought for in Europe. She could not risk Papa's freedom and his life by telling Adam.

"That's the last of them," said the farrier. He pulled a cloth from his pocket and mopped the sheen of sweat from his face.

"Thank you, gentlemen," answered Milton. "Best get home to your families now."

He ushered them through the doorway and into the

darkness beyond. When there was just himself and Frederick left in the cellar, Milton said, "Lock up after me," before he followed the others.

Frederick gave a sloppy salute. Once Milton disappeared, he closed the door that had stood open behind the displaced wine rack. Even in the dim light of the one candle left in the cellar, Catherine could see the wooden door was ancient, gray and pitted. It had clearly been in place a long time, longer than the fifteen years her family had owned the house. That Papa could not have ordered its installation was some small comfort to her.

The footman locked the door, leaving the key in the lock, then moved the wine rack on tiny wheels at its base and clicked it into place along the wall, hiding all trace of the door before he slapped his hands together, ridding them of the dirt and cobwebs of the cellar.

The slapping noise galvanized Catherine. He was the only man left, and he'd just sealed the secret exit, which meant he would need to come up the stairs and leave through the kitchen. If she didn't move, he would find her and then Lord knew what would happen to her.

As quickly and quietly as she could, Catherine climbed the stairs back to the kitchen. She almost tripped over her candleholder, which skittered across the floor. She snatched it up and clutched it to her chest, then looked around wildly, wondering where to go. With no time to get out of the kitchen and along the hallway before he came, she dived under the table and curled herself into the smallest ball she could manage. Moments later, Frederick left the cellar, locked the door, sauntered into the pantry, and came out a moment later chewing on a piece of shortbread. Then, looking as if he hadn't a care in the world, he went through the door into the main part of the house.

Catherine crawled from under the table and went to the door, opened it a smidgen, and peered through. Frederick made his way along the corridor and up the family's stairs as if he were the master, not a servant. He didn't look back.

Once she knew he was definitely gone, Catherine relit her candle at the stove and made her way back into the cellar. It was cold down here, and she could smell the damp air that had seeped in when the door was open, along with the dust that tickled her nose, and the musty fruit scent of old spilled wine. The shadows danced in the candle's flame, making grotesque shapes of the piles of contraband, the wine racks and the stained, chipped table where generations of butlers had decanted wine. The atmosphere was oppressive, almost alive, and Catherine shivered, not entirely from the cold.

It took a few minutes to figure out the mechanism that released the wine rack, but once it clicked loose its tiny wheels made moving it easy, and she soon faced the old, battered door. The key turned silently in the lock, and the door opened without a sound, revealing the dark, dark tunnel behind it.

"Oh, well," she said on a deep breath. "Here goes nothing," and she took her first step into the unknown.

Chapter Eleven

Catherine walked into a long, narrow tunnel dug out of the earth, its walls sheer slabs of clay, shored up every few feet by sturdy oak beams. The floor was uneven and pitted, its surface hardened under the impact of many years of use. She glanced over her shoulder, thinking, for just a moment, that it might be more prudent to give up this exploration and head back to the safety of her warm bedroom.

"Where you won't be able to sleep for thinking of it," she muttered. The words were hollow and echoey. She shuddered. Perhaps she should have waited and asked Adam to come with her. "Ridiculous." She shook her head, annoyed at herself. "Even if you needed him— and you don't—how would he get into the house without being seen?" The servants would be alerted to his presence before he even got to the cellar door, and if they saw Catherine and Adam going down the stairs together, without anyone else, the scandal would be horrific. No. She had to do this on her own.

After a few minutes, the tunnel changed. The clay walls turned to chalk, which made the candlelight go farther and seem brighter, although the walkway was just as narrow and the temperature dropped. Water dripped in a slow, steady rhythm, and a strong smell of damp chalk and mold filled the air. Several times, she trod in shallow puddles, soaking her thin slippers and chilling her feet. She wished she'd had the foresight to wear her boots, and chuckled at the absurdity of that thought.

"Because a woman should always be prepared for a midnight snack in her own kitchen to become a trek under the Sussex countryside," she whispered. It sounded far too loud.

The thought of being under the ground sobered her. She looked up but could not see the ceiling of the tunnel, just darkness beyond the circle of light from her candle. She had no idea how much land hung over her head, whether it was a few feet or several hundred. One thing she did know, though—even a few feet of soil and rock would be heavy if it suddenly came tumbling down on top of her.

A sudden panic quickened her heartbeat and made her breathing raspy and shallow. She swallowed, trying to calm herself. The tunnel had been here for years, she reasoned. Probably centuries. It had definitely been here since before Papa bought the house, and would likely be here for many years to come. She had no reason to think it would fall now, simply because she walked through it. The panic subsided, but it did not leave her altogether.

Catherine felt a strong urge to talk to herself out loud, rather than just in her head. She wanted, needed, to hear a human voice, even if it was her own, but she couldn't give in to that. Her whisper had sounded loud; if she spoke normally, her voice would positively boom, which would alert the men ahead of her. Even though she could not hear them, not so much as the scrape of a boot on the floor, she didn't trust that to mean they had all gone. So she carried on in silence.

After a long fifteen minutes, the chalk-scented air began to smell fresher. A breeze made the candle flame flicker, the chill of it patting her cheek and brushing strands of hair around her face, telling her she was nearing the way out. Relief made her smile, every muscle relaxing, every nerve end tingling. She would get out of here, alive. The fact that she would have to go back through the tunnel to get home again was something she did not wish to think about.

After the slight chill of the tunnel, the temperature outside felt icy. Wondering where she would come out, Catherine became aware of the smell of frost on damp earth, and of wet grass, and heard the roaring, hissing spit of fast-flowing water. She frowned. She must have come farther than she thought, because her home was nowhere near the river. No houses were built close to it for, at certain times of the year, when winter snow or spring rain came heavy, one could almost guarantee the river would breach its banks and flood everything nearby. The thought made her shiver, and she prayed the river level was not currently high, nor the tunnel mouth low enough to be within its reach.

The entrance was narrow, no more than a crack in the chalk, half covered with wild bushes, their branches pushed to one side, shaped by the bullying wind. Even now she could hear that wind whistle and moan, though the breeze on her face was gentle and the bushes hardly moved, as if to reassure her that the wind's howl was much bigger than its blow.

Realizing that if the smugglers were still nearby, the light from her candle would give her away to them, yet not wanting to blow it out and have to return through the tunnel in the dark, Catherine placed it carefully just inside the entrance, then stepped out onto a ledge about fifty feet up the sheer side of a chalk cliff. Below her, she saw the dark expanse of Marshy Meadow, its puddles shining in the moonlight, which shone more than enough for her to see quite well. The river was to one side of the meadow, roaring and growling like an enraged beast. The other side was the road, and beyond that, fields spreading off to the horizon. She could see nobody in the meadow, nor any way to get down to it. Instead, the ledge was part of a narrow path which hugged the wall and ascended to the top of the cliff.

Catherine blew out a heavy breath and saw white steam in front of her face. Her feet ached with cold and her skin prickled with goosebumps, and the tip of her nose and the edges of her ears stung. She pulled her wrap tight around herself, although it was far too thin to make any real difference to the cold. Holding it in place, she folded her arms tight across her body, her hands tucked into her armpits, as she took her first steps along the path toward the summit.

The freezing night was beautiful in its way. Thousands of stars shone brightly in a deep sky, sparkling and twinkling, mirroring the frost that covered the ground and caught in the moonlight. The cliff sides shone white, making the sparse plants clinging to them seem darker in contrast.

The path reached the top and sloped down again, moving away from the cliff edge, across the coarse grass. It wound between boulders, some the size of a man's head, others as big as Papa's desk. Bushes were dotted about, all wind shaped, and there was one gnarled, misshapen tree.

The murmur of voices and the pungent smell of tobacco alerted her that she was not alone, and she ducked behind the biggest boulder, a few feet from the edge. Thanks to its shape, she could peer over it without much risk of being seen, unless one knew when and where to look. The hem of her nightgown rested on the frozen grass, growing wetter by the second, making her colder. The soles of her feet were wooden blocks. She prayed that, if it came to it, she would be able to run. Her jaw trembled and she put her tongue between her teeth to stop them chattering as she peeked at the men.

There were eight of them, milling about, stamping their feet, their white breath mingling. A small orange-red circle glowed to one side of the group and she saw the farrier from Rotherton, smoking. To his side, another man held what looked like a lamp, but only a fine sliver of light escaped it. Was that a smuggler's lantern? Catherine had heard of them but had never seen one before.

"You ask him, won't you?" one of the men said.

"Said I would, didn't I?" replied the farrier. He threw the end of his cigar to the ground.

"Aye, well. This is the third time this month, and we ain't seen a penny piece yet."

"He's good for it."

Catherine frowned. Was "he" the leader of the smuggling gang? The man who oversaw everyone else and organized the entire enterprise?

Please don't let it be Papa.

She closed her eyes and prayed it wouldn't be. Just because half his staff were involved and they were using his cellar, it didn't mean he knew anything about this.

Please don't let him be involved.

"Here he comes. Look lively." Milton instructed the men, who stopped moving idly and showed more purpose.

148

"About time," said one.

"Just you ask him," said another.

"For God's sake, don't keep on," grumbled the farrier.

They formed a group behind the farrier, and Milton and all looked down the slope that led from the cliff top to the fields and roads outside Rotherton.

Somebody walked up the slope. Catherine moved slightly, trying to see who it was. The man was breathing heavily from the exertion of climbing, and as he reached the group, he said a word Catherine was not supposed to know. His voice was familiar, although for a moment she couldn't place it. His clothes were all black, and a floppy-brimmed hat hid his face. It wasn't until he pushed back the brim that she was able to see him. When she did, her jaw dropped and her eyes widened. There, breathing heavily from his climb, was Mr. Colbourne.

His jaw was set and his face looked grim as he looked from one man to another. Each looked away or bowed their heads, clearly unwilling to meet his eye. Some took a step back. Catherine didn't blame them.

"All right," he said, after a full minute of glaring had left them subdued. "What do you want?"

The men shuffled and mumbled. Then one of them nudged the farrier, pushing him forward. Mr. Colbourne turned his attention to the man, who suddenly looked very unsure of himself.

A second passed. Two. Mr. Colbourne never took his eyes from the farrier, who looked like a man about to go to the gallows. The others watched. Nobody moved. Nobody made a sound. Catherine shivered and gripped the side of her boulder.

One of the men nudged the farrier again. He half

turned to them and scowled, then turned back to Mr. Colbourne and raised his chin defiantly. "We want paying," he said.

Mr. Colbourne didn't move a muscle. His gaze stayed steadily on the farrier's face. The farrier swallowed. One of the men took another step back.

The farrier cleared his throat and said, "We, er, these men want to be paid. What they earned."

"I'm sure they do." Mr. Colbourne's voice was frighteningly soft. He looked from one man to the next. His actions were placid, but Catherine suspected his mood was anything but. "Could you not have picked somewhere a little more hospitable to do business?" he asked. "And perhaps a less ungodly hour?"

The men relaxed, seeming to take his even tone as a sign all would be well. Catherine was not so certain. There was something about his stillness, the easy way he held himself, which told her he was now at his most dangerous.

The farrier straightened and grinned as he answered Mr. Colbourne. "There's nothing else that's godly about any of this, so why should the hour be any different?" He glanced over his shoulder at the men grouped behind him, then, filled with bravado, he turned back to Mr. Colbourne, his head held high. "Besides, it don't hurt you toffs to get your hands dirty, now and then. Reminds you where the cash comes from."

Mr. Colbourne moved so quickly, Catherine barely saw it. He jabbed, and the farrier collapsed. He lay in a crumpled heap on the ground and did not move again.

The fear in the group was palpable. The other men stared at the farrier, disbelief on their faces. Nobody moved. Nobody tried to help their fallen spokesman.

"Anyone else want to say something?" Mr. Colbourne looked around, making sure to encompass every other man. Heads shook. Feet fidgeted. After a few seconds, Mr. Colbourne nodded, satisfied. He put his hand in his pocket and withdrew a pouch, which rattled and chinked when he bounced it on his palm, as if he was gauging its weight before he tossed it to the nearest man.

When the others gathered around, the man said, "Not here. My cottage." He bowed slightly to Mr. Colbourne and made his way down the slope. Others followed, until the only ones left were Mr. Colbourne, Milton, Sayer, and the farrier, who was now conscious but struggling to stand. Sayer reached out and helped him to his feet, where he swayed, unsteadily.

Mr. Colbourne watched the other men leave for a few moments, until their voices faded and they were completely gone from sight.

"Where'd you find them?" he asked.

Milton shrugged. "Not like I can advertise the positions in the *Times*, is it?" He held up his hands. "I do my best."

"Do better. There's too much at stake."

A cramp bit hard into Catherine's calf and she stiffened, pursing her lips against the agonized cry she wanted to release. She flexed her foot, trying to ease the seized muscle, and trod down hard on a patch of gravel. The pebbles crunched and skittered as she dislodged them, and the men turned sharply to her. She dipped down behind the boulder, thankful for once that her hair was dark, for the blonde she'd always wished for would have shone like a beacon in the bright moonlight.

"There's someone there," growled Mr. Colbourne, and he took a step toward her.

The cramp was nothing compared to the icy grip terror had on her heart. He was going to find her. There was nowhere to hide. Nowhere to run. Her ribs hurt as her stomach clenched. She couldn't move. She couldn't think. She couldn't breathe. She closed her eyes tightly and prayed.

Somewhere nearby, a fox barked. Catherine started and opened her eyes. It barked again.

The men laughed. "Just a fox," said Sayer. Relief sounded in his voice.

"Maybe," said Mr. Colbourne. He didn't turn away from where she hid. His stare was so intense, she thought he must be able to see her through the rock.

He took another step.

The fox barked again. Then a cockerel crowed, and Milton cried out, "There!" He ran toward the cliff edge, Mr. Colbourne right behind him. Catherine glanced over and saw Ned Fellowes, standing on the edge of the footpath, feet apart, arms akimbo, a silly grin on his face.

Move, Ned. Silently, she willed the lad to run before they reached him. Instead, he giggled, then barked again, exactly like a fox, before crowing like a cockerel. Sayer laughed.

They were nearly on him now. Catherine opened her mouth to cry out, though she didn't know if she actually would have done, or what she would have shouted if she had. She never got the chance. A hand clamped over her mouth, silencing her.

Chapter Twelve

She stiffened, ready to fight with all she had, until a man whispered against her ear, so quiet, she almost couldn't hear him. "It's me," he said. "Adam."

Adam. Panic subsided and she smelled his cologne, fresh and clean on the night air. He turned her so she was pressed against the boulder, and wrapped himself around her, his body acting like a blanket, warming her and sheltering her from the weather.

"Stay still," he whispered. She did.

"Don't let him get away!" yelled Mr. Colbourne. Running footsteps thudded over the footpath and onto the chalk ledge, making stones fly. They stopped abruptly. "Where'd he go?" Mr. Colbourne demanded, angrily.

"He just vanished." Milton sounded incredulous. "How can he just vanish?"

"He does that," called the farrier. His words were thick, and Catherine suspected he talked over a swollen jaw.

"It's only Ned," added Sayer. "He's no threat. He's one of them whatchamacallits. Lunatics. The boy can't even speak."

"That's right," said the farrier, and he groaned. Speaking obviously hurt him.

Farther away now, Ned giggled, then barked again.

"Be off with you, you halfwit!" yelled Mr.

Colbourne. Ned barked once more, then all was silent.

Cursing idiots who put themselves in the way of other people's business, Mr. Colbourne strode back from the cliff edge, followed by Milton. Catherine stiffened again. She was relatively well hidden here, behind this rock, but she was wearing white. If they looked over, they would see her for certain.

The men walked past and rejoined Sayer and the farrier. Adam relaxed, loosening his hold on her, and she turned her head to see him. Like Mr. Colbourne, he was dressed in black, his clothes coarse and woolen, such as a laborer might wear. He saw her watching him and winked.

It took her another minute to realize what he had just done for her. By draping himself across her, he had hidden her white nightgown and robe, and made it less likely she would be discovered. He had saved her from…whatever those men might have done to her. Gratitude flushed her cheeks, before she frowned and asked herself, why was he here in the first place?

Catherine's first thought was that he might be in league with the smugglers. Was he a part of the gang that had unloaded their goods into Papa's cellar? Or had he come with Mr. Colbourne for his rendezvous? He might be a lookout, perhaps, or he could be there to back the other man up should he find himself outnumbered and in trouble.

That wasn't something Catherine expected would happen to Mr. Colbourne often, not if the way he had felled the farrier was anything to go by. Still, it never hurt to have help when one walked into a situation one could not entirely control.

Yet from what she could see, Mr. Colbourne was

completely in control, and had been since the moment he'd arrived on the clifftop. So why would he have brought Adam?

It was feasible that they were working together. They were friends, after all. She frowned, realizing she hadn't actually seen much evidence of a close relationship between them, though they *were* both friends of Lord Hadlow, and they *were* both staying at his home, so it was possible.

She didn't know anything about Mr. Colbourne, other than that he was close to Lord Hadlow and had stayed with him at Hadlow Hall on numerous occasions. She assumed that he was, like his host, short of funds but, then again, on the evidence of this night, his friendship with the viscount would also be the perfect cover for involvement in the smuggling.

Which brought her back to Adam. He had made no secret that he was pockets-to-let. Could he be involved because smuggling provided income? Catherine had heard it was a lucrative business. It was said a laborer might be a Tubman for one night and earn several months' wages. It stood to reason, therefore, that those at the top would earn considerably more.

Of course, that did not answer the question of why Adam wasn't out there among the other men. Why was he lurking in the shadows, keeping himself invisible to them?

She was thankful he had not betrayed her presence to them. In fact, he had hidden her. But why? Catherine didn't think he would want to see her harmed, but at the same time, he must know that if he let her go, he ran the risk of her reporting these activities to Lord Rotherton. Then Adam, along with all the others, would be arrested and imprisoned, transported, or worse.

The idea that Adam Mason would swing made her shudder. She didn't want that, no matter what he had done.

He had saved her from discovery, so perhaps she could return the favor by not mentioning him when she told Lord Rotherton what she had seen.

But what if one of the others gave him up?

His hand softened across her face and he shifted slightly so he no longer pressed her against the rock, but was more to the side of her, though the right side of his body still covered her left, warm and comfortingly solid against her. She savored the feel of him against her, wishing they could stay like this forever, even as she knew she should make him move.

She turned her head and found him watching her. Their eyes met and he winked at her again. She raised her eyebrows, surprised at his flippancy, and he put a finger to his lips, warning her to be silent, then turned to watch the men on the clifftop. His jaw clenched, so hard and tense it was a wonder his teeth did not shatter, and his mouth thinned. He must have sensed her watching him, because he glanced at her. For a moment their eyes met and held, before he turned back to the group.

In that instant, Catherine knew she'd been wrong earlier. Adam was not a part of the smuggling gang. He was not their lookout, nor was he the support for Mr. Colbourne, although she could not have said how she knew this. Even so, she was absolutely certain. Adam was here tonight for the same reason she was: he had followed someone and was learning what he could of their plans. The only thing she did not know was whether he was, like her, here by chance, or whether he had watched and followed them by design. Perhaps Lord Rotherton had recruited Adam to go where the earl could not, and then report back to him.

Before she could ponder it more, Sayer hawked loudly at the back of his throat, regaining her attention. He spat at the ground and Catherine grimaced and felt slightly sick.

"That's all for now, is it?" he asked.

"Tomorrow," growled Mr. Colbourne.

Sayer groaned. "We've been out too many times lately. You get too bold, too greedy, they'll redouble their efforts to stop you. Before you know it, there'll be militia men from Rye to Brighton, so thick a mouse won't get through."

"We'll get through."

Catherine frowned. Mr. Colbourne's confidence and determination frightened her, because of what it might mean for the men ranged against him. She knew, as well as anyone in the area, the tales of the smuggler gangs and all they did. The Hawkhurst gang had been smashed fifty years ago, but they were still spoken of in hushed tones, their name held up as a warning to any who thought to oppose the "gentlemen." She made no doubt the modern gangs, while they might not be so brazen as the Hawkhurst men had been, would be just as vicious in their dealings with their enemies.

"Anyway," Mr. Colbourne continued, "it's just a little chore I have for you. Nothing to concern you in the least." He grinned. "Doesn't involve the ship. Nor even a trip to the coast. Not tomorrow, at any rate. Come to that, the job's not even to be done after dark."

Beside Catherine, Adam tensed. The other men grumbled, confused.

"The ship can't come until the night after tomorrow," explained Mr. Colbourne. His lips narrowed, his teeth gritted as if the news displeased him.

"You want us during the day?" Milton's voice was a high-pitched squeak, and he shook his head. "No, no, no. That won't do. I cannot—"

"Yes, you can." Mr. Colbourne's glare brooked no argument.

Milton seemed to shrink. Sayer spat at the ground again, and the farrier stared away over the Marshy Meadow to the cliffs on the other side, although he couldn't possibly see anything over there in the pitch darkness.

"The chest is coming from London tomorrow."

"To Hastings?" asked Milton.

"To here." Milton's eyes widened, and he shook his head. Mr. Colbourne ignored his objection. "I don't want it too far from me once it's been delivered."

What on earth could be so valuable to the man that he would want it near, though he intended to send it on a ship as soon as he could?

"I'll take it down to Hastings myself the next day," he said. "Before then, I need you to stow it safely at Hadlow Hall."

Hadlow Hall? Was Lord Hadlow involved as well? Catherine glanced at Adam. He did not return her look but focused on the men.

"Hadlow Hall?" Sayer was alarmed. "Are you mad? His lordship's in residence. And he's got guests with him."

"I know." Mr. Colbourne's smile was dangerously icy. "I'm one of them."

"Aye. You and two bleedin' fops."

Adam stiffened, presumably at being called a fop, but the movement he made was infinitesimally small, and quickly passed. Catherine wanted to reach out, touch his arm and reassure him he was no such thing. She did not do so. She didn't dare.

Mr. Colbourne sighed, as if the conversation wearied him. "Don't worry about them."

Sayer scoffed. "Easy for you to say. You're not the one they'll catch. He'll be all over us, demanding we explain ourselves. Which we can't. And I'm telling you now, I don't fancy killing a viscount. Not for you. Not for anyone."

An icy finger drew down Catherine's spine. She shivered. These men talked so casually about killing, or not killing. Sayer did not wish to kill a viscount, but he said it so matter-of-factly. The implication was that he would kill somebody lower down the social scale and never think twice upon it.

Adam must have felt her shiver, because he wrapped his arm about her shoulders, pulling her closer, sharing more of his warmth with her. Although it didn't rid her of the chill horror encasing her heart, his touch and his warming concern was welcome. She prayed he would not let go.

"Nobody's killing the viscount or anyone else," said Mr. Colbourne, his tone suggesting the very idea was absurd. Relief made Catherine's shoulders sag. "No need," he continued. "They won't know you're there."

"Says you," grumbled the farrier. Mr. Colbourne shot him a look of contempt, and the farrier took a cautious step back.

"They do have a point, Alfie," said Milton. Catherine had never noticed before how much he seemed to whine when he spoke. And how well did he know Mr. Colbourne, that he could use his given name?

Milton went on, "Hadlow is an idiot, but he's not stupid. He will wonder about these men bringing a chest full of gold into his house."

Catherine gasped. Adam glared at her. She bit her bottom lip and grimaced, apologetically. Thankfully, the men were too caught up in their plans and gave no indication of having heard her.

But…*gold*?

"He won't be there," said Mr. Colbourne. "He'll be at Offham, with his other guests, watching me knock seven bells out of this so-called Sussex Champion."

The farrier laughed. "All the oafs at Offham," he sneered, pronouncing the village name the traditional Sussex way of "Oafham," and not the way many of the visitors to the area pronounced it.

Mr. Colbourne rolled his eyes at the farrier's quip. "The point is, they will all be from the house. And since even Hadlow cannot possibly lose if he has the nous to put his blunt on me, we'll probably be there well into the evening, celebrating. Which will give you plenty of time to bring the chest in and stash it safely."

Catherine struggled to make sense of what she heard. It had confused her when she first realized they planned to load something onto a ship to be taken out of England, rather than the other way around. She had never heard of smugglers shipping things out, but once she knew it was gold they planned to send, it fell into place. It stood to reason the people who brought the contraband from France would want to be paid, and that was, doubtless, what this was. That it required an entire chest of gold to pay them confirmed what she had earlier

160

suspected. Smuggling was lucrative.

"Is everything else in place?" asked Mr. Colbourne. There was a chorus of "ayes" from the others. "And you're ready?" They gave him more "ayes."

Adam tensed at that. His every muscle was so taut now, Catherine thought he might snap. He made her tense, too, as she wondered what they had said to make him like this. What had he heard in their conversation that she had missed?

Mr. Colbourne went on, his tone warning. "We cannot have problems arising now. Not this close." He bared his teeth in a grin that frightened Catherine. "As soon as that gold reaches its destination, we must be ready to move." He rubbed his hands together. "This time, there'll be no Waterloo."

Adam pressed closer to her, pushing her harder against the rock. It was shockingly cold against her chest, and its rough surface snagged at her wrap, pulling threads, but the warmth of him at her back more than made up for it. She could smell the smoky sweetness of his sandalwood cologne, the night air, trapped in his clothes, overlaying the dusty chalk of the rock, the wet earth and grass, the ice on the soft air. His heartbeat was strong and fast against her back, and hers sped to keep time with his. His breaths, almost silent, caressed the back of her neck, making it impossible to listen more to what was said, or to make sense of what she did hear.

If only...

She closed her eyes and pushed away the inappropriate thought, angry at her own thoughts and feelings. Where was her common sense? Her self-preservation? There could be no "if only." Certainly not with a band of criminals standing six feet from them, plotting the-Lord-alone-knew-what, and talking nonchalantly of killing anyone who might stand in their way.

Besides, she clarified to herself, there would be no "if only," even if these men were not nearby. The chance of anything growing between her and Adam Mason had come and gone. All they had now were memories of more hopeful times, memories tinged with a cool and distant civility. They weren't even allies in tonight's endeavor, for if she hadn't been in danger of discovery, she was certain he would never have made his presence known to her. She needed to keep that in mind before she made a fool of herself.

Still, she couldn't help but savor everything about their closeness. She took in every detail, committing it to memory, so that she might relive it when he was gone from her life once more.

A few feet away, Sayer coughed loudly, cleared his throat, and spat. "Long as I get paid," he said. "That's all I care about."

Mr. Colbourne turned sharply to him, shocked. Tension built. It seemed to make the air crackle.

Sayer shrugged his shoulders, and tried to look unbothered, though the wariness in his face gave him away, even as he spoke in a relaxed tone. "I'm too bleedin' old to be impressed by armies and their silly little generals."

Mr. Colbourne was suddenly furious. He stepped forward, his shoulders squared, fists clenched. The farrier stepped back, his jaw dark and swollen, a reminder of what the gentleman could do.

Milton stepped into Mr. Colbourne's path, preventing him from reaching Sayer. "He's an old man,

Alfie," he soothed, his hand resting, placatingly, on Mr. Colbourne's chest. "He doesn't mean any insult."

Mr. Colbourne glared at Sayer over Milton's shoulder, though he made no attempt to move nearer to the head groom. The farrier looked from one to the other, nervously. Sayer rubbed his thumb and forefinger over the skin where the top of his nose met his forehead.

Beside Catherine, Adam's body seemed to thrum with the tension coursing through him. It made her shudder, her stomach swooping. She leaned closer into him, and he tightened his hold. She wished...oh, how she wished.

If they got away from here without falling foul of these villains, and if they didn't freeze to death in the meantime, she decided she was going to kiss him. She would hold him as close as he now held her, her arms around his neck, her hands stroking the hair that fell, a little longer than was proper, over his collar. Her lips would touch his, making her heart beat faster, her breaths come shallower, while the delicious warmth grew in her, and the strange, overwhelming ache between her legs, making her want...need...

Lord! She was a wanton! What would he say if he knew her thoughts? She prayed he could not read them on her face. Completely nonplussed by her own response to him, she turned her attention back to the men and tried to push the idea of kissing Adam from her mind. Easier said than done.

"I'm not that old," Sayer objected to Milton's description of him. "Although I'll admit I am too old for these shenanigans. This cold air is playing havoc with my arthritis."

For a moment, the men stood, staring at one another.

Then Mr. Colbourne straightened and his fists uncurled. "I can see it would," he said. He sniffed and added, "You should take care, really. Man of your age and infirmities. We wouldn't want anything happening to you, would we?"

Sayer looked up sharply, and the two men stared at each other for several seconds more before the groom turned away. Mr. Colbourne continued to watch Sayer for a few more moments. Finally, he nodded. "We'll meet soon."

He turned and walked away, down the hill, and was soon swallowed by the darkness. Catherine fancied the temperature rose after he had gone.

Once Mr. Colbourne could no longer be seen or heard, Sayer raised his hand, his middle finger extended in a contemptuous salute. Milton slapped his hand down. "What are you doing, you idiot?"

"He annoyed me. All that stupid talk." Sayer mimicked Mr. Colbourne. "There'll be no Waterloo." The groom spat on the ground. "The man's a bleedin' zealot."

"That he is," agreed the farrier.

"Be quiet. Both of you." Milton looked nervously down the hill where Mr. Colbourne had disappeared.

The farrier laughed, bitterly. "What's he going to do? Hit us?" He stroked his swollen jaw. "He doesn't need a reason for that. Might as well be thumped for a sheep as for a lamb."

Sayer nodded. "He can't do worse, can he? He can't kill us unless he gets the say-so from the paymaster."

"There's worse things than death." Milton looked as if he knew what he was speaking about.

"Not while he needs us."

Milton grinned wryly. "He won't always need you."

"I'll cross that stream when I come to it."

"He'll have to catch me first," said the farrier. "Soon as I get paid, I'll be gone." He shivered. "Somewhere warm, I think."

"You'll both be going somewhere warm, you keep goading Colbourne."

Sayer hunched his shoulders and thrust his hands into his coat pockets. "I'm home for bed," he announced. "I don't want to hear another word tonight about Colbourne and his little army." He walked away, stumbling on the uneven ground.

"Not worth going to bed," said the farrier, looking up into the dark sky. He moved down the hill in Sayer's wake, and Milton followed him. Soon, all three were gone.

As their voices faded, Catherine felt the tension drain from her body, leaving her aching and exhausted. She took her first deep breath in what seemed like hours, her lungs stinging, her chest tight, her shoulders on fire from being held stiffly for so long.

Adam pulled her upright and swung her around to face him. His jaw was clenched, his mouth a grim line. His eyes sparked with temper.

"Just what the hell—deuce—are you doing here?" he whispered, and there was no doubting his fury. "Do you know how much danger you've put yourself in?"

Chapter Thirteen

Adam had been terrified when he saw her crouched behind the rock, the moonlight making her white nightclothes shine like a beacon. If Colbourne had turned his head…Adam didn't even want to think about that. He had raced across the grass, risked giving himself away to the men he was watching, then thrown himself at her, using his own body to shield hers. At least his clothes were dark, giving him a chance to avoid detection.

It had taken time to get his fears for her under control. His heart had beaten so fast and loud, he was amazed everyone in Rotherton hadn't heard it, let alone the men on top of the cliff. What with the loud drumming it created in his ears and the struggle to control his breathing, already shortened by the steep climb following Colbourne, it was a wonder he could hear anything else at all.

He pressed against her for as long as he could stand to do so. Her body was slender beneath his, her curves delectable. He smelled her soap, an intoxicating lavender, out of place on the icy air. She trembled as the damp and cold seeped through her clothes, and he'd wrapped his arm around her, wanting to share his own warmth with her. His body reacted, growing uncomfortably and leaving her in no doubt what she did to him. Embarrassed, he'd shifted to the side, wanting to take the pressure away, and minimize the disgust she must have for him.

Time and place, Mason, he silently chided himself. He wished the rock they hid behind was bigger, for he could not move from her without giving away their presence, so he had to endure the feel of his right side against her, while his left pressed into the stone. Its cold, rough surface went some way to cooling his ardor, though nothing could make it dissipate completely. And all the time, he felt her next to him, curvy yet slight, soft and, at the same time, firm, rigid with bravery, even as her heart beat fast and fearful, like a bird trapped in his hand. Her hair was soft as watered silk and her skin alabaster smooth, and he was going to go to Hell for what he was thinking.

He took as deep a breath as he could without making noise, and fought to push away his desire, concentrating all his attention on his true reason for being here: the men in front of him, and their plans.

He was disappointed they didn't say more, which was ridiculous. He could hardly expect them to stand here and announce their plans in full detail to anyone who might be eavesdropping. What they had said had been, to an extent, incriminating, but he was aware that much of it was circumstantial and open to interpretation. Talk of gold to pay for an army was interesting, although nobody had mentioned France, or Bonaparte, specifically. Even the mention of Waterloo was not, in itself, enough to present to Lord Fremont as definitive proof, and it certainly wasn't enough to put a man's neck in a noose.

The one thing that had intrigued him was talk of Colbourne's paymaster. Colbourne may be socially superior to his fellow conspirators, but he was, apparently, just another cog in the machine, reporting to someone higher. Could that be Walter Ashton?

Adam closed his eyes and prayed it was not so. He didn't want to think of the wealthy Cit as a traitor. Not while Adam was pressed against the man's daughter, his body aching with the weight of his unholy thoughts about her.

He was definitely on the road to Hell.

Guilt at his unwarranted lust now combined with fear for her safety and exasperation at the risk she had taken, and his temper sparked. She could have been killed. Or worse. Those men would have made her pay for her inquisitiveness, and they would have shown no mercy. As his mind conjured all the ways they might have hurt her, his anger grew, until by the time they'd gone and he could confront her, it was all he could do not to shake her until her teeth rattled. He grabbed her shoulders and whirled her around to face him, his rage almost white hot.

"Just what the hell—deuce—are you doing here?" he'd whispered, the fact that he nearly swore in her presence a testament to his emotion. "Do you know how much danger you've put yourself in?"

Instead of looking cowed and ashamed, she lifted her chin and glared at him mulishly. "I could say the same to you," she answered. "And I suspect your being here was deliberate, which is worse."

"That is by the by." Adam hated the defensiveness in his tone.

"Is it?" She was less than convinced. "You ran a terrible risk, sneaking up that hill." She pointed to the steep slope leading from the clifftop to the road below. "Spying on men who, it is clear to me, would not have taken kindly to it if they'd found you. You have no right to scold *me* for accidentally doing what *you* did on purpose."

"Accid...how can you be here accidentally?" Was the woman going to try to persuade him that she "accidentally" left her home in the middle of the night—in her nightclothes, no less—climbed the hill, and lay in wait for the villains? More, to get here undetected by them, she must surely have arrived ahead of them, which meant she must have known they would meet here. Was that also an "accident"? Or was she in league with her father? That idea brought a searing pain to his chest, and he fought the urge to groan and massage it away.

"I heard something in the kitchen and followed the noise," she answered him. She continued speaking but he hardly heard her. *In the kitchen?* Her home had to be more than a mile away, even as the crow flew. A long-eared bat could not have heard any noises over such a distance.

"And when they'd gone, I followed them and found myself here," she finished.

He stared at her for a long moment, trying to make sense of what she'd said. Finally, he blinked, trying to work out if she thought him stupid or simply credulous.

"You don't believe me," she accused. "I will show you." She marched away from him, but she didn't head down the slope toward the road. Instead, she moved to the cliff's edge. "As I said, I did not know this was where it would come out."

She stepped down off the path onto a narrow ledge. Jagged in places, wide here and narrow there, it formed a path from the clifftop to the meadow below. It was where Ned had disappeared after he'd distracted the men

Adam spied on.

Catherine picked her way down cautiously. Adam followed. Far enough down the cliff face to be hidden from anyone at the top, they reached a bush which seemed to cling for dear life to the chalk. It narrowed the path and would not be easy to pass without losing balance, but Catherine made no attempt to go past it. Instead, she stopped and waited for him.

He was almost on top of it before he realized it was not growing into the meagre soil of the ledge at all. Instead, it was a free-standing mass of twigs and branches, shaped to look like a bush and placed so they hid a small crevice in the rock behind them. Narrow enough to be overlooked by anyone who didn't know of it, the gap was still wide enough for a man to get through, if he squeezed sideways. Behind the "bush" a tiny light flickered.

Catherine stepped past the bush, picked up the light, and held it up. It was a night candle, short and thick, in a small candleholder of the type people carried to bed because it was unlikely to topple and cause a fire. It looked as if it would last for another half hour or so.

Adam swore under his breath.

"Quite," she said, and his cheeks heated to know she had heard him.

"You came through here?"

"As I said." Her soft whisper echoed in the narrow darkness. She held up the candle, marginally increasing the circle of its light. He saw the rough walls, too close together for comfort, the uneven floor, the darkness that swallowed the ceiling above. "I didn't know it would come out here. I didn't know where it would lead. And there were times I nearly turned back and had nothing more to do with it, but, well, I couldn't bring myself to do that. So I just kept going."

He reached out to touch the walls. Standing in the middle, he could easily reach both sides. They were cold and had a slightly dusty feel. But something didn't make sense. One could not possibly keep secret a tunnel like this, considering the number of people using the kitchen daily.

"From the cellar," she corrected him when he voiced the thought. She gave him a sidelong look. "I said I was in the kitchen, I heard the noise and crept down to the cellar to find out what it was."

"My apologies." He remembered she had spoken more on the cliff, while he was lost in his thoughts and fears.

"I didn't know it was there before then," she continued. "I doubt anyone not involved in the…whatever this is," she waved a hand in front of her, "would know. I certainly would not have found it if I hadn't seen the men using it."

He nodded. "Show me."

Catherine hesitated. "First, can you answer a question of mine?"

Adam sighed. He didn't have the time nor the inclination to stand here in the cold and damp. The sooner he could learn everything and report back to Lord Fremont, the better. Besides which, they were both chilled through, and Catherine was shivering violently. If she didn't get back to her home and change into warmer, drier clothes, who knew how ill she might become? He did not want that on his conscience, no matter what her father—and she—may have done. "We should move on," he said.

She shook her head. "First, my question."

Stubborn little… He could see from the tilt of her chin that she meant it. On this, it would be quicker and easier to surrender. "Ask," he said.

"How is it that you came to be here? I know why I am here, but you…?"

He shrugged his shoulders. There was no need to lie about this part. "I followed Colbourne."

"Why?"

"When a man sneaks out after midnight, dressed in dark clothing and acting furtively, it raises suspicions that he may be up to no good. So I followed him to discover what he was about."

"He may have been going to meet a—lady friend."

Adam chuckled. "Then I would have sneaked away, my curiosity satisfied, and my lesson learned."

Catherine nodded. "Where did Ned fit in to it?"

"Excuse me?"

"Ned. I thought you were working together. How does he fit in with it?"

She was sharp, there was no denying that. "He distracted them when you—when it seemed they would discover you."

"You mean when I alerted them to my presence. You don't need to mince your words, my lord. I made a noise and was nearly caught. In my defense, unlike you, apparently, I have never been well versed in the art of subterfuge." He shifted uncomfortably. "Although I am not sure how I feel about you using that poor, benighted boy as part of whatever plan you had. It doesn't sit well to put him in danger when he can't understand what he is doing."

"He understands well enough," he told her. "And for

your information, I didn't use him as part of my plan. It was his plan."

She narrowed her eyes at him. "You expect me to believe Ned Fellowes came up with a plan, shared it with you, and then set it in motion? That boy cannot speak, my lord."

"But he can communicate very well when he wishes to do so." Adam thought back to those terrifying moments on the clifftop when Catherine had shifted her position and the men had turned toward the sound she made. Adam had frantically tried to think what to do. He knew he could not let them find her; he would die before he allowed that, but how would he get her out of harm's way?

Before he'd had a single useful thought, Ned touched his shoulder, making him jump. He'd winked, barked like a fox, put a finger to his mouth, grinned and gestured that Adam should go to Catherine. Then the lad had belly-crawled over the rough wet ground without so much as a whisper of sound. He reached the cliff edge, stood, and barked again, then crowed, distracting the men and giving Adam the opportunity he needed to reach her.

"He might have been hurt," Catherine mused now.

Adam suspected Ned had known that very well, and had come to her rescue anyway.

"Smugglers do hurt people," she continued, "if they get in the way. Don't they?"

Adam didn't really want to answer that.

Catherine paled, and the flame of the candle wavered as she shook. "They said..." She leaned against the wall as if all her energy had suddenly drained from her. Adam pulled off his coat and wrapped it around her trembling shoulders, as he should have done in the first place. And he called himself a gentleman?

The candle steadied. She used her free hand to pull together the lapels, burrowing into his coat with only the hand that clutched the candle outside of its warmth. "They said," she repeated on a loud swallow, "this time there would be no Waterloo." Her expression ran through myriad emotions as she thought about Colbourne's words and what they meant. "They're paying for an army, aren't they?"

"They're planning to," he answered.

"For…Napoleon."

He could not lie to her. She was far too astute. "Yes."

She took a deep, shuddering breath. "They are traitors."

"Yes."

Catherine sank to the floor. "Oh, God," she breathed. "I know them all."

He said nothing. What could he say?

"Half of them work for my father." She huffed sharply before she glared at him. "You knew."

Adam cringed, guilt racing through him. Though why he should feel guilty when he was doing nothing but his duty, he did not know.

"Is my father involved?" Her voice was tiny now.

That was not a question he had wanted her to ask, and it left him with a dilemma. Did he confess his suspicions, or not? If he did, would she race home and warn Ashton? How could Adam prevent her doing that anyway?

"You think he is," she decided.

"I've seen no evidence that he is." It was the only

truthful thing he could say. "He may know nothing of it." *Or he may know everything.*

She thought for a moment, then shook her head. "He would not be involved in anything like this. He loves his country as much as you or I do. He would no sooner turn traitor than he would—than he would—fly to the moon." Her voice broke on the last words.

Without conscious thought, he took the candle from her hand and set it on the floor beside her, then pulled her to her feet and into his arms. She fit perfectly there, her softness against the firmness of his own body, her head resting on his shoulder. Her hair was cold below his chin, and her breath was warm on his chest where his shirt was open. Her lavender scent pushed aside all the other scents of the dank tunnel, until he could almost taste her in the air, imagine his mouth on her soft skin, the luscious fullness of her lips, her tongue playing with his. His pulse sped up and his thighs stiffened, his trousers tightening. He heard her gasp and knew she had felt his arousal.

What was he thinking? He let go of her as if she had burned him, and stepped back as far as the narrow tunnel would allow.

It took him some while to force his brain to work again. Catherine watched him, but he couldn't meet her eye. She must be disgusted with him, with the thought that he would try to take advantage of their situation in such a dishonorable manner. He cleared his throat and bent to pick up the candle.

"It's freezing here, and you are in your night rail." He glanced at her, then looked away sharply. Even though his coat covered her, he fancied he could see her nightgown clinging to her shoulders, outlining her breasts, then falling in drapes to her ankles, tantalizing him with hints of what lay beneath. Hair that had escaped her braid fell on her cheeks and brought into focus the heart shape of her beautiful face. A face now filled with anger, her lips pursed and her eyes narrowed. He half expected her to slap him, and he couldn't say he would blame her. He absolutely deserved it, and more.

He swallowed hard, fighting to get himself back under control. "We must…" His voice sounded strained. He coughed once and tried again. "We must get you home before you catch your death. Lead the way." There. That sounded businesslike. Proper. Right.

For an instant, she looked as though she would argue, but then she changed her mind, gave him a curt nod, and took the candle from him. Holding it out in front of her, she moved through the tunnel, going deeper into the cliff. He took a deep, fortifying breath and followed her.

****

Catherine's head swam and her insides churned as she tried to make sense of everything that had happened this night. *Adam was not indifferent to her.* She had felt his reaction to her, pressing against her stomach. He had been affected by her nearness, and he'd wanted her just as much as she had wanted him. Even in the candlelight, she had seen the desire in his hooded eyes, and she had heard the catch in his breath, felt the racing of his heart, smelled the want on his skin…

No! This was not what she should be thinking about, here and now. There was far more to worry over than whether Adam Mason still desired her. She should steer her thoughts to things that were much more important, both to her and to her family.

That her father was loyal to his country she made no doubt. He would die before he turned traitor. Oh, he might buy a little brandy from "the gentlemen," not worrying too much that Frenchmen received the profits. For aught she knew, he was aware of the contraband in his cellar and turned to the wall, figuratively speaking. But treason? Not in a thousand years!

But Catherine wasn't stupid. Just because she knew, beyond doubt, that Papa was not involved in treason, it didn't mean others would see things in the same way. Others did not know him as she did, and they would be less than convinced by her assertions. Once it was known that his steward and his head groom were most definitely involved, and his under-footman and some of the outdoor staff may very well be as well, she knew it would not look well for him.

What would Adam do? Would he give Papa a chance to prove his innocence? Or would he report him as a suspect?

Lost in her thoughts, she walked through the tunnel in silence. Adam didn't try to speak either, though what thoughts occupied him she could only guess. The candle created a small pool of light directly ahead of her, but that seemed to make the darkness around them thicker, more impenetrable and suffocating. Catherine's mouth was dry, and she swallowed several times, trying to rid herself of the bitter taste of dread at the back of her throat. She could barely feel her feet now and didn't even flinch when she trod in the chill puddles. Her hair was heavy against her back, her nightgown wet, slimy with mud, and completely ruined. None of that mattered. All that mattered was finding a way to persuade Adam that Papa was innocent and should not be reported—or worse, arrested.

She still had not thought of a way to do that when they reached the door at the end of the tunnel. It was open, just as she had left it what seemed a lifetime ago but was probably just a couple of hours. The candle picked out the shapes of boxes and barrels, the dusty wine racks, the table for testing wines, the first few steps of the staircase that led up to the kitchen.

Behind her, Adam shut the door and locked it. Catherine turned to see him put the key in his pocket.

"They left that in the door," she whispered, and she moved the wine rack back into place.

One side of his mouth kicked up in a wicked smile. "If they can't open the door, they can't collect the merchandise."

"They will know we have been here."

Adam shook his head. "They'll think one of the others took it, betraying them." She blinked, surprised, and he explained, "When two or more men stand to profit from an illicit venture, they will suspect each other's every move. There is no honor among thieves, no matter what Shakespeare said. And it never hurts to sow discord among the enemy's ranks. Now, come on. Let's get you warm before your servants start moving around." He ushered her to the stairs.

In the kitchen, he built up the fire in the stove and made them both a drink of hot chocolate, and carried both cups up the stairs as he followed her to her bedchamber. Now that she was safe from Mr. Colbourne and his men, the energy that had sustained her on the clifftop seemed to drain away, leaving her bone-deep weary. She could barely put one foot in front of the other, and climbing the stairs required a gargantuan effort. She could not have carried her own drink without spilling it, and it was beyond her to object when Adam came through the door behind her, set the cups on her nightstand, and stoked the fire, which was all but out now. He added more coal, got the flames burning, then stood, wiping his hands together to get rid of the coaldust. Catherine wanted nothing more than to crawl into bed and go to sleep, but somehow that was a step too far, so she sat in the chair by her window instead.

"Right," he said, briskly, "that should get the room warm soon enough." He moved to her chest of drawers and pulled out a clean nightgown, then took a bath sheet from a pile on a shelf in her garderobe. "Let's get you out of those clothes."

"Pardon?" Catherine's eyes widened, and she was certain she had misheard him.

Adam's sigh was longsuffering. "I didn't think you would be missish about this," he said.

She bristled. "Behaving in a correct way is not being missish."

"It is if your modesty could kill you." He unfolded the bath sheet and held it up. "I know what I'm saying, Catherine. You need to get out of those wet clothes before you suffer harm. I've seen it happen to soldiers in the Spanish mountains. They got wet and cold, and their wet clothes cooled their bodies to a dangerously low degree. Before they knew it, they became ill. They stopped feeling cold, then they became sleepy, and once they were asleep, they died. I don't want that to happen to you. So take off those wet clothes, dry yourself, and get warm."

Catherine bit her lip. What he said made sense. Her clothes were wet and icy, clinging to her skin. It would be a blessed relief to get out of them. But the lessons in manners and decorum, and correct behavior, had been well learned, and it wasn't easy to overthrow them.

Adam laid the bath sheet and clean nightgown on the edge of the bed. "I will turn my back," he said, and he swiveled so that he faced the wall, clasped his hands behind his back and stared at an indifferent watercolor of a vase of flowers as if it were the most compelling thing he had ever seen.

Reluctantly, she pushed herself up from her chair and unbuttoned her nightgown. Although the buttons were at the front and did not require the services of a maid, Catherine still had difficulty. Those buttons were cold and wet, the material around them hard, and with her stiff fingers, maneuvering them was not easy. Once she had managed that, she peeled the gown from her chill body, while it tried to tangle itself around her limbs. More than once she was tempted to ask him for his help, but she struggled on, determined to the point of foolishness not to give in.

At last, she was dried inside the rough bath sheet, and able to slip the clean nightgown over her head. Her feet and wrists ached, and her calves stung, but she was no longer in danger of freezing to death.

She moved toward him.

Chapter Fourteen

It had taken all Adam had within him not to turn around while she undressed and dried herself. He told himself he was tempted to turn only because he was worried for her—she might need his help. He was a liar. He ached to see her, the way he had so often seen her in his mind's eye…the soft curves of her hips and waist, the roundness of her bottom, shapely legs, pert breasts. He wondered whether those breasts were tipped with a soft, blushing pink or if they were a deeper, almost brown color. Did her nipples stand to attention as she pulled the bath sheet over them? The way parts of him were standing now at the thoughts that filled his head. Once more he fought the urge to turn, telling himself over and over that he was a gentleman, until it became a silent mantra, going round in his head like a horse on a carousel he'd once seen at a fair.

He closed his eyes. It did not help. If anything, it made things worse, as his mind filled the visual void with more images of Catherine, her clothes discarded, every inch on show. He reopened them and gazed at the picture on the wall.

A watercolor. A lopsided vase with a bunch of flowers in it. Roses that didn't quite look like roses, and baby's breath which was little more than blobs of white. Fern fronds and other leaves of indeterminable shape and origin. And a signature. "Catherine Ashton. 1805." She would have been about eight years old then. That changed his perspective. The picture that was below par for an adult painter was noteworthy for a young child, well worth framing.

The rustling behind him took his mind from the picture once more. He swallowed, twice. He licked his dry lips and tried to concentrate on the childish art. She touched his shoulder, and he jumped.

"You may turn around now," she whispered.

He worked hard to do so slowly, trying not to seem too eager. When he saw her, he realized he had made a fundamental mistake. He'd chosen the wrong nightgown for her. He should have tried harder, found something thicker, something made of substantial linen, or wool. Anything but the diaphanous gown that skimmed her body, showing the outline of the dark areola surrounding her peaked nipples, and the patch of dark hair shadowing the juncture at the top of her legs. Her stomach was very slightly rounded, and her hips tapered into the narrowest of waists.

With a supreme effort, he raised his gaze to her face. *I am a gentleman.*

Her dark eyes watched him intently, and her top teeth worried at her bottom lip.

I am a gentleman.

"Thank you," she whispered. Adam frowned, confused, and she gestured vaguely toward the door. "For…well, for being there tonight." She smiled, shyly. "I was quite frightened, if the truth be known. But when you came, I felt…better. Stronger." She reached up and put her hand on his chest. It seared his skin, branding him. His heartbeat ratcheted up crazily, and his stomach clenched, while a shiver trembled through him. "I've missed you," she said.

He swallowed. "I missed you, too." His voice was croaky, strained.

I am a gentleman.

Her hand moved up over his torso. A muscle jumped, twitching his breast. His breaths were rapid and shallow. He clenched his fists and tensed his arms to keep his hands at his sides. *I am a gentleman.* She had had a dreadful fright, heard things that had distressed her. Only a blackguard would take advantage of her now.

"I always kept an eye on your progress, you know," she said.

My progress?

"I followed every troop movement the newspapers reported. Every battle. Every skirmish."

"You did?" He cleared his throat and tried to make sense of her words, as her hand travelled up, over his chest, skimming over his nipple, which jerked in response to her soft touch.

"I looked for your name in the lists of the dead and injured, and prayed I would not find it there."

"That—that's good to know."

Polite inanities. He was reduced to polite inanities. His brain wasn't working, that was certain. He needed to get out of there. Now. He should take his coat, which lay discarded by the chair where she had been sitting. He should get out of this room, out of this house, and away from her.

While he still could.

He stayed absolutely still.

The lavender scent of her was overlaid with the night air trapped in her hair, and the clean, fresh scent of her nightgown, the warmth of the fire, the wax candle, now burned down to almost nothing. Her dark eyes focused on him, capturing him. He could not have looked away if he had wanted to.

I am a gentleman.

He repeated his mantra in his head, over and over, faster and faster. He could no longer remember why it mattered. Her hands touched his shoulders, and she pulled him toward her. He went willingly and her fingers moved, slowly, softly, round to the back of his neck. He could hear her breaths, short and quick, and his own, rasping, hard to come by.

He couldn't say if she reached up or he bent down, but suddenly his mouth was on hers. It was not a gentle kiss. Their lips clashed together, their tongues tangling, driving him mad. He felt her fingers at his neckerchief, unknotting it, sliding it from him. His shirt was pulled from the waistband of his trousers and she found his skin beneath it. His muscles jumped as she caressed his stomach, his chest, his back. His trousers were painfully tight, and his legs trembled. She moaned softly against his mouth, and he thought he would embarrass himself then and there.

Somewhere, in the deepest recesses of his mind, a thought drummed like a tattoo. *I am a gentleman.* He wanted to push it away, ignore it. It took all his willpower to do the right thing.

"I am a gentleman," he murmured.

He felt her smile against his skin. "I know," she whispered.

"I cannot—take—ad—vantage of you," he said, each syllable harder to release than the one before.

"You aren't."

"But—"

"*I'm* taking advantage of you." She caressed his back, moved her hands down his spine. His nerves jumped. She squeezed his bottom and he groaned.

"You're killing me," he whispered. Of their own volition, his arms went around her, pulling her into him. He stroked her back, her neck, her arms. He cupped her breasts, his fingers finding her nipples, pinching them, rolling them, making them hard against his palms.

Somehow, he would never know how, they were suddenly both naked, their hands everywhere, as they reached her bed and fell onto it. He kissed her breasts, suckled her until she cried out in ecstasy, then he cupped her mons, used his fingers on the little ball of nerves at her center, stroking her, gathering her wetness. She bucked and squirmed and shook as he brought her to completion, kissing her and swallowing her cries as she shattered.

Afterward, he covered them with her blankets and held her close as she came down to earth.

"That was…" She swallowed. "That…I never dreamed…" She looked up at him, frowning. "What about you? You didn't…you know." He felt the heat of her blush. "You didn't take…pleasure."

Nor would he. He should not have gone as far as he had. That she had welcomed his touch was no excuse. She was an innocent, and under ordinary circumstances… Again, it was something he had seen before, many times. After the fear and danger of a battle, there was an overwhelming urge to celebrate survival, to affirm life, and it manifested itself in a need for passion. Tonight, she had been frightened for her life, and this was the result. He could not, would not use that for his own selfish purposes.

"I got my pleasure from your pleasure. It was enough," he lied.

"I don't believe you." Her hand drifted down and brushed against him. His hips bucked and she grinned, triumphantly. He pulled her hand away. She pulled back. "Let me," she whispered.

Lord, this woman would be the death of him. "Don't," he begged.

"Why not?" There was a mix of naughtiness and innocence in her tone.

Adam closed his eyes on the pain of temptation. "You're a maid, Catherine."

"And if I don't wish to be?"

He shook his head, every nerve within him tingling with desire, every muscle taut as he fought for control. "That's for your husband. Nobody else." To his own ears, his words sounded strangled.

She chuckled. It was the most sensuous sound he had ever heard. "I'm not getting a husband," she said. She laughed again, but he heard the pain behind it. "Haven't you heard? I'm going to be an old maid. The parish spinster."

"Catherine…"

"Two Seasons. No offers."

He stilled. "That's not true."

"I know."

He heard what she didn't say. He had offered for her, but Society did not know that. She had refused him because he wasn't suitable. His offer had not been good enough. It didn't count.

And just like that, his ardor cooled.

He rolled out of bed, strode across the room to where his clothes lay in a heap, and started to dress.

Catherine sat up, the blankets gathered around her, covering her. "Adam?"

"I should go."

"What?"

He pulled his shirt over his head. "It's getting late. Early. I shouldn't be here."

"Adam…"

"You should—" He took a deep breath. "You should refrain from…following smugglers through tunnels."

She scoffed. "You should stop following your friends on their after-dark assignations."

"I can take care of myself."

"And I can't?"

He couldn't resist looking at her then, trying to use his expression to say what he did not want to put into words. No, she couldn't take care of herself. If not for him, and Ned Fellowes, she would have been caught tonight, and then, who knew what would have happened?

Clearly, she thought the same, because she looked away. Her bottom lip trembled, and his heart hurt. He felt like the worst of villains—but, he told himself, it was for the best. If he stayed, he knew what would happen, and it must not. She would thank him. One day.

And if he told himself that often enough, he might come to believe it.

She sighed. "What will you do now?"

Adam concentrated on stuffing his shirt into the waistband of his trousers so he didn't have to meet her eye. "Your servants will be about shortly," he said. "I'll leave before they find me here and you are forced to marry me."

Catherine clicked her tongue, impatiently, as he pushed his foot into his boot. "I meant what will you do

187

about what we saw and heard?" He turned to her then. She looked troubled, a deep frown creasing her brow. "When I followed them," she went on, "I thought they were merely smugglers. But they weren't, were they?"

"No."

"I can't believe Milton would…" She breathed deep, pushing down her emotion. "And Sayer."

And Colbourne. Adam had followed him, suspecting him of being in league with a band of smugglers. He had thought to find their contraband and tip the wink to Lord Rotherton, to help the earl ease the pressure he was under. It had never crossed Adam's mind that the man was one of the traitors. And, from what the man had said, not just an ordinary traitor, the kind who betrayed his country for money. No. Colbourne was, it seemed, a true believer in Napoleon's cause.

But he was not the leader of the band. Sayer had mentioned a paymaster, someone Colbourne reported to. Could that be Catherine's father? The thought of that possibility left a taste like ash in Adam's mouth. He did not want to ask her his next question, but he knew he must. If he didn't, others would, and they would not be gentle. The man's senior servants were involved, so it could not be ignored.

"Milton and Sayer," he said, carefully. "How long have they worked for your father?"

Catherine thought for a moment. "Since we bought the house. They worked for the previous owners, and Papa just kept them on."

Adam nodded. "And the tunnel… Do you think your father knows of it?"

She hesitated, just for a fraction of a second. It gave him an answer he did not really want. Then she glared at him. "No," she said. "He wouldn't have anything to do with any such thing."

"Hmm."

She sat up straighter. The blanket shifted, exposing the curve of her breast. She grabbed it and pushed it more tightly around her. "You cannot think he would…" Her face changed, horror widening her eyes. "You do!"

"No, I—"

"Don't lie to me, Adam Mason. I see it in your face. You believe my father is involved in all this—this—whatever this is."

He grimaced.

"How could you? How can you even think for a moment…? You know him! You know he's…" Her eyes narrowed and she laughed bitterly. "I see what this is. Well, you certainly play a long game, I'll grant you that."

Adam frowned, confused. "I don't know what—"

She stood, the blanket still wrapped around her, her eyes sparking with fury. "This is your revenge on him. On me."

"My revenge?" For a moment, Adam could not think what she meant.

"I refused your suit. So now you'll what? Blacken our family name? Ruin us? See my father hanged?"

"No! I would never—"

"Get out!" She snarled at him and pointed her finger at the door.

"Catherine…"

"Get. Out."

He stood there, trying to figure out how things had gone so badly wrong so quickly. He could not allow her to think…

The truth. He *was* here because her father was a

suspect. And while Adam still had his doubts, he knew his superiors in Whitehall did not.

She turned and marched over to her writing desk, her blanket trailing her like the queen's train. She looked regal, proud, magnificent, and he could not help but admire her. Right up to the moment she snatched up her letter opener and brandished it at him like a knife.

It was a paltry weapon, blunt and short, and he would find it easy to disarm her. He didn't try. With his stomach in knots and a lump in his throat, he nodded curtly at her, opened her door and, with a quick look up and down the corridor to make sure the way was clear, left the room.

****

After Adam had gone, Catherine slumped against her desk, all energy drained from her. The letter opener slid from her numb fingers and hit the floor with a soft clack. She looked down at it and huffed. What kind of weapon was that? How foolish she must have looked, brandishing it at him, when it was about as deadly as a sausage. If Adam had truly been a threat to her, that would not even have given him pause.

But he was a threat, was he not? Not because he would physically hurt her, of course, but because he thought Papa was a traitor. She had heard it in his oh-so-casual questions, seen it in the way he tried to hide what was in his eyes. His denial of suspicion had been half-hearted too, made to appease her rather than because he believed it the truth.

But could she fault him for his thoughts? Had she not hesitated herself before her common sense took over and allowed her to see Papa would never do such a thing? Her father would be appalled that anyone under his roof could even contemplate it. She knew that, and she could not understand why Adam could not see it, too.

She swiped away the tears that tickled her cheeks, and sniffed. As her governess had been fond of saying whenever something dreadful happened, she could wallow in self-pity or she could set to and do something to improve the situation. Although what, in this case, she had no idea.

She ought to tell Papa everything she had learned. He would know what to do about it. A man of the world, he must have some idea of how one should deal with the likes of Milton and Sayer.

Still, telling Papa meant confessing what she had done this night. He would be horrified to think she had put herself in danger, and furious that she had risked her reputation—at the very least!—by wandering around the countryside in her nightclothes. And if he should learn that Adam had been there, pressed against her, touching her in ways no man had ever touched her before...

There would be pistols at dawn.

Besides, when the militia came to call, Papa's best defense might be in his transparent ignorance. If he was obviously surprised at what was happening, if he could convince the authorities he knew nothing of it, that would be for the best.

Wouldn't it?

Oh, Lord, what a mess! Catherine prayed Papa's genuine surprise and ignorance would be enough. She knew Adam would not keep quiet about what they had heard. He would never allow treason to go unchallenged. Nor should he. It was the most heinous of crimes, and she, too, would want to see the guilty punished. But *only* the guilty. Mayhap she could speak to Adam, ask him...

Ask him what? To delay reporting the crime? There was no time for that. Mr. Colbourne's gold would arrive tomorrow and be shipped out a day or so later. There was no room for delay.

Even if there were, could she really ask that of Adam? It would run contrary to all duty and honor, all that he was, and it would tear him apart. Catherine loved him too much to ask that of him.

She stopped. The breath caught in her throat and every muscle tensed. She stared across the room without seeing anything clearly and let her thoughts circle slowly in to land like a gull from the sea.

Catherine loved Adam Mason. She had always loved him, and always would. It didn't matter who he was: son of a farmer or peer of the realm, half-pay officer struggling to make ends meet or as rich as Golden Ball.

That thought made her giggle, which in turn caused a few more tears to run over her cheeks. "Rich as Golden Ball," she scoffed. That was something he certainly was not. He wouldn't be in Rotherton on a repairing lease, availing himself of Lord Hadlow's hospitality, if he was rich. Which might matter to her father, but, she could admit now, was of no consequence to Catherine.

One could not choose whom to love. A person's status and position, wealth and prospects did not enter into it. All that truly mattered was who they were within, and how they made one feel.

Adam Mason made Catherine feel in love.

Which did not mean he was in love with her, of course. In fact, she was certain the opposite was true. He despised her. Not only had she callously turned him away and told him he was not good enough for her two years ago, but she had just ejected him again, at the point of a knife—well, a letter opener shaped like a knife. On top of which, he suspected her father…

Suddenly, the weight of the world pressed upon her. It forced her down, draining her of all her energy until it was all she could do to drag herself across the room to her bed. The bed where he had made her feel so alive, so wonderful. Loved.

Until she had spoilt it all by asking too much of him. She had wanted to pleasure him, to have him feel what he had made her feel. She had wanted—truth to tell, she wasn't sure what she had wanted but that hadn't stopped her reaching for it, playing the wanton in her bid to entice him. The only thing she had succeeded in doing was giving him a disgust of her.

Tears ran freely now, making her face itch and leaving a salty taste on her lips. Her neck was tense and a headache was building. She climbed into bed, hoping the cool bedlinen would alleviate the hot pain pulsing through her. Her pillow smelled of him: sandalwood and night air, mixed with the musk of their desire.

She buried her face into it and sobbed.

Chapter Fifteen

The morning came far too soon. Adam's eyes were scratchy from lack of sleep and his body felt heavy and sluggish. He did not want to get out of bed, although he knew that staying beneath the blankets would do him no good. Sleep was not about to come, no matter how he wanted it.

He joined Freddy, Bertie, and Colbourne in the breakfast room and put up with the friendly teasing about how rough he looked.

"Hope you're not keeping all the excitement to yourself," laughed Bertie. "Who was she?" He thought as he chewed on a piece of honey-coated toast. "Let me guess. Not Hannah Grey. She married last year and her husband would *not* be understanding. Rosie Waddington's got a baby…Susie Turner." He snapped his fingers as if he knew he'd hit on the right answer. "Susie Turner." He nodded. "Careful, old boy. She will wear you out." He wiggled his eyebrows and laughed heartily.

Adam said nothing, although he reflected that if he had been with the barmaid from the Golden Goose, he would not have tossed and turned for hours, replaying in his head every moment of their time together, wondering what he could have done or said differently, berating himself for touching her, before admitting he did not truly regret it for an instant and, given the chance, he would do it again. Which led to more self-recrimination, because she was a lady and he, despite all evidence to the contrary, was supposed to be a gentleman.

Then there was the other matter, the one that should have been foremost in his mind. Walter Ashton and his connection to whatever plot was being hatched here.

Catherine was adamant her father was not involved. Adam wanted to believe her, regardless of the evidence which seemed to be building against him. Damning as it may look, none of that evidence was more than circumstantial. but Adam knew men were convicted on far less, and that did not sit well with him. Had his own sire not been a peer, he might have hanged for a crime he hadn't committed. With that in mind, Adam was reluctant to judge a man unless his guilt was irrefutable.

As Colbourne's was.

Adam studied the man as surreptitiously as he could. He was not dressed today in the tailored clothes of a gentleman but wore the same dark coat he'd worn last night, homespun and cheaply made. His breeches were looser fitting than usual, and he wore a kerchief instead of a carefully folded cravat over his coarse shirt. There was stubble on his chin and his hair was tousled, giving him an unkempt air. The coffee cup looked tiny in his meaty fingers, and a sense of menace hung around him.

He drained the cup and moved from the table, and Adam saw his boots were worn and scuffed. "Best be on my way," he muttered. "I'll hire a hack from the stables in Rotherton, and I'll see you all later."

"When we shall not know you," said Bertie, and he tapped the side of his nose. The gleam in his eye said he was thoroughly enjoying himself, unlike Adam, whose conscience bothered him. He knew there were few, if any, rules to these gatherings. Two men met, one pummeled the other into the ground, and other men wagered on the outcome. Provided nobody died, the authorities tended to turn a blind eye and everyone crawled home at day's end, full of alcohol and eager for the next time.

Still, he couldn't help but feel uneasy. Actual rules there may not be, but it didn't seem fair to wager when your challenger was, effectively, a ringer. If the locals worked that out, if they felt cheated, Adam did not want to imagine how they might react. Not that he would blame them.

"Don't expect me to come straight home after I've creamed him," Colbourne told them.

"You expect trouble?" asked Freddy.

Colbourne shrugged. "Wouldn't be the first time I was followed afterward. Sometimes, it's someone who fancies his chances at stealing my purse. They tend to lose a few teeth and crawl away. But sometimes, it's because they're curious. Suspicious, maybe. Want to know where I came from." He chuckled, but there was no humor in the sound. "Them, I lead a merry chase. Take 'em miles, then grab their boots and their rides and leave them to walk home."

"No matter," said Bertie. He waved his hand through the air dismissively. "Long as I have my winnings, I'll be happy to see you whenever you get here."

"Same here," grinned Freddy.

"What about you, Abberley? Do you have a stake?" Bertie asked. "If you're completely broke, I can sub you a couple of guineas to start you off."

"I have some blunt," Adam answered. "Thank you."

"Well," said Bertie, as he watched Colbourne leave, "if it's any consolation, you'll not be throwing away what you do have. Today is a sure thing."

That really wasn't a consolation to Adam. Guilt churned his stomach and left a taste of ash and bitters in his mouth. It would take him a good while to be easy about taking money from people who weren't in full possession of the facts as he knew them, and he especially baulked at cheating hardworking men who could ill afford the loss. Freddy had shrugged his shoulders when Adam had said so, seeming not to understand Adam's scruples. He pointed out the men at Offham intended to gamble their cash away anyway, whether Adam was there to win it or not, but that, he felt, was a poor excuse.

"You don't have a choice, I'm afraid," Freddy had declared when Adam had voiced his concerns again this morning. He'd woken his friend at dawn to tell him what he had seen in the night, then confessed his feelings about today's outing. Freddy had tried to alleviate his guilt. "We're supposed to be inveterate gamblers, rusticating to avoid the dunners. We'll gamble on anything, with anyone."

"I know," Adam had replied. But he didn't have to like it. He began to wonder if he was really the right man for this sort of job.

They set off for Offham in Bertie's coach. It was a glorious day, the sun shining brightly in a flawless sky, although there was still a sharp nip in the air, reminding them it wasn't quite spring yet, regardless of the buds on the branches and the green shoots appearing in the soil.

The atmosphere in the coach was light. Bertie could barely contain his joy at being able to indulge in his passion, especially with more than an even chance of winning. "I think I'll just lay a few pounds down on this champ for the first few rounds," he said. "Make it look good, increase the amounts gradually. Then, when Alfie steps forward, I'm planning to lay down a ton."

"A hundred?" Freddy's eyebrows rose. "Bit rich for this crowd, isn't it?"

"Not by then, it won't be. And anyway, I have to make the most of it. I need this win."

"Yes, but a hundred…"

"I reckon a ton will bring me a monkey, and that makes the day worth my time."

Freddy frowned. "You expect to win five hundred from one? You think that's what the odds will be on Colbourne?"

"At least."

Adam stopped listening to them and stared out at the passing scenery. They moved along a narrow lane, the ruts and potholes keeping their speed down so that the journey to Offham, which should take an hour, was more likely to take two. The drystone walls around Bertie's fields were higgledy-piggledy, bowing out of shape in places, tumbled in others, but as they moved past land owned by other people, the walls became straighter and better tended, the fields cared for, some filled with sheep and cows and the occasional horse, others brown and bare, ready for planting.

An image came to him of the Shropshire farm where he had grown up. Like most of his neighbors, his father—no, his *uncle*—had kept sheep and poultry, but many of his fields were used for cereal crops, and Adam felt a wave of homesickness rush through him as he thought of those fields now, ploughed and ready for sowing, just like these ones. He hadn't visited the farm, or contacted his uncle, since learning of his true parentage just over a year ago.

He had been so angry then. Angry at having been lied to over the whole of his life, and at what he saw as his father's abandonment of him. He had been confused and hurt, and in no mood to listen as he slammed from the house and rode away as fast as he could.

Perversely, he had then been even angrier when his uncle made no attempt to come after him. At the time, Adam had seen it as more evidence that he hadn't really been wanted, he had been brought up on that farm by these people because they felt a duty to do it rather than because they wished to care for him. Now that his temper had cooled and he had had time to think, he saw things more clearly. Perhaps they did owe him apologies and deeper explanations. But he owed apologies, too.

Things could have been worse for him, he knew. He only had to look at Freddy to realize that. The spare second son of an earl, Freddy may have grown up knowing who his ancestors truly were, but he was also painfully aware that he was surplus to requirements, of no real use beyond an insurance in case something happened to the heir. Adam had never felt as if he was an encumbrance the way Freddy had. He hadn't been ignored and pushed aside, miserable through every single day of his childhood.

Adam sighed and pushed away his musings. Returning to Shropshire and rebuilding the bridges there was for the future. Today, he had other things to do.

They passed Marshy Meadow, the sodden field enclosed by the towering chalk cliffs. Patches of green stretched across the cliff walls where gorse bushes and other hardy vegetation clung to the rock, and in the daylight he could make out some of the cracks and crevices. None of them looked big enough for a man to squeeze through, let alone find a cave and a tunnel behind, which made them very clever hiding places indeed. The revenue men would never find them, neither from here on the ground nor looking down from the cliff edge. If Catherine had not shown him, Adam would still not know of them. He would have had to follow Colbourne and his cohorts back down the hill and along the road, riding his luck and praying he would not be discovered as he made his way home behind them. He certainly would have had no concrete evidence of their smuggling.

He had not suspected Colbourne at all. From talking with Freddy, he knew he wasn't the only one who had been fooled by the former bare-knuckle boxer turned gentleman. If Adam had not been looking through his bedchamber window, checking all was clear for him to make his way to the forge, he would not have seen Colbourne slip furtively from the house and across the park. He would never have discovered all that he had, and he would not have been there to protect Catherine.

Catherine. She'd looked so lost, so frightened as they listened to the conspirers. Her fear had grown when she realized the implications for her father, then had changed to anger at the questions Adam asked, once she knew he was trying to discover the extent of Walter Ashton's guilt.

Or otherwise, Adam added quickly. There was still a chance Ashton was innocent, no matter what the evidence pointed to, or what Lord Fremont believed. Until such time as the proof was irrefutable, Adam refused to make judgment.

Not that Catherine believed that. She had made it more than clear she thought he sought only to prove her father's guilt. For revenge, no less! Simply to return the hurt of her rejection of him two years ago.

If that was truly her opinion of his character, he thought now, she had never known him at all, and mayhap it was for the best that they had not married. If she had loved him the way he loved her, she would never have believed him capable of hurting her like that.

He started, as if coming to from a nap, and blinked until he got his bearings. Freddy grinned at him but said nothing, and Adam turned back to the window. The road was wider now, and curved, trees on one side of it, dipping down into a valley, while a steep hill climbed away from them on the other side. Perhaps he had dozed off after all.

But asleep or awake, he couldn't escape what had just gone through his mind. He loved her. Adam Mason loved Catherine Ashton. The truth of it was like a hammer blow, knocking him off balance. If he hadn't been sitting, his back against the squabs of Bertie's coach, he would have collapsed into a heap on the floor.

He loved Catherine Ashton. It didn't matter that she did not love him back, or that she had turned him away, not once but twice now. He didn't care that her father may well have been up to no good, working his neck into a noose over a lost cause. Adam loved Catherine. Always had. Always would. And when this was all over, regardless of the way things fell, he would come back for her. If she would have him.

Chapter Sixteen

"At last!" cried Bertie as the coach slowed to a stop outside their destination.

The Blacksmith Arms was a substantial inn built about fifty years before. Its frontage bordered the road from Lewes to Burgess Hill, ensuring plenty of passing traffic and a steady income. Its yard was on the north side of the inn, with a wide entrance that allowed for two carriages, one going in and the other coming out, both at the same time. Today, however, Bertie's coach had no hope of entering the crowded space, and the three gentlemen disembarked at the roadside before the coachman pulled away, presumably to find somewhere safe to park the conveyance.

Men moved about the stable yard, mingling with friends, warily eyeing rivals, and drinking pints of ale served from a table erected under a canopy at the inn's door, where the landlord stood, arms crossed, watching with satisfaction as barmen prepared drinks that barmaids delivered with wide smiles, ribald comments, and saucy winks. The customers ranged from a few well-dressed gentlemen to laborers in smocks and woolen breeches, their calves bare above crudely made shoes. At the roadside, a couple of scantily clad women stood, hips thrust provocatively forward and cleavage on show as far as decency and the law would allow. They smiled, curling their lips in a vain attempt to hide rotten teeth, their faces covered in paint that didn't quite hide the pock marks and sores.

"Penny for a good time, me lord?" said one of them as Bertie passed her. Bertie gave her a scathing look and moved on, as the landlord came from behind his makeshift bar and crossed the yard at an impressive speed, considering his girth.

"I warned you, Molly Trickle," he said. His fists rested on his hips and he glared at the woman. "You're bothering my customers. You are not welcome on my property."

The woman cackled. "They ain't your customers yet," she argued. "And we are not on your property, neither." She stamped the ground with her foot. "King's Highway, this. I can stand here, and you can't stop me."

The landlord glowered at her, then turned to Freddy, Adam, and Bertie and bowed. "Welcome, my lords," he said, using a completely different voice to the one he'd used with Molly. "Were you wanting a private parlor? As you can see, we are busy today, but they're all out here for the mill. Inside's only available to my more respectable customers, so it's comfortable, and quiet."

"I'm sure it is, my good man." Bertie grinned. "But we are not here for the quiet. Where will we find the Champion?"

The landlord said the champion had not yet made his appearance, but the ring was at the back of the yard. Then, with an order for three pints of ale and three meat pies, he scuttled away. Adam and Freddy followed Bertie through the crowd, inching past men who turned their heads to scowl at them, even as they moved aside.

Finally, they reached a small area at the very back. A raised platform had been erected and roped off, allowing everyone to see. On the platform at present, three acrobats tumbled through the air, jumping over one another, balancing on each other's shoulders and falling into somersaults. Some of the onlookers applauded them, but most ignored the show.

Nearby, on another raised dais, a juggler kept several balls in the air at once, while another man swallowed fire. Next to them, a young woman in a red costume that left little to the imagination called, "Come to the fair tonight at Lewes. All these performers, and many more. Thrills galore. One night only!" She held out a small bowl containing a few farthings and ha'pennies, with one or two pennies. Most people ignored her. Adam tossed in two pennies and she gave him a wide, bright smile.

They drank the ale and ate the pies Bertie had ordered, mingled with the crowd, and engaged in meaningless chatter with friendly strangers as they waited. Adam heard nothing of any note, but he had not truly expected to.

After about an hour, a rotund man in a puce waistcoat and an emerald green jacket strutted onto the platform. The acrobats headed for the small garden at the rear of the inn, and the man held up his arms and yelled for attention.

"Gentlemen, please." The crowd surged forward, eager to be as near to the action as they could. Bertie made his way forward along with everyone else, pushing his way to the bookmakers at the front as the promoter used as much pretentious language as he could to introduce, "the pugilistic sensation of the southern counties, the epitome of exuberant exaltation of anatomical perfection." The crowd whooped and hollered at his words. "Deserving of all approbation," he continued, "I give you, the undisputed Champion of all Sussex, Tumultuous Tom Springson!"

The crowd cheered wildly as the Champion stepped into the ring. He was big, well over six feet tall, with broad shoulders and a massive chest, which was bared to the crowd. His arm muscles flexed, proudly, and his skintight breeches were designed to show off his muscular thighs. He held up his arms, loving the adulation, and there was a flurry of activity around the bookmakers.

"He's a big lad," muttered Freddy.

"Isn't he just?" agreed Adam.

"Reckon Alfie can take him?"

Adam shrugged. "What do you think?"

"I think it'll be one hell of a fight," said Freddy.

"The undisputed king of the ring in Sussex issues a proclamation," yelled the promoter. "If there be anyone in this gargantuan gaggle who thinks they can take the pugilistic crown from him today, they should step forward and make themselves known. It'll cost a confident and cogitable contender a tiny trifle, a three-penny bit, to enter his name, but if he stays the course for three magnificent and monumental minutes, he will be awarded five golden guineas. And if he can put Tumultuous Tom down for a complete and uncontested count of five, he will win not only his venerable title, but a prodigious, portentous, phenomenal, and, I am sure, *welcome* purse of twenty guineas!"

The crowd cheered. There were shouts of, "Go on, Fred," and, "you can do that, Joe." Tom Springson strutted around the ring, daring anyone to come forward. Adam watched the crowd. Someone was bound to take the challenge. That prize, more than a year's wages to most of these men, was too good not to tempt someone.

A man ducked under the rope and climbed up onto the platform. His friends cheered, and his grin widened. Almost as tall as Springson, the challenger was not in such good shape. When he removed his smock, his flesh was flabbier, not so sculpted. His arms and shoulders, though strong, did not have Springson's definition.

"Three to one," shouted a bookmaker, and the gamblers surged forward.

The fighters circled, slowly, their gazes locked on one another. The crowd shouted encouragement. Some called out advice and instructions. The challenger jabbed and Springson ducked. The challenger came in closer and jabbed again, following through with his other fist. Neither blow landed. They circled again. Bertie stood by the rope, urging Springson to hit the challenger. Springson made no move to do so. Adam saw Colbourne standing to the side of the ring, watching carefully.

Freddy touched Adam's shoulder and spoke quietly into his ear. "Shall we mingle?" Then he headed through the mass of bodies toward the drinkers near the bar. Adam slowly moved toward the garden, stopping every few feet to make a show of watching the fight.

The challenger tried to hit Springson again, and this time, Springson responded. His fist connected with the challenger's jaw with a loud crack. The noise of the crowd died. For perhaps three seconds, nobody moved. Then the challenger corkscrewed to the ground and lay still.

Shock rippled through the crowd. Then some cheered and others groaned, and the bookmakers paid out to the winners. Bertie grinned broadly as he held out his chit. Colbourne leaned against a post, looking utterly relaxed.

A second challenger came forward, and met his fate in much the same way as the first had done. A third ducked and weaved and danced about. Springson watched him, his eyebrows raised in bemusement. When he'd had enough of the man, he simply hit him and knocked him out.

The fourth challenger made everyone laugh. A tiny man, he would struggle to reach five feet if he stood on tiptoes, and so slight a stiff breeze might blow him over. His ribs showed through milky skin, his arms and legs like twigs, no discernible muscles whatsoever. Springson looked over at the promoter in astonishment. The promoter shrugged his shoulders.

The little man ran around the champ, fast, making no attempt to hit him, or even come close to him. Springson tried to keep an eye on him, but he couldn't turn that fast without risking becoming dizzy. The crowd laughed and cheered. Then the little man swooped down and kicked out, his legs taking Springson off balance and bringing him down. Colbourne stiffened. The crowd gasped. Bertie froze mid cheer, his triumph turning to anxiety.

As quick as he fell, Springson bounced back to his feet. The little man looked frustrated, then began running again. Springson grinned. The crowd cheered and joined in with the fun.

This time, the little man jumped onto Springson's back and hugged his neck, as if trying to choke him. Springson staggered around the ring for a couple of turns, then pulled the man off his back the way he would have pulled off his shirt. He held the little man out at arm's length. The little man tried to hit out, but his arms were nowhere near long enough to reach Springson, and he simply punched air. The crowd roared their approval. Springson grinned.

The promoter rang a bell, signaling that the bout had lasted three minutes. The crowd cheered wildly as Tom stood the little man on his feet and shook his hand. The promoter handed him a coin bag, and the little man waved his joined fists above his head in triumph. Springson joined in the applause for him, before the next challenger, a more serious contender, stepped up.

By now, Adam had reached the back wall of the inn, where he stood, sandwiched between a small group of laborers, drinking and joking with each other, and the trio of acrobats, who watched the fights making the occasional comment about technique.

The champ hit his new challenger and the laborers groaned. "There's got to be someone who can put him down," moaned one. "Weren't worth coming, otherwise."

"Not this day, there isn't," replied another, grinning.

"Is that your boy?" asked Adam, and the second man nodded, his pride evident. "Aye, it is," he said, his Sussex burr making his vowels round and long. "Tom Springson, Sussex born and Sussex bred."

"Yup," said the man next to him, whose broader accent marked him as Kentish. "Long in the arm, and short in the head."

"Leave off," scoffed Sussex. "That's you comer-inners from over the border."

"Over the border?" Kentish laughed. "North, South, East, West, Sussex loses, Kent is best."

"South, North, West, East, Sussex first and Kent is

least."

They laughed, and Kentish held up his pint pot. "I'll drink to that."

"Good," nodded Sussex, draining his own drink. "Because it's your shout."

Kentish took his friend's pot and made his way to the bar. Sussex eyed Adam. "You thinking of betting against our Tom, then?"

"Not on what I've seen so far."

"Sensible. He's never been beat, you know. Not in more'n ten years."

"Truly?" Adam looked suitably impressed.

"Truly. Though I reckon this next one might give him a bit of a run for his money." He gestured at the ring and Adam turned to see Colbourne climbing onto the platform. There were cheers and shouts of encouragement from the crowd, aimed at both fighters.

From the other side of him, Adam heard one of the acrobats murmur to his friends, "Don't bet on the champ. Not against him." Adam pretended he hadn't heard, and fixed his attention on the ring.

Colbourne peeled off his coat and handed it to the promoter, who looked at it as if unsure what to do with it before he hung it on a corner post. He draped the shirt and neckerchief Colbourne handed him over the coat, then stood back and rang his bell to signal the fight could begin.

The betting became livelier as the crowd got their first proper look at Colbourne. He was shorter than the champ by some inches, but no less muscular, with broad shoulders and a barrel chest, darkened by a layer of hair. His arms were massive, his stomach muscles well defined. Whatever else his elevation to Society might have brought him, it was not soft living.

Springson seemed to understand instinctively that this opponent was in a different class to all who had come before. He straightened a little, preparing himself for a fight rather than mere entertainment. The crowd quietened and seemed to collectively hold its breath.

"That geezer might actually win," whispered Kentish, handing Sussex his refilled pot.

"Nah," said Sussex. "Springson'll wipe the floor with him."

The champ moved in and tried to deliver his roundhouse punch, the one that had downed most of his other challengers, but Colbourne had been studying him and easily avoided the expected blow. Some spectators cheered, while others groaned. Then Colbourne made a move of his own, jabbing at Springson. It wasn't a particularly hard punch, certainly not as powerful as the one he'd landed on the farrier last night, but it was lightning fast, and accurate.

"What was that?" laughed Kentish. "That's not a hit. That's a gnat bite."

"All part and parcel of it," Sussex replied. "Makes it more of a spectacle for them what's watching. Ups the betting."

A quick glance at the bookmaker showed the truth of that. Men were handing over money in a frenzied fashion. Adam saw Bertie hand over a heavy-looking bag.

In the ring, Colbourne's jabs seemed to rattle Springson, who snarled and looked ready to pounce, then seemed to think better of it and took a step back instead. Colbourne darted in to hit him again and Springson hit him, knocking him down. The crowd roared.

"Yes!" yelled Sussex.

Colbourne sprang back to his feet before the count could begin. He grinned, wiggled his jaw from side to side, then pointed at Springson, acknowledging the hit. Springson nodded once, respect for his opponent plain upon his face.

The fight went on. Both men got in hits. Both went down and got up again. Neither slowed, although both now glistened with sweat. The crowd's roars grew louder.

"Who is he?" asked Sussex, awed.

"I heard at the bar he's come down from London," answered Kentish.

"A long way to come," Adam said.

"Not for twenty guineas, it isn't," Kentish replied. "That's nearly two years' wages to me. We're not all like you toffs, with your fancy clothes and your money to burn."

Adam grinned good-naturedly. "We're not all like that, either. Some of us don't have two ha'pennies for a penny."

Kentish laughed loudly. "My heart bleeds for you."

Adam spoke with the men a little longer, then turned, hoping to speak to the acrobats, but they had disappeared, so he moved across the yard toward the bar. By now, both Colbourne and Springson sported swollen jaws and cut lips, and the champ had a black eye that was swelling impressively. Adam suspected Colbourne could have ended the bout several times by now, but he continued to fight, never actually landing the killer blow. Either he was playing to the crowd, which was now baying like a pack of dogs on the trail of a fox, or, more likely, he was keeping the match going for as long as he could, to keep Bertie from going home and finding men stashing a chest full of gold in his cellar. Adam doubted even Colbourne knew exactly when the chest would arrive, so the longer the house stayed empty, the better.

At the bar, the landlord looked like a cat that had found a vat full of cream, as his barmen brought up another keg from the cellar. Men were leaning into each other now, their eyes glazed and jaws slack as they told improbable tales in loud, slurred voices, sloshing ale over themselves as they gestured wildly to back up their claims. Barmaids ducked and weaved in between them, laughing with their mouths and not their eyes as they avoided grabbing hands, smiling more sweetly at those men who handed them coins, which disappeared quickly into the women's bodices.

Adam bought his new drink and moved aside, standing next to the fire eater and the fairground girl who'd made the announcements earlier. She now wore a long brown cloak which covered her scanty costume, and she looked bored. The acrobats and other performers seemed to have left.

"You're in Lewes tonight, then?" Adam asked.

She nodded. "Just for one night. Tomorrow, we're in Hastings, and from there, Brighton."

"Is it good business for you there?"

The girl shrugged. "Better in the summer, but it is what it is. And we'll do well tonight, at least." She gestured at the crowd.

"You go around the whole country, with the show?"

"More or less."

"See a lot of fights?" She frowned and he clarified, "Prize fights."

"A few. Why?"

Adam shrugged. "I heard your friends talking. They seemed to know the challenger."

"Did they?" She was wary now.

He smiled, trying to seem unthreatening, his questions casual. "One told the other not to bet on the champ for this bout. I took his advice."

"Then you'll be in the money."

"They look fairly well matched," he argued.

The girl chuckled. "Trust me, they're not." She studied Adam for a moment before she continued. "We saw him, up round Colchester way. We were doing a show up there and we provided the warmup to the main event, just like today. That bloke was there. Mind, that was for a much bigger purse. Not that this one's to be sneezed at, but that one…"

"What happened?"

She folded her arms tightly across her chest and stared over at the ring. For a few seconds, Adam thought she wasn't going to answer him. He turned back to where Colbourne and Springson were still trading blows, though both men were slowing now as they tired. Then she took in a deep breath and exhaled sharply.

"He played with his opponent," she said. "Just like he's doing now. Then, when he'd had enough, or, when his cronies in the crowd had won enough, or whatever it was he was after, well, then, he ended it. All but ended the other poor fighter, too. Vicious, he was." She shuddered. "I know that you…" she curled her lip in contempt, "*gentlemen* like to see a bit of blood and what not, but that was way too much. He had no call to go in on him like that."

Adam frowned. "He didn't kill the other man, did he?"

"Not far off. Shouldn't think the other bloke ever fought again." She huffed, but there was no humor in it. "It'd be a wonder if he ever even walked again. Nor used his hands properly."

"Wow." Adam watched her, and the disgust on her face said she was neither lying nor exaggerating. "Seems excessive," he said. "Why would he do that?"

She sniffed. "Perhaps it was personal. Or he just likes doing it. Makes some men feel better to hurt others."

Their eyes met and Adam knew she spoke from personal experience. He dipped his hand into his pocket and pulled out a guinea. "That's for you," he said. "Not for your collecting bowl. You."

She looked wary. "I ain't that kind of girl."

"If you were, I wouldn't have given it to you."

The girl studied him for a moment longer, then turned back to the fight. "And there it goes," she said. "You can collect your winnings now."

Adam turned and saw Colbourne and Springson. They stood, facing one another, fists raised. Colbourne was perfectly still. Not a muscle twitched, not a hair moved. In front of him, Springson swayed back and forth, rhythmically. The crowd was silent. Time seemed to stand still.

Then, in a strange slow motion, the champ fell backward like a chopped-down tree. He hit the platform with a thud, and lay still. The promoter approached slowly, his face ashen. He glanced at Colbourne, then Springson, then Colbourne again, before he reluctantly began his count. He reached five and the crowd erupted in a mix of cheers and boos, elation and objection, shouted threats and cries for calm.

On the platform, Colbourne picked up a cloth and wiped his sweaty face and neck before rubbing his underarms with it. He threw it contemptuously onto the unconscious Springson's face, took his own clothes from the corner post, and swaggered away, as if he hadn't a care in the world.

It was only because Adam was watching him so closely that he saw the almost imperceptible nod Colbourne gave to a man in the crowd. The man nodded back and moved away from the ring. Adam looked around the crowd, found Freddy, and gestured for him to follow. Freddy nodded and made his way across, joining Adam as he discreetly followed the man.

The man pushed his way through the boisterous clusters of people trying to leave the inn yard. He was a nondescript individual, which was presumably why he'd been chosen for this task. Of average height and build, his hair was mousy, a color that would be hard to describe, and his clothes were no different to fifty other men who'd been here today.

The crowd thinned as they left the yard and headed along the road and around the bend. A hundred yards from the inn, a pony stood, tethered to a tree. The man looked over his shoulder, saw them behind him and quickened his pace. Freddy and Adam sped up, too.

By the time he reached the pony, the man was running, but they had closed the gap on him. There was no way he could mount up and ride away before they were able to stop him, but that did not mean he wasn't going to try.

He put his foot in the worn stirrup and tried to swing up into an old saddle that had seen better days, but Freddy pulled him back to the ground and turned him around to face him. The man stumbled, unnerving the pony, which grumbled and fidgeted. Adam went to its head and held the bridle, murmuring softly to soothe it.

"Oi! You let go of me!" yelled the man in a strong South London accent. Other men stopped to see what was happening.

"Freddy," murmured Adam, in warning.

Freddy nodded. "I know." He turned his attention to the man. "Why did you run?"

"Who wouldn't? Two useful-looking geezers chasing him down the road, any man'd run. I thought you was going to rob me."

"Do we look like robbers?" Freddy sounded incredulous. Adam watched the other men, who gathered closer, showing more interest in what was happening.

"I don't know, do I? Anyone can dress like a dandy. You might have stole those clothes."

Some of the spectators murmured agreement. Adam realized this could get very ugly very quickly if they weren't careful. Besides which, it was hardly subtle, arresting the man in sight of every Tom, Dick or Francis who cared to take notice. Adam kept a weather eye out for Colbourne, or anyone else who looked too invested in this.

"You're not from around here, are you?" asked Freddy, seemingly unbothered by the audience that made Adam so nervous.

Some onlookers said Freddy was right, the man being detained was a stranger, and anyway, robbers would have waited for a quieter stretch of road.

"What's it to do with you?" demanded the man, struggling to free himself from Freddy's grip on his coat.

"There has been a spate of housebreakings and other

crimes in these parts over the last week."

This was the first Adam had heard of this, although some in the crowd agreed it was true.

"So?" asked the man. "Nowt to do with me. I wasn't even here."

"You're certain about that, are you?"

"Course I am. I come to watch a fight. Let me go!"

"What makes you think it was him done them houses?" called one man. Adam looked over at him. He wore ill-fitting breeches and a leather jerkin. His friends nodded agreement with him.

"I don't," admitted Freddy, easily. "It may not be him. That's why I wanted to talk with him and find out."

"Sounds reasonable," said the onlooker.

"I didn't do it." The man in Freddy's grasp tried to pull free again.

"Thing is, we *know* the housebreakers are not local men," said Freddy, and the onlookers sounded relieved and happy about that. "We know that, because they're the work of a burglar who has committed crimes in other towns too, And they always coincide with prize fights."

The crowd sounded shocked now. There were even people telling their friends they'd seen this man acting strangely around the town.

"And since you know the fighter who just won the prize…" Freddy let the sentence hang in the air. The man paled and swallowed as the crowd expressed outrage.

"Trouble, Mr. Finch?" Lord Rotherton pushed through the onlookers and stood near Freddy. Beside him were two burly members of the local watch.

"My lord," Freddy acknowledged. "Those crimes we spoke of?"

Rotherton glanced from Freddy to Adam, to the

man, and back. "What of them?"

"I had nowt to do with them," insisted the man.

"Mr. Finch seems to think you did."

"He's mistaken."

Now that the acting magistrate was there, together with the watch, the crowd began to thin, many unsure whether they would be rounded up for having been at an illegal prize fight. Adam knew Rotherton wasn't in the least bit interested in arresting any of them, but he wasn't sorry to see them leave. The less attention they attracted, he thought, the better. Soon, only the drunkest and most belligerent of the crowd still stayed to watch.

Rotherton smiled at the man Freddy held. "Thing is, my good man," he told him, "I know Mr. Finch. I don't know you. So now, why don't you come with me and we can remedy that? I'm sure we can have this little matter sorted in a trice." He signaled to the watch, who took the protesting man from Freddy and led him and his pony away. Freddy whispered to Rotherton, who nodded and followed his men.

"What now?" asked Adam, quietly, as he and Freddy walked back to the inn.

"Rotherton'll hold him for as long as we need him to. Hopefully, he'll sing like a canary to save his neck. Even if he doesn't, it's one we don't have to worry about."

"I say," called Bertie, coming round the bend toward them. "What are you two doing out here?"

"There you are," Freddy replied. "How did you do?"

Bertie beamed. "Won seven hundred and fifty on Colbourne alone. With the other bets I won, I'm up by over a grand."

"Good for you." Freddy slapped Bertie's shoulder.

"Let's get back to Hadlow Hall and celebrate, shall we?"

And hopefully, thought Adam as he followed them, we'll find a chest of gold there before Colbourne can spirit it away again.

He climbed into the coach after Bertie, who was cock-a-hoop at his profitable morning. "A few more days like that," he said as the coach made its way back through the lanes to Rotherton, "and I would be completely out of Dun territory." His face creased in thought. "Do you think Colbourne would enter into a partnership with me? One of these fights a month, we'd never need worry again."

"I rather think that would be cheating, don't you?" Freddy gave Bertie a mock stern look, and Bertie's upper lip curled in disgust. "Besides, even Colbourne can't win every time."

"Based on what we saw today, he's got a lot of fights left in him." Freddy and Adam exchanged glances and Bertie frowned at them. "Why? What do you know that I don't?"

"Nothing." Freddy smiled, benignly. "Just a feeling I have. I shouldn't be surprised if his days as the champion are numbered."

Bertie grimaced. "It'd be a pity if they were. Still…" He cheered. "Mayhap I can make this thousand into five at Lord Percival's later. He has a card game going all day."

Adam rolled his eyes and looked out of the window.

Freddy argued with Bertie. "You could just quit while you are ahead," he said. "That must be enough to pay your most pressing debts."

"Not really." Bertie looked rueful for a moment, then gave a naughty grin. "Besides, what fun would that be?"

True to his word, the viscount left again the moment they reached Hadlow Hall. He didn't even get out of the coach, merely set down Adam and Freddy, then called to the driver to take him to Lord Percival's as fast as he could. They watched him go.

"Percival will take the shirt from his back," predicted Freddy. "You'd think a grown man would know better."

"I don't think he can help himself," answered Adam. "It's like a sickness with him. He will never stop, not while there is breath in his body."

"Then let's hope he never wins big. If he won a huge sum, then threw it away again, I think the devastation would kill me."

Adam smiled sympathetically. He knew Freddy was not as flush as most of their friends. Although the Seaford title was old, the fortune behind it was not a large one and, as the second son, Freddy's allowance was limited. He was not working for Fremont simply for something to do with his time, nor because of a sense of patriotic duty like Adam's. Freddy needed the salary. Since Adam also knew how it felt to have little or no money, he understood how much it hurt his friend to see Bertie squander it.

"Where do you think they'll have put this chest?" he asked, more to change the subject than anything else. He turned to the house.

"Your guess is as good as mine," answered Freddy. "Cellar?"

"We can start there." Adam led the way into the hall.

Chapter Seventeen

Catherine woke at dawn, feeling as if she had not slept at all. Her eyes were hot and swollen, her cheeks blotched. Her head ached and her neck was tense. It did not take much to convince Mama that she did not feel up to accompanying her on her visits to other families in the neighborhood.

Although staying home in self-pitying seclusion was not a good thing, either. Her head was awhirl with all that bothered her, which meant she could neither rest nor concentrate on anything else.

She told herself, over and over again, she would not think of Adam Mason. What they had done last night was shameful and never to be repeated. Even as she thought that, though, she knew it for a lie. What had happened between them in this room, in this very bed, had not felt in the least bit shameful, either at the time nor, if she were honest with herself, at any moment since. Far from shameful, it had been…wonderful. More than wonderful. It had felt right, and natural, and bound to happen. Bound to happen last night. Bound to happen again, if they ever were alone together. There would be no fighting it, no gainsaying it. Just the memory of it now filled her with a delicious ache that started in her belly and worked its way outward, to her most private places, shocking her with an almost overwhelming urge to touch herself there.

Nor could she be angry at Adam for the feelings and sensations that had awoken within her. He had not seduced her. *She* had seduced *him*. Her face heated with the memory of her behavior last night. She had been wanton. There was no other word for it. And she did not regret a moment.

That wasn't true. She did regret the way they had parted. She had thrown him out. Again. Rejected him when he might have had reason to expect better. And this time, she had threatened him, too. With a letter opener. Catherine rolled her eyes at the absurdity of that. It certainly wasn't the effectiveness of the weapon that had sent him on his way when she'd brandished it.

He had plainly seen how very angry she was with him. He'd gone too far with his questions, all of them designed to cast suspicion on Papa and justify Adam in whatever he intended to do.

But Adam *knew* Papa. He knew he wasn't a traitor. Or at least he should have known. Yet there he had stood, willing to believe the worst, asking her questions in hope that something she said would consolidate his suspicion. Asking her those questions after they had done…*that*.

How could he? If he had felt even a tenth for her what she felt for him…

That was, she supposed, one problem she could solve. It should not be difficult to prove Papa had nothing to do with any of the nefarious goings-on. She would find the proof and take it to the blasted Baron Abberley and rub his sanctimonious, judgmental nose in it. And after she had done that, she would walk away with her head held high, and never have to acknowledge his suspicious, conniving face again.

"He'll be sorry then," she muttered. "He'll grovel

for my forgiveness, and he won't get it." She felt her mouth pucker into a childish pout and made an effort to stop it. "Catherine Elizabeth Ashton," she scolded herself, "you are a grown woman, not a child of five. Behave like it."

Pushing away thoughts of the horrid man who had caused such immature emotions to surface, she flung back her covers and climbed out of bed, determined to prove her father a loyal Englishman, once and for all.

Papa, she learned when she went down to breakfast, had gone to Tunbridge Wells on business and would be there for the whole day. Catherine took the opportunity to look in his private study, but quickly realized she would find nothing there. The proof, if there was any, would be found in a place the real villains accessed, which meant she needed to search the estate office.

The office was in a small stone building with a slate roof, the sash windows set either side of a narrow and ill-fitting wooden door. It was just beyond the kitchen gardens and looked out toward the stable buildings and the park beyond. Catherine approached it with some trepidation, uncertain what excuse she would use for being here, should Milton happen to be present. She prayed he wouldn't be, and she had hopes of this, since she was sure she'd heard Papa say the steward was to visit the tenants today, collecting rents and information on necessary repairs. That should keep him away all day. Still, unwilling to take anything for granted, she approached the office hesitantly.

It was empty. The key was positioned on top of the lintel, left there so the maid could get in to clean. Catherine grabbed it and, a moment later, slipped inside and looked around.

Milton's desk took up much of the space. It was positioned against the wall, underneath one of the windows, from which light shone over the desk's dark wood top. A blotter was positioned centrally on it, and to one side stood an inkwell and pen stand, a paperweight, and a carriage clock. There were no papers on the desk.

On the other side of the room were shelves which held books and ledgers. They stood in neat rows in size order so that the tops sloped tidily down from largest to smallest. None of them leaned. One shelf even held a wooden bookend, carved in the shape of a horse's head, ensuring that the books stayed upright. Milton was, clearly, a neat and meticulous man.

And so it proved. Each book was in pristine condition. Each ledger was carefully ordered, the writing within done in a small, precise hand with no crossings out or noticeable errors. All columns of figures were neatly added up.

Catherine was careful to check each book, aware the proof she needed might be nothing more than a slip of paper tucked between pages. There was nothing. The desk drawers also yielded nothing. One was filled with pencils, pens, a knife to sharpen them, a ruler and other measuring instruments, all neatly stacked. The second drawer held plain paper, and more sheets for the blotter, all neatly arranged. Milton took pride in his workplace to an incredible degree, she thought sourly, and wished he might be a little less fastidious. A man this precise was hardly likely to be careless in leaving useful evidence where she might find it.

After about an hour, her search had yielded nothing. Hands on her hips, lips pressed together in frustration, she stood on the rag rug in the middle of the office and turned a full 360 degrees, looking for somewhere she had missed. Other than the fireplace, there was nowhere. She hardly thought Milton—or anyone else—would be stupid enough to hide anything in the chimney where it would be vulnerable to the flames of the fire.

It pained her to admit she hadn't found anything. But then, if she had not found proof of Papa's innocence, mayhap there would be nothing to suggest his guilt, either. That was something, she supposed, although she had hoped to take away all doubt, and she was upset that she had not done so.

She spun on her foot and the rug rucked beneath her. Her heel caught on something underneath it, almost toppling her. The floor was uneven, she thought, which was probably why the rug had been placed there in the first place. Using her foot to smooth down the rug again, she hit something that was more than just an uneven or loose floorboard. It was hard and solid, and sounded heavy. Frowning, she pulled back the rug and found a metal ring, attached to a small trapdoor in the floor. At about eighteen inches square, it wasn't big enough for a man to squeeze through, so she guessed it was some kind of storage space.

Catherine pulled open the heavy trapdoor, exposing a small cupboard under the floor, in which were nestled two thick ledgers. She lifted them out, rested them on the desk, and opened them carefully, hesitantly, as if they might bite her.

The first one was full of loose leaves, which she quickly discerned were letters, not in English. At first, she thought they might be in Latin, a language she could not read. But when she looked more closely, she saw a phrase she knew: "Je vous en prie." *I beseech you.* Not

Latin, then, but French. Other phrases jumped out at her. "Soyez pret." *Be ready*. "Nous viendrons…" *we will come*.

The phrases were not, in themselves, damning, although her rudimentary French meant she could not read the whole letter, and therefore could not find the context, which might make a huge difference. There were a list of places named, too: Lewes, Nottingham, Portsmouth, London.

She turned to the second book, and found it much easier to read and understand. It didn't take her long to realize it was a second set of accounts, pertaining to the estate, and it was proof that Milton was systematically stealing from her father. A quick perusal suggested a loss to Papa of more than three thousand pounds—a substantial amount, but taken in small enough amounts over a long enough period of time that it was likely to have been unnoticed for a while yet.

Catherine bit her lip and thought through what these books meant. That treason was afoot, she was certain. These letters probably all but clinched it. And she now knew fraud was happening too. Did that help to exonerate her father? After all, he would hardly defraud himself, would he?

Lord Rotherton might not see it like that, of course. She didn't know the earl well, but he always seemed cynical and jaded, as well as indolent. He might find it easier to arrest Papa along with everyone else and sort through the details at his leisure. Catherine could not stomach the thought of Papa languishing in prison because she had presented evidence without ensuring it proved him innocent.

But she could not hide these books and pretend she

hadn't found them. They were tangible evidence of treason, and Catherine could not, would not, allow the villains to succeed if she could prevent it, not even if it would make life easier for her family. She had no choice but to share them with someone.

Adam. He would know what to do about them. He would probably be able to interpret the letters better than she had, too. Yes, he had questioned Papa's innocence last night, and she had accused him of malice, but here in the light of day, faced with this cold, hard evidence, she did not believe he would stoop so low. His honor would never allow him to send an innocent man to the gallows, no matter how much he held a grudge against him. If he could do that, Catherine would never have fallen in love with him. She knew that now. She had known it, even as she levelled her accusations at him and threw him out.

She had maligned him last night, called his integrity into question. He would probably never forgive her for that. But he would put his personal feelings aside and see justice served properly. He'd have to. It was the man he was.

The man she loved. The man she had lost. And she had no one to blame but herself.

Her eyes stung as she closed the trapdoor and rearranged the rug over it, locked the office and carefully replaced the key, and taking the two books with her, headed down the lane toward Hadlow Hall.

****

The cellars at Hadlow Hall were cold and musty and covered in cobwebs, some of them so thick they were almost solid. The wine cellar held a few bottles, but little else. Mindful of what he had seen at Ashton's home,

227

Adam checked the walls, the wine racks, and the floorboards, but found no hidden tunnels.

The coal cellar held a few nuggets of nutty slack, and the pantry was almost bare. Having satisfied themselves that there was nothing to be found in any of these places, Freddy and Adam moved on, searching the rest of the house. The kitchen was easy, for there was little in it. The other parts of the house—the dining rooms, drawing rooms, parlor, music room, and ballroom, together with the numerous bedrooms, dressing rooms, and servants' quarters—were more time consuming, mostly because the furniture was draped in heavy Holland covers, all of which had to be moved and looked under. Every cupboard was checked, as were the tumbledown stables, the dilapidated gardeners' sheds, and other outbuildings. It was late by the time they had searched everywhere. There was, alas, no evidence of the chest, nor any telltale marks in the dust to say it had ever been there, nor that anyone had even walked through most of the rooms recently.

"We've run out of places to look," said Adam as he closed the door on the last outbuilding.

"You're sure he said it was to come here?"

"I'm sure. One said something like, 'Hadlow is an idiot but even he's going to wonder about men bringing a chest full of gold into his house,' and Colbourne answered that Bertie—and we—would be at Offham when it arrived, so we wouldn't know."

Freddy raised his arms, then slapped them down again in frustration. "I fail to see where."

Adam followed Freddy back through the house to the largest drawing room. It was the only public room, other than the small dining room and the billiards room, where the furniture was uncovered and in use, and where the fireplace was primed and ready. There was a chaise longue and several armchairs, all covered in a velveteen which had seen better days, and three card tables topped in green baize, each surrounded by wooden chairs with ladder backs. The floor was unpolished, the veneer worn in places, and some of the floorboards bounced when they were trodden on. The curtains were dotted with tiny holes, and the paint on skirting boards and dado rails needed retouching. In the corner, an occasional table held bottles of brandy, whisky, and port, and it was to here that Freddy went, to pour them both generous measures.

"Where do you suggest we look next?" he asked, and he took a large gulp of his drink.

"Could they have moved it already?" Adam sipped from his glass.

"Anything's possible." Freddy sat down wearily in one of the armchairs. "If that's the case, we haven't a prayer of intercepting it. We don't even know where it's sailing from."

"Hastings."

"That's a big stretch of coastline. It goes from Bexhill in the west almost to Rye in the east. There are plenty of coves and inlets all along there. We don't have the manpower to search them all. Not in time."

Adam thought for a moment. "What if we just start rounding them up? If we get a few in the cells, put the fear of God into them, someone might tell us something."

Freddy shook his head. "Most of them are cannon fodder. They're in it for the money, so they won't be trusted with anything big. And the ones who do know the details, they are zealots. They would die before they betrayed their cause." He finished his drink and put down his glass, carefully and deliberately. Then he crossed one leg over the other and swiped his hand over his thigh as if removing dust from his breeches. "Although, I suppose, Ashton might be persuaded."

Adam grimaced. "I am still not convinced he's involved."

"You mean you don't want him to be involved." Freddy laughed, but the sound was bitter, devoid of all humor. "She's a pretty girl, Adam, I'll grant you that. But she's not for you."

That was true, thought Adam, ruefully. Catherine was most definitely not for him. After their encounter last night, what he had done, how it had ended, she had nothing but contempt for him.

She had accused him of wanting to see her family ruined, her father arrested and perhaps even hanged. And if he did turn out to be the notorious Miller who led the area's traitorous plotters, that was exactly what would happen to him. But if Ashton was innocent…Adam gritted his teeth, remembering the way she had hurled words like weapons, each wounding him deeply. Malice, she had called it. Revenge.

How could Catherine think that of him? True, he had been angry two years ago, when she had rejected his suit after giving him every indication she was ready and willing to accept him. He had blamed her parents, knowing they had put pressure on her to push him away and hope for something better. He had seen the triumphant smugness on Ashton's face when he had watched Adam stalk from the morning room where Catherine had just given him his congé.

Catherine had been adamant that her father was innocent. Of course, that was only to be expected; she was his daughter and if she did not believe in the man, who would? But Adam thought there was more to it than family loyalty. She had seen what happened on the cliff, knew her father's senior servants were involved. She knew how heinous the crime was, and what the stakes were. She would not have stood in the way of justice for anyone, he was certain of that. He had watched her last night, as her quick mind worked through the possibilities. Her dark eyes had clouded with uncertainty and her lovely face was marred by a frown as she thought it all through, and made her decision about her father on her powers of reasoning, not on her emotions.

If only she had been as willing to do the same for Adam.

She had been wrong about Adam's motives, but that did not mean she was wrong about her father. She knew him better than Adam, or Freddy, or Fremont, so she was more likely than they were to be able to tell whether he might be guilty of such a crime. And if she truly believed he was innocent...

"What if it isn't Ashton?" he insisted.

Freddy raised one eyebrow in mocking surprise. "Of course it's Ashton. Who else would it be?" He stood and looked squarely at Adam. "The goods are stored in his cellars," he said, counting the points off on his fingers. "They were carried there through tunnels that can only have been dug for that purpose. Tunnels that go nowhere else."

"Tunnels that were built long before his time. They're at least a hundred years old, Freddy. You can't blame Ashton for them being there."

Freddy laughed. "If you're suggesting our ringleader is the man who built the tunnels, we'll need to dig up the graveyard to arrest him."

"Freddy!" Adam was not in the mood for his friend's facetiousness. "You know very well what I mean. Ashton has no history with the place. He bought it long after the tunnels were built. He inherited his steward and most of the other servants from the previous owner. Who's to say he knows what they're doing, or that he is even aware there are tunnels."

"We are looking for a miller. Ashton bought the estate with the proceeds from his cotton *mills*. His woolen *mills*. The man is a *miller*."

"Not the only miller in Sussex." Adam was clutching at straws now, and he knew it. "What if "Miller" does not refer to those kinds of mills? There are other types. Water mills, windmills…"

"How many water and wind mills are owned by men with the means to pay for an operation the size of this one? And how many millers have the authority to command so many other men?"

Adam sighed. Freddy was right. The evidence was building against Walter Ashton, and it wasn't going to disappear just because Adam wished it would.

The front door banged loudly, startling them both. Freddy reached into his coat pocket, to the pistol there. Adam moved to the fireplace, ready to grab a poker as a makeshift weapon. Footsteps sounded in the hall. One pair of boots. They were sure and steady and made no attempt at stealth. The door pushed open, and Bertie stopped on the threshold.

"What's the matter with you two?" he asked. "You look as if a whole army of housebreakers was coming for you." He looked around and sniffed. "Not that they would be too interested in coming here. Far richer pickings in other houses. Indeed, a housebreaker with an ounce of compassion might feel compelled to leave some of his loot behind for me, when he realized how little I have."

Adam replaced the poker and moved away from the fireplace. "At least you know we were prepared to protect your property," he said, trying to sound nonchalant, though his heart still beat too fast, and every nerve and sinew was tensed. Freddy pulled his hand from his pocket and went to pour himself another drink.

"Hold that thought, will you?" said Bertie. "It may prove useful. Because I…" he grinned broadly as he sauntered into the room and gestured that Freddy should pour him a drink, too, "have finally hit my stride." He pulled a money bag from his pocket. It looked heavy.

"You won?" Adam could barely keep his astonishment from his voice.

"Yes, I won," answered Bertie. He tried to look affronted that his friends would question his ability to do so, but his happy mood was too much to suppress. "Nearly trebled my money. I've got a pocket full of IOUs as well. I haven't worked it all out yet, but I reckon I have cleared about ten grand today. What's more, please note, I left the table without putting my winnings back into the pot. You should be proud of me for that, at the least." He took his glass from Freddy and downed the drink in one long swallow. "I'm going to put it in my safe for now," he said. "Ten grand! I bless the day I met the Miller." He turned to go. Freddy and Adam exchanged puzzled looks.

"The Miller?" asked Freddy.

Bertie turned back, one eyebrow raised. "Colbourne," he said, as if that should have been obvious. "It's what they called him in his fighting days. The Miller. Not just because he fought at mills, but because he ground his opponents to dust, like grindstones crush wheat. The Miller. See?" He weighed his money bag in one hand, then tossed it into the other, grinning happily. "I thought you knew that. Though, I suppose, why should you? He hasn't been a professional fighter for some years now. Just has the odd bout to keep his hand in." With that, he left the room.

Freddy and Adam stared at each other.

"The Miller," whispered Freddy. He shook his head to clear it. "Looks like you were right about Ashton."

Adam nodded. He wished he could run to tell Catherine. Not that she would let him. She wouldn't want to see him, let alone listen to him. She believed he'd thought her father guilty. He'd made no effort to disabuse her of that, and now there was nothing he could say, no apology he could give, that would lessen her anger.

Which didn't mean he wouldn't try. As soon as this business with the gold was resolved, he would seek her out, get down on his knees and grovel, if that's what it took. He would earn her forgiveness.

Even if it took him the rest of his life.

Chapter Eighteen

The books were heavy in Catherine's arms. She wished she could have brought a footman to carry them, but she didn't know if she could trust any of them. She knew Frederick was involved with the smuggling, even if he wasn't party to the other business, and thus he would be unwilling to help stop Milton and, undoubtedly, his own income. There was Peter, of course; she hadn't seen him with the smugglers last night. Which did not mean he wasn't in league with them.

She cursed, realizing for the first time how much easier her life was made because she had people to fetch and carry for her. She hitched the books so they were more secure in her grasp, vowing not to take her easy life for granted again, and moved on.

Cutting through the woods took over a mile off her journey. Unfortunately, it also meant travelling along the narrow bridleway, misshapen and uneven from countless horses. The middle of the path was gouged, leaving a narrow channel between two equally narrow shelves of higher ground, which made walking difficult as she was forced to either shuffle along with her feet either side of the channel, or in a lopsided manner, one foot hitting the ground eight inches lower than the other. Mostly, that ground was hard and dry, but here and there, puddles of clay sucked at her feet, coating her boots with slimy mud and trying to hold her fast, so she almost fell when she pulled herself out. Her arms grew numb with the weight of the ledgers, and her nose was stung by the cold, fresh air. She ducked low branches so she wouldn't snag her hat, and found herself wondering if the distance saved by coming this way was actually worth it.

Finally, she came out of the woods and onto the lawns at the side of Hadlow Hall, which were more like a meadow than the formal garden they should be, the grass long and unkempt, interspersed by giant dockweed and henbit, burweed and shepherd's purse. A stone statue had fallen from its plinth and sat, lopsided, in the grass, the stone spotted with white lichen. A small herd of deer grazed near the tree line but looked up nervously at her approach, then gathered together before hurrying away. Catherine ignored them and moved toward the house.

She reached the wall and the stone path that hugged it. The paving stones were spotted and dingy, some cracked. Blades of grass grew between them, while ivy climbed the wall. She made her way along the path to the corner at the front, intending to walk around and knock loudly on the front door. It was a little late to think of it, she knew, but she wondered if Adam would actually be at home. She had the horrid suspicion that today was the day when Mr. Colbourne was supposed to fight someone, while the others wagered on the outcome. With Catherine's luck, she would have hauled these heavy books all the way here, only to have to take them home again.

Almost at the corner, she heard voices coming from the driveway at the front.

"What are you doing here?" Mr. Colbourne asked somebody, and Catherine stopped dead. He was someone she definitely did not wish to encounter. Even if she hadn't been carrying the incriminating ledgers, she did not wish to be near him. For one thing, he frightened her more than a little. For another, she doubted she could successfully hide her disgust now she knew the truth of what he was doing.

Carefully, she peered around the side of the house, thankful for the ivy, its leaves changing the outline of the wall from stark, square brick to a less defined edge that camouflaged her better.

She saw a long drive that ended in a circular carriage stop, all pockmarked and rutted, clumps of couch grass pushing through the surface. Mr. Colbourne stood in the circle, feet apart, arms akimbo. He wore the same dark, homespun clothes he'd worn last night, and a rundown pair of boots. His face was slightly swollen, his eye black, but he did not look as if the injuries bothered him much. If anything, he looked more dangerous than ever. Catherine shuddered at the sight of him.

Beside him, speaking in low, urgent whispers, was Milton, while the farrier looked on. Catherine could not hear what was being said, but Mr. Colbourne nodded as he listened.

"Come with me," he said, after a moment. All three men went inside the house.

No! No, no, no! How would Catherine reach Adam safely now, without alerting Mr. Colbourne and Milton? They would see the books and know exactly what she had found.

A word Catherine was not supposed to know came into her mind and would have made it out of her mouth if someone hadn't touched her shoulder. The touch was soft, but enough to make her jump and spin around,

237

barely controlling her frightened squeak.

Ned Fellowes sprang back, alarm on his face as he raised his hands in surrender. Catherine breathed out hard and closed her eyes against the shock he had given her.

"You scared me," she murmured, willing her heartbeat to slow and her breath to even.

Ned hung his head, contrite.

"Never mind." She smiled. "Thank you for saving me last night."

He grinned broadly, showing teeth that were more gray and black than white, with large gaps. His hair stood in clumps and his thin frame seemed barely enough to support the ragged clothes he wore.

"Why are you here?" she asked, then grimaced at her own idiocy. Everyone knew Ned could not speak, so what purpose did it serve to ask him inane questions?

Ned crouched, narrowed his eyes and peered from side to side, furtively, and Catherine realized Adam was right, Ned could communicate what he wished to say very well, when he wanted to do so.

"You're keeping a look out," she interpreted, and he stood taller, his pride evident. "For Adam?"

He cocked his head to one side, as if trying to make sense of her words.

"Lord Abberley," she clarified.

Ned grinned.

"Is he in the house?"

He nodded.

"But so is Mr. Colbourne, now."

Ned growled, low and menacing, like a dog warning away a threat.

Catherine chewed her bottom lip while she thought.

"Do you know a way to get to Lord Abberley without meeting Mr. Colbourne?"

Ned looked around, as if checking they were alone and unremarked, then he touched her wrist gently and pulled at her. Instinctively, she pulled back and he frowned, before he pulled her again. This time she went with him. He let go of her arm and led the way toward the back of the house.

Around the corner, there was a terrace that stretched the width of the house. It was bordered by a stone wall with ornately carved balusters and stone steps that led down to what must once have been a pleasant garden. Along the terrace, at regular intervals, were deep, wide windows and, here and there, a French door. Ned moved silently across the terrace to the first window, peeked in, then beckoned Catherine to come to him. She followed, warily, wondering what he intended to do next.

A moment later, she was astonished to see him pull a long, thin wire from inside his shirt. He threaded it into the gap between the window and the frame, jiggled it up and down until something clicked, then withdrew it and put it back into his shirt before pulling the window open.

"Ned!" she breathed, horrified. He grinned at her and swung his long, skinny legs over the low sill and disappeared into the room.

Catherine bit her lip, not really wanting to follow him. She had planned to go in through the front door and confront Adam with her proof, all open and honest. What Ned was doing was housebreaking, and she had just become his accomplice. If they were caught…

Would Lord Hadlow have them prosecuted, even though they did not intend to steal anything? That is, Catherine didn't intend to steal anything. She could not speak for Ned, though she hoped he wouldn't do anything stupid. And if Lord Hadlow did wish to press charges, would Adam stand up and dissuade him? Or would he think it served her right, and leave her to her fate? After the way she had treated him, how could she blame him if he did?

She jumped as Ned leaned back out of the window. He put a long, dirty finger against his lips and beckoned her to follow.

"In for a penny," she whispered, and handed him the ledgers before she, too, climbed in.

They were in Lord Hadlow's dining room. The table was set for four places, with plain cutlery and chipped side plates. A brass candelabrum sat in the center of the table, mismatched with the silver condiment pots. The top of the credenza was bare, and there were marks on the walls where pictures had been removed.

Ned handed her one of the ledgers, though he held on to the other. He mimed swinging it like a bat, then acted as if someone had hit him around the head, before giving her a thumbs up and a querying look.

Catherine nodded. She could do that. If she was threatened, that was, and there was no other way to escape. And provided the person who needed to be hit didn't see the blow coming in time to counter it. She had seen the speed and power with which Mr. Colbourne had downed the farrier last night, and she knew the only way she could hope to beat him was through surprise.

Ned moved to the dining room door. Catherine took a deep breath and braced herself, pushing down the butterflies swarming inside her, then followed him.

****

Freddy stared into the fireplace. The fire wasn't lit

now, but it had been last night and the ash was still in the grate, its cloying, stale smell permeating the room. The marble surround was sooty too, a testament to the fact that Bertie was doing his own menial work, and not doing it well. There was a small hole in the hearth rug, its edges singed, legacy of the first time he had tried to light the fire and ended up with a hot piece of timber falling out and almost setting the house ablaze.

"Do you think Bertie is involved, too?" asked Freddy, quietly.

Adam shrugged. "I don't know. I think not, but…" He shrugged again. "I don't know."

"Colbourne wanted him out of the way when he had the chest delivered."

"True."

"Or," continued Freddy, "was that to get you and me out of the way? We followed where Bertie led, did we not?" He put one hand on the dusty mantelshelf and leaned heavily against it, hanging his head, sad and tired. "Going to Offham was Bertie's idea."

"Which doesn't mean there was anything sinister behind it." Adam sympathized with Freddy, who now faced the same questions and feelings about Bertie that Adam had had about Catherine's father. Although, for Freddy, it was worse. Adam had hated the thought of Ashton being guilty, yes, but the man had not been an old schoolfriend he liked well.

"Colbourne may have wanted Bertie out of the way because he didn't trust him with the gold," mused Freddy.

Adam didn't believe that. "Bertie's no thief. If you're going to play devil's advocate, at least make your argument convincing. And besides, remember who told us that Colbourne is the Miller. Why would Bertie do that if they were in cahoots?"

They sat down together, one on either side of the fireplace. Both crossed their legs and stared at the cold grate, and the absurd thought hit Adam that they looked like a pair of bookends. He wanted to laugh out loud at the idea but did not, recognizing it from his years on the battlefield as a reaction to the stress of the situation.

After a few more moments of morose contemplation, Freddy took a deep breath and sat up straighter. "Let's recap," he suggested. "We know that Colbourne is the leader of the smuggling gang, and he's using that position to—"

He stopped when Bertie laughed, loudly. "What are you talking about, Freddy?" he asked, striding into the room, his grin wide, eyes dancing. "I've never heard such utter rot in my life. Whatever you're drinking, I'll have one." He continued past his friends to the table in the corner and poured himself a generous measure of brandy.

"Bertie." Freddy stood and approached his friend, who gave Freddy an "I-can't-believe-you-said-such-a-thing" look. Freddy sighed. "I'm sorry, but—"

"You should be sorry, maligning a man that way. Colbourne? Leading smugglers? I never heard anything so ridiculous in my life."

Adam saw the exasperation on Freddy's face and wondered whether he should say something too, then decided to stay silent until he was needed. Freddy knew Bertie far better than he did, so it stood to reason he would know better how to handle this.

Bertie sipped at his drink. "I like Colbourne as much as I like anyone. But I can tell you, you're barking up the wrong tree." He tapped his forehead. "He hasn't the nous to lead anything. Good with his fists, and enjoyable company, and all that. There's a lot to recommend him. But...leader? No. Just...no." He chuckled again. "Absolutely famous. Colbourne as leader of a gang of smugglers." He shook his head.

"It's worse than that," said Freddy.

Adam raised his eyebrows, although he wasn't overly surprised. Now that Bertie knew this much, it was as well that he know the rest.

"Worse than smuggling?" Bertie was puzzled. "What's he been doing, then? Stealing the silver? Well, if he finds any in here, I hope he tells me about it. I've already hocked everything I know about."

Quietly, Freddy answered, "Treason."

Bertie stopped, his glass almost at his mouth. He stared at Freddy, then at Adam, astounded.

Adam nodded. "It's true."

There was a moment of silence. Bertie stared at one, then the other. He downed his drink in one large gulp and frowned, sternly. "Dammit, you two," he said. "That is not funny."

"No," agreed Adam, "it isn't."

"Say that to the wrong person, you could ruin the man's reputation. His life, even. Good God, he could swing!"

"Bertie..."

"Why would you say such things? What's he done to deserve that?"

"He planned an insurrection," answered Adam. "And the restoration of Napoleon."

"Which would lead us into another war," added Freddy. "As if we haven't had enough of those."

Bertie sank down onto the chaise longue. His forearms rested on his thighs, his hands together, clutching his now empty glass as he stared at them, stunned.

"We have to stop him," Adam said. "Especially now we haven't found the gold."

Freddy nodded. Bertie blinked. "Gold?" he asked. "What gold?"

"Colbourne's gold for Napoleon's army," Freddy told him.

Bertie looked down at his glass. "I've drunk too much," he murmured.

Freddy turned to Adam, his face grim, his manner that of a superior officer. "Fetch Rotherton," he commanded. "Tell him to summon the militia. I'll wait here for you, with Bertie. If Colbourne comes, we'll delay him…"

A loud click stopped Freddy mid-sentence and he whirled to face the door. Adam stood up sharply, startled to see Colbourne standing there, pointing a pistol at them. Behind him, also holding weapons, were Milton, the farrier, and two men Adam didn't recognize. They wore the rough breeches and leather jerkins of working men.

Colbourne smiled, regretfully. "I'm afraid I must put a damper on your plans, Finch." He moved farther into the room, allowing Milton and the farrier to follow. The other men filled the doorway behind them, as if they were unsure they had the right to come into a room their betters used.

"What gave me away?" asked Colbourne. He sounded calm and collected, as if he was talking of no more than the weather.

"Does it matter?"

"Not really." He turned to Adam. "You were with the halfwit last night, weren't you? I should have been more thorough in my search."

"Alfie?" Bertie stared at his friend, his mouth agape, eyes wide. "You're a traitor?"

Colbourne's laugh was bitter. "That depends on your perspective. One man's traitor is another man's patriot."

"But you...how could...I don't understand."

"You wouldn't." Colbourne spat the words, contempt darkening his face and curling his lip. "It's always been so easy for you, *Lord* Hadlow." He emphasized Bertie's title. "Feckless fop. You sail through life without a second thought for anybody but yourself. Nothing touches you. Or if it does, what of it? You simply stop paying your bills. What do you care if that means the little people starve? Just as long as you can carry on gambling and drinking and carousing. Well, *Lord* Hadlow," he leaned in, his face menacingly close to Bertie's. Bertie shrank back on the chaise longue. "My father was one of those 'little people' you like to cheat. I watched him struggle to feed his family because people like you thought they were too good to pay up. I started fighting for prize money when I was twelve years old so I could help him put bread in my sisters' mouths. I watched him grow old before his time. He worked himself until he was ill, and he died because your kind threw away his money on the turn of a card."

Adam watched Colbourne intimidate Bertie and tried to move slowly forward. If he could get himself into a better position, he could tackle the man, use him as a shield against his co-conspirators. He knew Freddy was also waiting for the split-second opportunity to act. Between them, perhaps they could…

He stopped dead when the farrier pointed his gun squarely at him. The man moved nearer, his pistol never wavering, until the muzzle of the gun poked Adam's side just above his hip. Milton also moved, his gun pointed at Freddy.

"I'm sorry," Bertie told Colbourne. "I didn't know."

"You didn't care to find out."

"You're right. I should have. I should have paid my bills. We all should. But Alfie? Treason?"

Colbourne scoffed. "You still don't get it." He raised his gun to point at Bertie's face. Bertie's entire attention narrowed to the end of the barrel.

"What do you hope to gain?" Adam asked the question to distract Colbourne from pulling the trigger. Outnumbered, outgunned, he could not immediately see how any of them were going to survive this, but he wasn't about to give up until he had to. Colbourne straightened, Bertie seemingly forgotten as he glared at Adam, so Adam continued. "What will you get out of this? Any of you?" His gaze took in the other men, too. "You think you'll be given position? Power? Money?" He scoffed, trying to sound as if he mocked them, while inside his heart beat painfully fast and his stomach roiled. There was a feathery feeling at the base of his throat, and every muscle was tensed, ready. "Bonaparte will never reward you. Not as much as you hope."

Colbourne snarled and Freddy joined in, dividing his ire and, hopefully, sowing doubt in his men. "He's right," he said. "Bonaparte will want rid of you as soon as you've served your purpose. Nobody wants a turncoat behind him."

Milton laughed. "That's what you say. You know nothing."

"Our turn to have it all," agreed the farrier, "while men like you go to the gallows."

"Or the guillotine." Milton's smile was malevolent.

"How do you expect to succeed? You'll have every man, woman and child in England against you." Adam was saying whatever came into his head now, in an effort to draw out the conversation. The longer he could keep these men talking, the longer he and Freddy had to come up with something that would save them. That one of them lived was of paramount importance, for nobody outside of this room knew the danger England was in. Nobody, that was, except for Catherine.

The thought of her made him falter. That she would report what she knew to the authorities, he had no doubt. But would they believe her? Fremont was convinced her father was the ringleader of this band. Would that make him unwilling to take Catherine's word? Or would he suspect her of being involved as well? The thought of her being interrogated by Fremont's men made Adam feel sick. He had to get to her, to protect her and make the truth known. Though how he was going to do that was, at present, a mystery.

"You'd be surprised," said the farrier, his mouth close to Adam's ear, the muzzle of his gun poking Adam painfully in his side. It took a moment for Adam to realize the man was answering his comment about everyone in England opposing them. "There's a whole army of people out there who're just waiting to join us—"

"Be quiet!" Colbourne interrupted. "Your jaw flaps more than an old biddy at a tea party. They don't need to know everything." He glowered at Adam. "Not another word from you."

Adam stared back at him, and hoped his eyes conveyed his silent contempt.

"Just put a ball in his brain and have done with it," suggested Milton. His face filled with eager anticipation as he pushed the barrel of his own gun into the underside of Freddy's chin, making Freddy tilt his head back.

"Not here." Colbourne sounded weary, as if dealing with his underlings was too much trouble. Adam didn't think these men would live long enough to collect their reward once their usefulness was past. "We cannot leave any trace of them here," continued Colbourne. "We don't need the authorities to begin an investigation before we're ready. And I, for one, do not wish to lug their dead carcasses away when, alive, they can walk."

"And then what?" asked the farrier. "Where will we take them?"

Colbourne raised his eyebrow at the man, as if he could not believe his stupidity, but it was Milton who answered his question.

"They'll board the ship with the rest of the cargo," he explained. "But they won't reach the French coast."

Adam and Freddy exchanged glances, silently agreeing to be ready.

Chapter Nineteen

Catherine followed Ned out of the dining room and into the hall. The floor was covered in black and white ceramic tiles that had probably once been highly polished. Now, there were dull patches where the varnish had worn away, and some of the tiles were chipped and cracked from heavy use and too much neglect. The walls were bare, no pictures on display, only the tall doors to various rooms breaking the line of the plasterwork. At the far end was the front door, firmly closed. To one side, a wide staircase led up to the rest of the house. About halfway along the hallway, Catherine saw two men looking through an open door. They both held pistols.

She clutched her ledger tightly against her chest. It seemed dreadfully inadequate as a weapon now, especially since she knew these two men were not the only threats in the house. She could hear Mr. Colbourne, although she could not make out his actual words. However, the timbre of his voice told her he was not pleased.

Ned turned and put a finger to his lips. She nodded and resisted the urge to roll her eyes. She wasn't stupid. She frowned as she realized Ned might say the same, yet he probably had to tolerate such patronizing treatment every day. People treated him as if he were a child, and not a particularly bright one at that. Yet there was a wisdom in him that many who were considered more clever lacked. Shame filled Catherine as she realized she had treated him in that way more than once. She vowed to give him more respect from now on.

Silently, Ned made his way along the hallway, keeping to the shadows near the wall, which camouflaged his movements, although she guessed the men in the doorway were so intent on whatever was happening within the room they probably would not have noticed him anyway. She followed, walking on tiptoe so her boot heels did not sound against the floor. Her fingers hurt where her grip on the ledger was so tight, the knuckles of her gloves stretched thin enough to tear. Her heart beat eighteen to the dozen, painful against her ribs. She had to remind herself to breathe.

"I should have paid my bills." That sounded like Lord Hadlow. Was he involved in the villainy here, or was he its victim? The men at the door were certainly threatening someone.

"You still don't get it." That was Mr. Colbourne again.

"What did you hope to gain?" asked Adam.

Catherine's heart missed, then sped up until the beats became one long thrum in her tight chest, and a noise like rushing water filled her ears. Her breath caught in her throat. Every nerve tingled, every muscle tensed.

Adam was in that room with Mr. Colbourne, and probably Milton and the farrier, too. He was outnumbered, even if one counted Lord Hadlow as his ally. From what Catherine knew of the viscount, she didn't think he would be much use in a fight. Not only that, but at least two of the men against them were armed. If they shot into that room…

She stopped dead, her legs refusing to move forward

as panic threatened to engulf her. Adam was in there!

"Put a ball in his brain and have done with it." That was, unmistakably, Milton. Advocating killing…Adam?

No! She held her breath and bit her lip for a second, certain she had screamed the word out loud. They could not kill Adam! The idea was too horrible to even think on. A world without Adam in it, even if he was no longer hers, was not a world she could bear. She would rather die herself than let him be killed.

Ned touched her arm gently. She stared at him, coming back to the moment, then nodded. He turned away from her and moved on with a liquid smoothness, somehow managing to slither past the two men at the door. Catherine held her breath, waiting for someone to spot him and raise the alarm. No one did.

She sneaked closer, until she was almost on top of the nearest man.

"They won't reach the French coast," said Milton ominously.

Ned gave her a look that asked if she was ready. She swallowed, hard, and nodded. Both of them raised their ledgers high, and then Ned growled.

He sounded like a very large, very angry guard dog. The men in the doorway turned, clearly startled, but before they could complete the move, Ned swung his ledger, catching the man nearest to him full in the face. There was a thump, and a sickening crunch as his nose broke.

The sound galvanized Catherine, and she swung at the man near to her. The ledger came down hard on the back of his head. He stumbled forward and she hit him again, knocking him to his knees. The gun fell from his hand and hit the floor, but she heard no clatter of metal and wood hitting clay. She heard nothing but the rage within her, roaring like a winter wind, loud and overpowering.

From the corner of her eye, she saw Ned swing again and his man toppled. Catherine hit out once more, and her own victim slumped to the hall floor and lay unmoving.

Through the door, the room was in a strange, silent chaos. Adam grappled with the farrier, each trying to wrest a single gun from the other. Mr. Finch fought with Milton. They tugged and pushed at each other, knocking into walls and furniture. A table covered in bottles of alcohol toppled, sending bottles everywhere, breaking glass and spraying walls, floor, and men with pungent liquid. A chaise longue lay on its side and two card tables were snapped and broken, their chairs fallen. Lord Hadlow and Mr. Colbourne faced each other near the chaise longue. Lord Hadlow's eye was swelling and his cheek was a hot, vibrant red where Mr. Colbourne had hit him, but the viscount was still on his feet.

There was a pop, like a large bubble bursting in Catherine's ear, and sound raced back in. She heard furniture snapping and glass breaking, flesh hitting flesh, and the grunts of men struggling with each other. Her own breathing was loud and ragged, and her heart beat like a drum in a military parade. And a cockerel was crowing.

Catherine blinked. Why would there be a cockerel? Confused, she turned and saw Ned, standing on one of the inert men in the hall, clutching the ledger and crowing triumphantly. She shook her head to clear it. Ned crowed again, then barked like an overexcited dog.

"Traitor!" yelled Lord Hadlow, lunging at Mr.

Colbourne, who hit out at Lord Hadlow, making him stagger backward toward the doorway where Catherine stood. He grabbed the door frame to keep himself upright and she saw the anger and determination on his face. His eyes were full of hot fury and his jaw was clenched. "Traitor!" he said again, the word clipped and sharp. He lunged again, landing a blow on his opponent. Although it had no impact on Mr. Colbourne physically, not even knocking him backward, the man looked shocked. Catherine guessed he did not get hit very often.

He recovered and hit Lord Hadlow again, much harder. The viscount smashed into the wall beside the door.

Mr. Colbourne retrieved a pistol from the floor and Catherine heard a click. It sounded loud, drowning out the crashing and banging of the other fights and the animal noises Ned was making.

Time crawled. Everybody moved unnaturally slowly but extremely clearly. She saw Adam take a swing at the farrier, his fist hardly seeming to move through the air. Mr. Finch's hands were at Milton's throat, Milton's hands around his attacker's wrists. They seemed frozen there. Lord Hadlow pushed away from the wall an inch at a time. Mr. Colbourne raised his gun.

There was a deafening bang and an echo that seemed to go on forever. Then, for the longest of moments, there was nothing.

Time sped up. The farrier dropped to the floor and lay still. Adam dove at Mr. Colbourne, knocking him sideways before both men fell over the upturned chaise longue. Ned stood still as a statue, making no sound, watching, wide-eyed. Milton's grip slackened on Mr. Finch's wrists and his body went limp.

Catherine turned to Lord Hadlow, who still stood by the wall, a look of astonishment on his face as he stared down at his chest, and she followed his gaze.

For a moment, all she saw was a small black mark on his silver silk waistcoat. Then something red seeped through and spread over his front.

Lord Hadlow looked up and his eyes met Catherine's as his knees gave way, his legs crumpled, and he sank to the floor. She ran to him and fell to her knees, catching him as he fell sideways, his head landing in her lap, her arms going around him, holding him. His breaths were shallow and labored, each one hard fought for, and there was a strong smell of copper, mixed with the alcohol he had drunk and the tobacco he had smoked.

He sobbed, once. "Miss Ashton," he whispered. "Why are you…?" He took in a breath. "You'll get…blood…blood on…your dress." He laughed, then groaned.

"Hush," she said. "Be still." She frantically looked around the room for help. Adam was fighting Mr. Colbourne, who was giving him a pasting, but Adam was not giving up. Mr. Colbourne grinned, as if this was a game.

"Your…" Lord Hadlow swallowed. "Your rep…repute…" His face was a gray-blue white, the bruise growing on his cheek huge, and his lips unnaturally red against the pallor of his skin. His eyes were dull, and getting duller by the second.

"Just lie still," she said. Somewhere in the back of her mind, she recalled being told one must put pressure on a heavily bleeding wound. She ripped open his waistcoat, scattering buttons as she searched for the exact spot to press down on. His shirt was covered in a sticky red, the smell of it so strong she could taste it. Bubbles frothed, more with each breath he struggled to take.

"I've...rue...ruined   your...rep...but   I...I can't...marry you." He huffed a pained laugh that turned into a breathless cough. "Pity."

There was a crash. Catherine looked up to see Adam on his back on the floor between two chairs. They blocked him in, preventing him from getting up. Mr. Colbourne stood over him, brandishing a knife. Adam scrambled back on his elbows and heels, but he couldn't go far.

"No," whispered Catherine. "No."

Mr. Colbourne jabbed. Catherine opened her mouth, perhaps to scream, but no sound came out. Her heart stopped.

There was a loud bang. Catherine jumped and clutched tighter at Lord Hadlow. Mr. Colbourne swayed, half turned and corkscrewed to the ground, then lay still. Behind him, Mr. Finch crouched, a gun in his hand, smoke rising from the end of its barrel.

****

Adam looked around, dazed. The room was carnage. All the furniture was upended, most of it broken. Shards of glass littered the floor, glittering incongruously in the chaos. Milton lay, gasping for breath, one hand massaging his throat, the other arm hanging, useless and broken. Cuts and nicks on his face and hands showed where glass was embedded in his skin.

The farrier lay still, his head bleeding from a large gash where he had fallen against the marble hearth. Colbourne was heaped in the middle of the room. From the unnatural angle of his limbs and the utter stillness of his body, it was clear he was dead.

The smells of strong spirits, cordite, smoke, and blood threatened to overpower him and, for a moment, Adam was back at the crossroads at Quatre Bras, where he had taken a bullet, rendering him useless for the bigger and more decisive battle at Waterloo two days later. Cannons boomed around him. Men yelled, horses screamed, and the reports of small arms punctuated every breath. He fought his way to the surface, pushing through the battle's smoky fog, through blood so thick it tasted on the air, and the excruciating pain as the ball ripped through his shoulder, knocking him backward to the unforgiving ground…

"Adam?" Catherine called to him.

He frowned. Why was she here? She did not belong here. She should be safe in England, away from all this.

"Adam!"

Her voice broke through. The Belgian battlefield disappeared. He was in Bertie's home in Sussex. The traitors were defeated, the Miller dead, and Catherine sat at the wall, half her hair hanging around her shoulders, her face and coat spattered with blood.

Fully back in the moment now, Adam scrambled to her. "Catherine? Where are you hurt? Are you shot?" Eyes stinging, brain racing through a million dreadful scenarios, he reached out, and only then registered the viscount in her arms, his shirt almost completely red.

"He needs a doctor," said Catherine. Shock made her voice flat and quiet.

"No," argued Bertie. "Doctor…no good."

Freddy knelt the other side of Catherine, put his hand on Bertie's shoulder and squeezed. His eyes glistened with his tears, and he pressed his lips together to stop their tremble.

"Did we…win?" asked Bertie.

"We won."

Bertie smiled. "Been my…day for…winning." He coughed once, sighed, and was gone.

After that, things moved swiftly. Ned was sent to fetch Lord Rotherton, who brought the local militia to herd the surviving miscreants from the house. They were taken to the secure jail at Haywards Heath where they would be interrogated by men Rotherton described as, "far more adept at it than I am." Even so, Adam doubted they would gather much information from them. Even Milton was little more than a foot soldier, so it stood to reason their knowledge would be limited.

Catherine's father arrived and bundled her away, having received the promise of every man there that they would never tell a soul she had been present. Adam watched her go, swathed in a long, black cloak that hid her bloodied clothes, her face wiped clean, her hair bundled up into the best hairstyle her father could manage. She had sat and let Ashton pin it up without demur, suffering his unpracticed attempts to push in her pins without making a single sound. Her father had talked nonstop, his tone one he might use for a skittish horse, his words nonsensical, a testament to his love and concern for his daughter. He nodded an uncomfortable acknowledgement at Adam as he steered her out of the dining room where they had gathered, away from the mess of the battle. Adam nodded back and watched them go, wondering if he would ever see her again. He thought it unlikely. Her parents would see to that. If they had thought him unsuitable before, they certainly would not approve of him now, after she'd almost been killed because of him.

His eyes burned and the lump in his throat threatened to choke him, and his heart hurt.

It was for the best, he told himself, a thousand times over. She could do so much better than him—a minor baron from a family mired in ancient scandal, and a servant of the Crown whose work involved nothing but subterfuge and lies.

She looked back at him as she was led away. He smiled at her. She did not smile back. The pain in his heart grew, and threatened to bring him to his knees.

Freddy clapped him on the shoulder, but said nothing. They stood together like that for a long time, silent in their grief.

Chapter Twenty

Tuesday, 2ⁿᵈ April, 1818

It was a cold, wet day with dark gray clouds hanging low over the landscape. A fitting day, Catherine thought, for a funeral. The gentlemen of Rotherton and its surrounding villages had gone to the church of St Simon and St Jude in the hamlet of Crompton Hadlow to bury Robert Featherstone, eighth Viscount Hadlow, alongside his ancestors in the family crypt.

Ella Forbes-Smythe, who had known Lord Hadlow since childhood, had desperately wanted to go to the service but it was not something respectable ladies did, and his friends had dissuaded her, pointing out he would not have wanted her to compromise her reputation for him. So she, along with the other ladies, had gathered at Hadlow Hall to await the return of the men.

The house looked a lot different to the last time Catherine had been here, just a week ago. Lord Rotherton had taken control with ruthless efficiency, arranging for an army of cleaners to work their way through the entire building. They had removed all trace of the battle, replacing the broken furniture in the drawing room with the best they could find in other parts of the house. The windows glistened and the woodwork shone, carpets had been beaten back to their original colors, and all cobwebs had been removed from every nook and cranny. Throughout the house, the walls had been washed, the floors polished, and the most pressing repairs done. The place smelled of beeswax and fresh herbs. The underlying decay was still there, and there was no disguising the general state of the neglected building, which would take thousands of pounds to restore, but, on the whole, it was presentable for those who would visit today.

"I still cannot believe he's gone," said Mrs. Potter, placing her tea cup carefully into the saucer on the table beside her. "He was such a…" She sighed, and her hand fluttered as if she tried to capture words to convey her meaning. "He was so full of life."

Ella sniffed and Miss Potter reached out to her, stroking her arm.

"Who succeeds him to the title?" continued Mrs. Potter, seemingly oblivious to Ella's distress.

"I believe he has a cousin," answered Mrs. Bell, and she sipped at her own tea. "Not a first cousin, of course. Lord Hadlow had no really close relatives. This is a second, or is it a third cousin. Removed."

"Does it matter?" Her daughter, Amelia, gestured with her eyes that Ella was upset, and her mother should be more circumspect. Mrs. Bell looked contrite.

"Well, of course it matters," retorted Mrs. Potter. "The man will be a landowner in the area, and landlord to all the tenants on the Hadlow estate. He will be an important part of our society. It matters very much who he is and what he is about."

"All I can say is," answered Ella, "I hope he takes his duties more seriously than Bertie did. He drove me mad with his devil-may-care attitude and his neglect." Her tone was acerbic, but Catherine was not fooled. It was Ella's way of combatting the grief that might otherwise overwhelm her.

"Miss Forbes-Smythe!" Mrs. Potter was appalled. "It does not become you to speak ill of the dead, who are not here to defend themselves."

Ella snorted. "He never defended himself to me when he had the chance. I say nothing here that I did not say to his head, and he would be the first to admit his…" She bit her lip and stared down at her hands in her lap. Amelia and Miss Potter sat either side of her, gently rubbing her arms in comfort.

"One would have thought the new Lord Hadlow would have been here today," Mrs. Potter went on. Her daughter glared at her, but she did not seem to notice.

"I heard he was on the continent," said Miss Burgess. A prim and trim woman in her thirties, she was sister to the curate who served the churches at both Rotherton and Crompton Hadlow and who was, even now, conducting the funeral service. "We must pray for his safe return to his ancestral home, and that the Lord will make him a fit man for the job." She nodded her head and smiled, serenely, at them all. Her hands were clasped together as if she was ready to make those prayers right now.

"Yes," answered Mrs. Bell.

"The Lord has His ways of providing for the comfort and well-being of His people," continued Miss Burgess. "Whether those people are in agreement with Him or not."

There was a moment of awkward silence.

"How go the arrangements for your wedding, Miss Bell?" asked Catherine's mother, and the conversation turned to the plans for Amelia's wedding to Josh

Summersby, which would take place in May.

Catherine, however, did not take in many of the details. Although she wished the couple happy, she found it hard to concentrate on their upcoming nuptials. She found it hard to concentrate on anything, if the truth be told.

She had been distracted since the day Lord Hadlow was killed. For the past week, she had taken little part in any conversations, saying no more than she must and hearing even less. She had done nothing of use with her time, either. She tried to read, but gave up after a page when she did not take in the sense of a single word. Her embroidery was a disaster that Mama had needed to unknot for her. She had not walked outside, or ridden, or visited her neighbors, nor had she been at home when they called. Her appetite was depleted, although Cook prepared her favorite dishes to tempt her.

Mama and Papa decided privately that it was the natural reaction of a gently bred woman to the dreadful ordeal she had been through. Publicly, they said she had taken Lord Hadlow's death hard because, as they said, "Catherine has never known anyone who died before," and, "It was such a shock, the way he died, to one of her delicate sensibilities."

There was, Catherine supposed, an element of truth in that. She had never expected to see a man murdered, or to have him die in her arms. Not that anyone other than her family, and those who had been there, knew she had cradled Lord Hadlow as he passed from this world. Her reputation had been carefully shielded from the gossip, although Catherine herself found it hard to care.

She hadn't seen Adam, either, since Papa had wrapped her in his voluminous traveling cloak and led her from Hadlow Hall to his carriage. By that time she had slipped into a state of numbness, and she was grateful for that—the pain and anguish as Lord Hadlow died had been too much to bear. Her head had pounded, thoughts racing through it at a mile a minute, while her stomach churned and her heart cracked, spilling despair over everything she did or said or touched. Numbness had been a blessed relief.

Adam had watched her go. He said nothing. His face gave no indication of his thoughts and emotions, and Catherine had been too drained at that time even to guess at what they might be. In the days since, of course, she had thought of little else, her mind replaying those moments, examining everything about him—the way he'd stood, the set of his mouth, the intensity of his eyes, the squaring of his shoulders. Over and over, she wondered if he was happy to see her leave, and she had asked herself a thousand times, did he still want her as much as she wanted him?

Given that he'd made no attempt to call on her since, she surmised the answer was no.

And now he would be leaving. He and Mr. Finch had only stayed this week to attend Lord Hadlow's funeral. They had given their statements to Lord Rotherton in his capacity as magistrate, then moved themselves and their possessions out of Hadlow Hall and taken rooms at the Golden Goose Inn instead. From there, they had done what they could to honor their friend, making sure the entire neighborhood knew the viscount had died a hero, fighting the enemies of his country.

Lord Rotherton's investigations were complete now, and the prisoners had been taken to London to await trial. After today, there would be nothing to stop Adam and Mr. Finch heading to Town and resuming their lives there. She could see no reason for them ever to return to this area and, with her Seasons firmly behind her, Catherine doubted she would visit London in the foreseeable future. Which meant that, in all probability, she would never see Adam Mason again.

She tried to ignore the sharp pain the realization caused her.

****

The wind howled across the graveyard as if it, too, mourned the man they had laid to rest. It whipped at Adam's coat, lifting his capes, and threatened to tear his hat from his head. The weathervane atop the church steeple creaked and shrieked, spinning round and round, far too fast. Adam narrowed his eyes against the grit in the air as he walked along the narrow path from the little church to the road that led to Hadlow Hall.

"Strange service, wouldn't you say?"

Adam turned to see that Walter Ashton had caught up to him. The man's coat was buttoned tight against the bullying wind, and there was a strange expression on his face, not quite puzzled, not quite troubled, but something in between.

"Yes, it was," agreed Adam. There had been an atmosphere in the church, as if the curate, Mr. Burgess, did not want to be there and felt it was an imposition on him that Bertie needed to be blessed and laid to rest. He hadn't seemed to know much about Bertie, either, although, in fairness, that was not much of a surprise, as the late Lord Hadlow had not been a regular attendee at Sunday services. He was never out of bed in time for the start of them. Mostly, he was still in bed by the time they finished.

Not that that had worried Bertie. "I won't bother God and his church," he had said, "if they don't bother me. I give the fellow a living, to supplement what he gets from Rotherton. If he takes my money, he can leave my soul alone. And if he wants my soul, he can do without the money." He'd laughed then. "Now, there's an idea," he'd added before raising his glass and making a toast to the man he called "that confounded cleric."

"It was as if Burgess didn't want us there," continued Ashton, pulling Adam out of his memories of the irreverent Bertie. "As if he had somewhere else he would rather be."

"I daresay we all had something we would prefer to be doing," answered Adam, irritably. The damned cleric should do his job and make the deceased and those who had loved him his priority. "Especially Lord Hadlow."

"Quite." Ashton shook his head sadly. "Taking holy orders should be a calling. Not a dumping ground for surplus sons of the landed gentry."

They left the churchyard and headed along the tiny street at the center of the hamlet. As well as the church and its vicarage, the street comprised of several houses, a small inn, and a bakery. On the road ahead of them, Freddy walked with Lord Rotherton and Josh Summersby, who pushed a bath chair in which sat his father, Viscount Frantham. The older man had looked frail and tired in the church, and was swathed in blankets against the cold day.

Behind Adam and Ashton, several other gentlemen talked quietly as they walked from the church. Adam looked back over his shoulder and was surprised to see Mr. Burgess had not come with them but now stood in the church porch, hands tucked into his surplice and a look on his face which suggested disdain for them all, though why that should be Adam could not begin to guess.

He turned back and put the curate from his mind when Ashton cleared his throat. "Finch tells me," said the older man, hesitantly and clearly uncomfortable, "that I was under suspicion for a time."

Adam nodded but said nothing.

"He also said you were my champion. That you were adamant I was innocent."

"It made sense." Adam did not wish to talk about this. He had no desire to spend time with Catherine's father, knowing the man did not consider him good enough to be his son-in-law. More than that, Catherine herself had rejected him not once but twice now, and the memories and might-have-beens were brought painfully to the fore by the man's presence. He wished Ashton would leave him be.

If it were up to Adam, he would not return to Hadlow Hall, where he could not avoid seeing Catherine among the lady mourners. He had no choice but to do so, of course, though he hoped that once he had paid his respects he could leave unremarked, after which he would return to his room at the inn, pack his bags, and make ready to leave this place once and for all. Then, perhaps, he could finally forget her and start life anew.

And, perhaps, pigs flew through the air backward, using their tails to steer.

"I am not a traitor," said Ashton, bringing Adam's attention back to their conversation. The statement was, Adam thought, unnecessary, since nobody thought Ashton guilty any longer. "Nor am I involved with smugglers." Since Rotherton had rounded up most of them and Ashton was still free, that too, was a given. "But I am a fool." Adam glanced at him, puzzled, and Ashton smiled, sheepishly. "I have always prided myself on my ability to read people. I consider that ability central to my success in business. Yet I read you wrongly from the start, and because of that, two years ago, I treated you very badly."

Two years ago, or even two months ago, for that matter, Adam would have agreed with the man. Now, he knew better. "You did what was best for your daughter," he said.

Ashton shook his head and chuckled ruefully. "I did what I *thought* was best for her, that is true. What I thought, and what was…? I was wrong, and I apologize."

Adam did not want this conversation. Apologies changed nothing. Besides, the man had not been wrong. "You were right to dissuade her from accepting me," he told him. "I was a soldier on half pay, with no prospects of preferment. I could not have kept a wife and, had she married me, she would have been unhappy. As they say, love flies out of the window when the bills come in through the door."

"But things are different now, are they not?" Ashton smiled. "I do not believe you were rusticating to avoid your creditors. You were always frugal before, and a leopard does not change his spots. Am I right?"

It took Adam a long time to answer. He thought about denying it, letting the man think he truly was a ne'er-do-well who had thrown away a fortune within months of inheriting it, but he could not do that. Although it should not matter, it did, and he did not wish Catherine's father to think him so feckless.

"No," he said, at last.

"How do you now feel about my daughter?"

I love her. I always will. If I could, I would spend every moment of the rest of my life with her, making sure she was in no doubt of that.

Aloud, he said, "She doesn't want me."

"You are sure of that, are you?"

Adam frowned and turned to look at the man, who was grinning. "You think she does?"

"I am not the one you should be asking. Nor, I think, am I the one you really wish to be speaking with at this moment."

Hope flowed through Adam, His chest felt lighter, as if a weight had lifted from him. Could it be? Could she possibly…?

"Go, boy. Don't keep a lady waiting," said Ashton. Adam did not need to be told twice.

It took just a few minutes to reach Hadlow Hall, though it felt like a lifetime to Adam. With every step, he tried to think of what he would say to her, but the words would not come, and in the end, he decided he would just see how it happened.

The first gentlemen had shed their coats and gloves and were gratefully accepting warming cups of tea from their ladies. Footmen, borrowed from nearby homes, circulated with trays of wine and maids held plates of sweetmeats and tiny cakes and sandwiches, or carried in fresh pots of tea and coffee. The chatter in the room was still subdued but growing louder by the moment.

Catherine sat by herself near the corner. She watched the other mourners mingle, her face devoid of expression, giving him no clue what she thought. Adam swallowed, unsure. What if her father was wrong? What if she did not want his attentions? What if…?

He stared at her for a long moment, his feet stuck, not allowing him to move closer. His heart beat loud and fast, drowning out the rest of the gathering.

She wore a high-necked dress in black crepe, the neckline and sleeve cuffs decorated with black lace. Over her shoulders a black shawl ensured her warmth, and there were black ribbons in her hair. The unremitting darkness of her clothes made her face seem unnaturally pale. In turn, her eyes, ringed as they were by bruise-colored circles, seemed incredibly large.

A minute went by. More men arrived and moved past him, eager to get to the refreshments. Adam did not take his eyes from Catherine. Then, she turned her head, saw him, and returned his stare.

As if drawn on an invisible string, he moved to her. She stood and gave him a polite curtsey, and he answered with a small bow.

"Miss Ashton," he murmured. "Catherine. I—" His mind traveled back to the last time they were together in this room—the chaos, the broken furniture, the blood and death and destruction. She might have been killed!

The thought almost drove him to his knees. A mixture of anger, relief, and panic flooded him and he clenched his teeth. His words were forced out between them, stark and raw, driven by emotion, with no rational thought holding them back. "What were you thinking?" he ground out. "Do not ever put yourself in danger like that again."

She raised an eyebrow, shocked.

"The man you hit was twice your size," he went on. "Do you know what he might have done to you? If your blow had not hit true, or if you had not hit hard enough, he might have—and then to come into the room—you might have been injured. You might have been shot!"

Catherine pulled herself up to her full height and glared at him. "I do not need to be scolded by you, sir. I bid you good day." She made to step away from him. He reached out and his fingers encircled her wrist, stopping her. She looked pointedly down at his hand. He had seconds to make this right, to make her see…

"Forgive me," he said. "I didn't mean…that is not what I meant to say." His tongue seemed too big for his mouth and his thoughts tumbled over one another, pushing coherence away. "I—it took ten years from my life to see the woman I love put in the way of such… Catherine, you must know I could not bear it if anything happened to you."

Catherine looked from his hand to his face. The anger he'd seen in her eyes was gone, replaced by uncertainty and—hope? His pulse skittered, out of control, and his breathing shallowed. Beneath his fingers was the watery cold of her dress, the rough edge of the lace, the warmth of her skin.

"You love me?" she whispered.

He swallowed. "I do. I always have."

She nodded, once. "Good."

That made him frown. What did she mean? "Good?" he asked, not certain he wanted her answer. What if she told him it served him well to suffer unrequited feelings?

"Yes, good. Because I love you, too."

Adam's lips curved into a smile, and his eyes warmed as relief filled him. "Enough to marry me?"

She looked thoughtful. "That depends."

The hope and joy that had begun to spread through him shuddered to a halt. "Depends?" *Please don't let me lose her again. I will do anything. Please.* "Depends on what?"

Her eyes widened in false innocence and her lips twitched. "On whether you ask me."

A chuckle broke from him, part humor, mostly relief. Then he knelt before her, took her hand in his and said, "Miss Ashton. Catherine. I love you so very much. Please will you make me the happiest of men by consenting to be my wife?"

The room fell silent. Everyone watched. A moment passed. From near the fireplace, Mrs. Potter said, "Well, really! At Lord Hadlow's funeral!"

"He would have been delighted," answered Freddy. "The Bertie I knew would have called it perfect."

"Yes, he would," agreed Ella.

Catherine was silent for another moment, just long enough to cause him anxiety. He did not know how he would survive if she rejected him again.

Finally, she nodded. "Of course I will marry you."

There were oohs and aahs. A smattering of applause. Adam stood holding Catherine's hand, smiling, happier than ever before in his life.

Outside, the rain stopped and the sun came out.

A word about the author...

Caitlyn Callery lives in Sussex, southern England, near the Regency towns of Brighton and Tunbridge Wells. She is passionate about writing and suffers withdrawal symptoms when she takes a few days away from her work.

Before becoming a full-time writer, she worked in banking, as a waitress, in the motor repair industry, in a call centre, and for a charity. As part of this last job, she helped build a school in Kenya and drove a vanload of wheelchairs from the UK to Morocco.

She also loves reading, knitting, walking by the sea, the theatre, and spending time with her family.

CaitlynCallery.com

Thank you for purchasing
this publication of The Wild Rose Press, Inc.

For questions or more information
contact us at
info@thewildrosepress.com.

The Wild Rose Press, Inc.

www.ingramcontent.com/pod-product-compliance
Lightning Source LLC
Chambersburg PA
CBHW070102030726
47506CB00002B/560